THE
TUDOR PRINCE

The second Mary Fox adventure

By
Jonathan Posner

Published by Winter & Drew Publishing

ISBN: 9781739184940

CONTENTS

ACKNOWLEDGMENTS

I would like to thank all those who helped me make this book happen. Jane Rayner, Maggie Saunders and Angie Chadwick of my Devon Novelists critique group, whose constructive comments helped smooth out many of the rough edges in early drafts – and for constantly challenging me on the history and character motivations; Sinead Kelly for her thorough editing, questions and encouragement (as always), and to Carolina de Vivo for proofing.

I would also like to thank the following who read the book in beta, and were kind enough to give me their honest feedback and support: Marta Emmitt, Kate McCormick, Michal Strutin, Shirley De Vivo, Linda Ulleseit and Lisa Gentry.

I used a number of research sources, but the most informative by far was Beverley A Murphy's excellent book *Bastard Prince: Henry VIII's Lost Son*.

Finally, thanks to you for buying this book. I do hope you enjoy Mary Fox's latest adventure!

INTRODUCTORY NOTE

This book follows on from Mary Fox's first adventure, **The Broken Sword**, although I have tried to ensure it stands alone if you've not yet read the first book.

This new story sees Mary impersonating Prince Henry Fitzroy, the illegitimate son of Henry VIII. Fitzroy was a real person, as was his mother Elizabeth 'Bessie' Blount. She was King Henry's mistress in 1519, and bore him the boy when she was aged around nineteen. After her relationship with the King ended, she was married off to Gilbert Tailboys, 1st Baron Kyme, who died in 1530. For this reason I have decided she should be referred to throughout the book as 'Lady Kyme'.

The King acknowledged his son, and was likely to have considered legitimising him as heir to the throne. Equally, Fitzroy's very existence was used by the King as proof that he could father sons – enabling him to put the blame on Katherine of Aragon and Anne Boleyn for not giving him any legitimate boys (at the time when action of the book takes place, he had not yet had his son Edward, by Jane Seymour).

Henry VIII showered honours and titles on Fitzroy from an early age, bestowing on him the dukedoms of Richmond and Somerset, as well as the earldom of Nottingham and the Order of the Garter. There were several other titles, positions and honours, but it was the King's acknowledgement of his illegitimate son that has led me to refer to the boy throughout as 'the Prince'.

I have substantially simplified the Prince's household – which in truth would have had many servants, gentlemen attendants and other officials. My concern was that if I represented the reality of this, it would add greatly to the complexity of the story. So I reduced the household down to Lady Kyme, Marcus Kytson – the fictional gentleman attendant – a fictional steward and a few servants. The household would in fact have moved frequently between the Prince's many houses throughout the country – but, again for simplicity, I have chosen to focus the action primarily on his London residence, Durham House.

There are a number of real events in the Prince's life that I have weaved in throughout the book, although I have, as you would expect, put a 'Mary Fox' spin on them.

It has been a lot of fun researching and writing this book, and spending time getting to know even more about my feisty heroine.

Once again, I hope you enjoy reading her latest adventure as much as I did bringing it to life!

Jonathan Posner
Exeter, January 2024

THE SECOND MARY FOX ADVENTURE
BY
JONATHAN POSNER

DISCLAIMER

No part of this publication may be reproduced, stored or transmitted in any form by any means; electronic, mechanical, photocopying or otherwise, without the prior written permission of the publisher.

Jonathan Posner has asserted his right under the Copyright, Designs and Patents Act, 1988, to be identified as the author of this work.

This is a work of fiction. References to real people, events, establishments, organisations or locales are intended only to provide a sense of authenticity and are used fictitiously. All other characters, and all incidents and dialogue, are drawn from the Author's imagination and are not to be construed as real.

THE BROKEN SWORD
THE FINAL SCENE

Mary Fox has just escaped into the night after some desperate fighting, and is trying to untie the horse from a wooden cart, so she can ride off – who knows where…

In horror I watched as a ghostly dark figure appeared in the moonlight, galloping towards me from the direction of the inn.

Desperately I fumbled with the traces, but my fingers could not get the knots undone, and the man was upon me, his horse rearing up as he pulled it to a halt.

"Mary Fox?" he called down, and my breath caught as I realised it was not one of my pursuers. Thank the Lord, it was not Hal, Tom or even Tobias!

"Yes?" I answered, relief mixed with caution as to what this stranger who knew my name could possibly want with me.

He leapt down from his horse and swept off his cap, bowing low.

"Marcus Kytson, mistress, at your service."

He stood up and I saw him more clearly in the moonlight. He was tall, maybe a few years older than me, with blonde hair that fell across his forehead and clear eyes above a trim, dark beard.

"Yes, Master Kytson?"

He replaced his cap. "I was in the Sun Inn this evening," he said, "and I saw how well you handled yourself."

I admit I had not seen him, for I am sure I would have recalled his strong face and broad shoulders, but then I suppose I had had other things to occupy my mind at the time.

"From the moment when you swung in past that horse's head, then disrobed that boy with swordplay that few could have mastered as well, then leapt to the roof like an acrobat and dispatched that scoundrel with a kick, before swinging backwards onto the stair – t'was a magnificent display!"

I found myself warming to this Marcus Kytson for the boyish delight he took in my actions. "Thank you, sir, but I was only trying to get away from those who would do me harm." I turned back to the traces and continued to untie the horse.

"So I warrant," he replied. "Then you fought that Sir Reginald on the roof of this cart and conspired with the horse to dislodge him…" he shook his head and smiled. "'This girl,' I thought to myself, 'is the one I need for my task.'"

The traces came away and the horse was freed. I grasped the reins and turned back to him.

"What task is that?" I asked. "I do not seek a new task."

"But you are perfect," he answered with a small laugh. "Dressed in boy's garb you are perfect in both physique and face for the task."

"You would have me play a role?"

"That I would." He became serious. "My need is most pressing, and I would reward you with a substantial sum of money."

"I am not motivated by money, sir." I pulled myself up onto the horse and settled on his back.

"No?" He also swung into his saddle, and we faced each other in the moonlight. "But money can buy you freedom, for a woman of means has more choices as to how to live her life." He paused. "I am offering a hundred sovereigns."

I looked up at the clouds thudding across the night sky. A hundred sovereigns! True, a woman was always the property of a man – her father then her husband – but with that kind of money I could set up home for myself. Or I could stay on the move, able to pay my way with ease as I went about the country…

"What would I need to do for that?" I enquired.

"I have a friend who has a son, and he has gone missing," he answered.

"And you want me to find him?"

"No, I want you to pretend to be him, for a visit by his father."

"You would offer me a hundred sovereigns to fool this boy's father that I am his son?" I asked. "Would the father not know his own son?"

"Not this father. The boy was born out of wedlock, and he has not seen his son more than once or twice since he was a babe."

"So the boy is a bastard. Then why is the visit so important?"

"Because of who the father happens to be. And because he is considering making the boy his legitimate heir."

I paused. Should I take this further? Or should I just ride away now and make my own adventures? I will admit, I was intrigued…

"And this boy's name?"

"Henry Fitzroy, son of Elizabeth Blount.

"And his father?" I needed to hear it said, although I fancied I already knew.

"His father is King Henry the Eighth."

The moon shone down on his expectant face. "Will you do it, Mary Fox?" he asked. "Will you be the Tudor Prince for me?"

I smiled.

"Yes, Master Kytson," I said. "Yes, I will."

The story continues…

I

A MONASTERY IN ESSEX

September 1533

The dormitory was on fire.

Brother Ignatius and I stared open-mouthed as a flame burst out of the furthest window of the building, roaring into the night sky like a vengeful demon. Another blew out the window beside it with a shower of glass and sparks.

I clutched his arm. "Is Master Kytson up there?" I shouted.

"Yes," Brother Ignatius answered. "After all the wine he had drunk, we carried him up to sleep."

For a moment I stared at him in horror, then I let go of his arm and started to run towards the burning building.

"Mistress Fox!" he called. "Do not go inside! It is God's will if your companion perishes!"

Ignoring him, I ran up the steps and into the dormitory building. There was a short stairway before me, which I assumed led up to the men's dormitory rooms. A couple of monks were on the landing, unhooking a carved wooden crucifix from the wall opposite. They staggered down the stairs with it, just as another monk swept up two silver candlesticks from the shelf below.

As the monks hurried out through the front door with their treasures, I ran up the stairs.

Several men that I took to be other travellers ran past coughing. But none was the tall, broad figure of Marcus Kytson.

"Help me!" I shouted as they went past. "My companion is still up there!"

But none stopped, or even acknowledged my presence. They ran down the stairs with wide, staring eyes, almost tripping and falling in their haste to get out.

With a curse at their unchristian selfishness, I ran to the top of the stairs. On the left was an open door with black smoke pouring out and the flicker of flames visible through the darkness. I could just make out a line of wooden cots down each side of the chamber, with only a narrow space up the middle. All the cots at the far end were heavily ablaze, and I nearly retched at the sight of a dreadful twisted shape silhouetted on top of the furthest one.

By God's good grace, the flames had not yet reached the closest end of the room. The cot nearest the door was untouched and there was a man-sized shape under a thin blanket.

Putting my mouth into the crook of my elbow and breathing through my sleeve to avoid the worst of the smoke, I ran to the foot of the cot. The flames were mercifully still two cots away. Which meant I had but a few moments before they made the final leap and consumed this one.

I leant over the figure. The blanket was pulled over his head and must have kept the worst of the smoke from his mouth. I whipped it back, to reveal Marcus. With a heartfelt prayer of thanks, I shook him hard.

"Wake up! In Heaven's name!"

He grunted and moved slightly.

The flames were now at the next cot, and it was burning fast.

I shook him again, harder. "Wake up, Marcus!"

He grunted once more, and his eyes opened briefly, then fluttered closed.

A stray spark landed on the wooden frame of his cot and a small flame burst into life. There was a pitcher on a shelf above, so I snatched it up and threw the contents across the frame. There was a hiss and a cloud of steam. The flame was doused. For now.

"WAKE UP!" I screamed.

With another curse, I ran round to his back and forced my arms under his shoulders, then started to pull him away.

I am a slight girl, while Marcus is a broad-shouldered man – so in truth there should have been no possible way for me to carry him even a few feet. Yet somehow I found enough strength to get his upper body off the bed. I gritted my teeth and pulled once more. He grunted as his feet slid off the bed and dropped to the floor. I felt him stand, if somewhat unsteadily, and start to cough.

"Come!" I yelled. The flames had returned to his cot and were now starting to consume it. "Run!"

I took in some air through my sleeve, grabbed his hand and pulled him staggering out after me.

By God's further grace we made it to the door and out into the corridor beyond. Flames were already licking around the lintel. Then the wood panelling beside the door burst alight.

I dragged him to the stairs. Together we stumbled down, coughing uncontrollably, until we made it out of the front door and fell together onto the lawn, still unable to breathe clearly.

"Art whole?" I asked Marcus eventually. "No burns?"

He patted his legs then shook his head. I supposed that his streaming eyes and smoke-blackened face must be the worst he had suffered. And were presumably also a mirror of my own.

But he then gave another deep cough, turned onto all fours and vomited heavily into the grass.

"Is that the wine or the smoke telling its tale, Master Marcus Kytson?" I asked, the relief of our escape giving me some levity. He flopped onto his side and stared at me with red eyes. "Well?" I added with a thin smile. "Pray tell."

Before he could answer there was the sound of a footstep behind my head. I craned my neck round, to see a pair of old leather sandals and broken yellow toenails in the moonlight.

I struggled to my feet, which caused me to double over with another bout of coughing. Eventually I could breathe again, and stood straight. It was Brother Ignatius; worry written deep across his fleshy features.

"By Heavens, Mistress Fox," he said, stepping away from Marcus and the contents of his belly. "How in the name of all that is holy did you get your companion out?"

There was a sudden crash. He flinched and looked past me. The whole of the dormitory building was now ablaze; flames bursting from every window, and even from the front door we had just come through. One half of the wooden roof had collapsed, and as we watched, the rest of it fell in with another crash and shower of flaming sparks, right onto the place where Marcus had been sleeping only minutes before.

My levity disappeared as fast as it had come. I shuddered at how close we had been to disaster. "With God's help, Brother," I replied. "God gave me the strength to lift Master Kytson from his bed and get him out." Then I recalled the awful, twisted shape I had seen. "But I fear the one who slept at the far end is lost."

He crossed himself. "Oh no, the poor man. That must be old Godfrey Fletcher, who we have allowed to stay for many years. He has… had… a book of prayers he liked to read before sleep, but his failing eyesight meant he would oft hold a candle too close. Belike he fell into a slumber and set his book alight." He stepped back as several monks ran past with buckets of water. "It seems his lack of care has cost him dear." The monks threw the water at the fire in high arcs that hissed and steamed, but seemed to have little effect on the blaze. "A worthy effort," observed Brother Ignatius, shaking his head, "but I fear unlikely to help." He looked across at the rest of the buildings, that were mercifully untouched by the fire. "At least God has seen fit to send a wind that bears the flames away from the main monastery."

Marcus struggled to his feet and came over.

"It seems you owe Mistress Fox your life, sir," said Brother Ignatius.

Marcus nodded. "That is so," he said in a hoarse whisper, giving me a weak smile; the cockiness and bluster that I had observed on our travels so far seemingly knocked out of him. "I am most grateful to Mistress Fox." We looked over at the burning building in silence.

There was a hiss as the monks threw more water at the fire, and after a time it began to reduce down to glowing embers and smaller flickers of flame. Other monks and some of the travellers were standing round in small groups. A couple of monks were picking through a pile of ornaments laid out on the grass, including the cross and candlesticks I had seen them rescue earlier.

"Why were you not abed yourself, Mary?" Marcus asked. "You must also be most weary after our long ride."

"Brother Ignatius was walking me to the other dormitory, the one attached to the nunnery," I replied. "We had just set off across this lawn when we saw the inferno."

"Yes, I am most sorry for the destruction of your building." Marcus turned back to Ignatius. "What will you do? How will you restore it?"

The monk shook his head. "I very much doubt that we will do any such thing," he said. "King Henry and his servant Master Cromwell have given word that we are to be turned out soon, and our monastery given over to the enrichment of some godless lackey of the crown. Maybe Our Lord has seen fit to devalue our property with this fire before such a transaction takes place." He gave a small, slightly hopeful smile. "It would be a sign from God that he favours us over this King."

"Indeed," Marcus said.

"We must be away soon," I observed.

"Nay," said Brother Ignatius. "Not until you are fully recovered and can breathe clear. We will find you a bed in the nunnery," he glanced at me. "And you, Master Kytson, one in the main monastery. You can rest a few days until you are fit to travel." His fleshy features were set in an expression that brooked no argument. "I will not allow otherwise."

I wondered what he would do if we ignored him and continued on our journey anyway, but then I heard Marcus coughing again. It was clear we needed time to recover.

"Thank you," I said. "We do not deserve such care."

Brother Ignatius observed me silently a moment. "All God's children deserve it," he said. "Even a strange young man and a headstrong young woman dressed in men's attire, who arrived this afternoon seeking shelter on their journey, so tired that they almost fall from the saddle." He gave Marcus a significant glare. "Such that they are not able to hold more than a few glasses of the monastery wine." He paused a moment. "I would know the purpose of your journey?"

"I am sorry, Brother," Marcus said with a ghost of a smile, "but we are not at liberty to tell."

I caught Marcus's eye and gave him a small nod of support. Our journey was in part on the King's business – so it would hardly be appropriate to share it with a monk who had just expressed his opposition to the King's policies.

Marcus had recruited me to stand in for a missing prince, after the boy had been kidnapped. This much I knew; little more. I had asked no questions on our journey thus far, as I had only just escaped from grave danger when Marcus had accosted me, and needed time to gather my thoughts.

"I see," Brother Ignatius nodded. "A clandestine mission. So be it." He looked at each of us with his eyes narrowed in the moonlight. "Then I would enjoin you both to proceed with the utmost caution. Whatever is your purpose, I suspect it will place you in the gravest danger." He looked hard at me. "You have demonstrated remarkable bravery already, Mary Fox. But what if you face even greater dangers in the days to come? Are you ready for these?"

I took a deep breath and met his eye.

"Yes, Brother," I said. "I am."

2
LADY KYME

Three days later, our journey to London continued once again.

"Tell me of your recovery," I said to Marcus as we rode through the monastery gate and onto a little Essex lane. "The nuns would give me no information on how you were doing, and indeed, looked horrified when I said I would come over to the monastery to see you. I feared they would secure me to the cot with ropes."

He gave a small grin. "Ah yes. They were determined to imprison us with their kindness. The monks said as much to me as well."

I had spent the three days and nights in the care of a kindly but firm old nun called Sister Assumpta. "I would never see another bowl of thin pottage," I observed with a grimace.

"But good for your soul, eh Mary?"

"Perhaps."

He gave a small chuckle as he rode. I was beginning to understand him a little better; a confident-seeming man a few years my senior, with blonde hair to his broad shoulders and a trim, dark beard. But there was much about him I still could not fathom. And I still needed more information on this mission.

"Tell me of yourself, Master Kytson," I began. "As we are thrown together on this venture. How do you come to be seeking a double for the King's son? Who is he to you, and you to him?"

"I' faith, Mary, that is a big question for a small girl."

This flippancy seemed most condescending. "As Brother Ignatius noted, there is much danger," I snapped. "I need to know. Pray be so good as to tell me."

"Very well." He was silent a moment, no doubt collecting his thoughts. "You asked me to tell you of myself." He nodded, as if confirming that this was the best place to begin. "I am the youngest son of Sir Robert Kytson of Huntingdon, in the Diocese of Ely. At the age of eight, I was presented to the royal court by my father, who was at the time an advisor to Cardinal Wolsey."

"A good position," I observed.

"Indeed so," he replied. "The King had been married to Queen Katherine for around ten years, but she had been delivered of only one surviving child, the Princess Mary. So when the King met a young beauty called Bessie Blount, he made her his mistress. One time, I was at Richmond with my father, and had been placed for the day in the royal nursery, no doubt to keep me from mischief."

"How old were you?" I asked.

He grinned. "I suppose nine or ten. I was something of a wayward child, always cheeking and getting into scrapes." He added a small chuckle. "On that occasion I was making play with the little princess, when Mistress Blount came by. As was my way, I thought it most fun to prank her, so I said I was Prince Franz of Austria, here on a secret visit."

"Tell me she did not believe you?" I exclaimed.

"She did at first, yes. Then my father came to collect me, and my deception was soon revealed."

"So she thought it amusing?"

"In part," he admitted. "But it introduced me to her, and from then on she seemed to find my companionship pleasant."

"A grown woman with a young boy?"

He shook his head. "She was but a few years my senior. Scarce more than a young girl herself. When she was later delivered of the King's son, Prince Henry – named 'Fitzroy', son of a king – I became a member of her household. I have been with her ever since, as a friend, a confidant and a problem solver when required."

"I see." I glanced at his tall, broad frame as he sat easily in the saddle. "And this arrangement has been acceptable, even when she was married?"

He shrugged. "I have always been but a friend, if that is what you mean. Her husband Gilbert Tailboys, Baron Kyme, accepted me as such. When he died three years ago, I was there to help and support his widow."

"So, as her problem solver, Mistress Blount," I paused, "sorry, Lady Kyme, charged you with the substitution of her son when he was kidnapped?"

He smiled. "Nay, she charged me to find him. I was following up a possible sighting when I came upon you fighting like a demon in that tavern in Dedham. Your resemblance to the Prince astounded me – as if you were his very twin. So in that moment I formed the plan to have you take his place. If the boy himself could not be found, then why not use a double in the meantime? As I mentioned back in Dedham, his father the King plans to visit soon."

We rode on in silence a while as I considered this. By sheer fortune I had been recruited to stand in as the Prince by virtue of my close resemblance to him, and the fact that I had been dressed as a boy at the time. Could a seventeen-year-old girl truly play a fourteen-year-old boy?

For his father, the King?

Marcus said, "But to the business at hand. The good monks and nuns have held us up with all their fires, restorative care and suchlike. Fun though that was, we have lost three days in our travels." He glanced across at me. "I was expected back at the London home of young Fitzroy some two days ago."

"I am sure Lady Kyme will understand," I replied.

"Perhaps," he said with a cryptic smile. "But… perhaps not." He hesitated a moment. "The visit by the King is most important, as His Majesty was considering making the boy his heir."

I shifted to get comfortable in the saddle. After three days of enforced bed rest, I did not want to get sore on the ride ahead.

The ride to – what?

To meet with the King, posing as his son.

To deceive the most powerful man in the land?

The enormity of this suddenly hit me, and I nearly pulled my horse up. Had I become soft in the head? Agreeing to such a foolhardy escapade, which could cost me my life if I was discovered?

I swallowed hard. The trees seemed to fade away, to be replaced by a frightening vision.

A cold dungeon. Rats scuttling by my feet. Being led to a hangman's noose.

Why in the Lord's name had I accepted?

For a hundred sovereigns – the reward Marcus had offered? There was no doubt the money would be useful; it could buy me some measure of freedom. But it was not that. On the night when Marcus had proposed this scheme, I had just escaped from Sir Reginald de Courtney and his men. They would have forced me into their cramped little wooden cart and taken me back to Marchington Manor, home of my tyrant of a stepfather. There I would be made to wear constricting gowns and be subservient to his capricious whims. One of which had been to marry me off to de Courtney, a controlling bully of a man.

I grimaced. In the final fight with de Courtney, I certainly had not submitted to his control. Indeed, quite the opposite, and we had ended up sword-fighting on the roof of the same cart he would have put me inside for the journey back to Marchington Manor.

Marcus's proposal had seemed like the ideal opportunity to keep moving and see where fortune might take me. A fortune that was mine and mine alone.

No. There was no going back for me – I was committed to this itinerant life. Committed to making the best of it. Always moving on. Not getting close to any man, but hopefully leaving things better than I found them.

With that thought I urged my horse forward into a trot.

"Come," I said over my shoulder as I passed Marcus, "if we are running behind schedule, then we had best make good speed, had we not?"

—0—

The dark, narrow streets of London were an unwelcome change after the bright leafy lanes of Essex. The tall houses loomed over us on both sides, cutting out most of the sunlight. The channels that ran up the middle of each street stank with their content of human waste, so that I must stop and buy a lavender nosegay to press to my face as we rode. It was also not possible to make any sort of pace. We were continually being held up, such as by men who stopped their carts in the road, women using the street to meet and talk, or small boys shouting as they kicked an inflated pig's bladder to each other.

"We must proceed to the Strand," said Marcus, pushing past a vendor selling bread.

I glanced at the fellow, who looked up as we passed. And nearly fell from my horse in shock.

He had a deep scar down one side of his face.

Just like a man called Jacob Cruddon.

A one-eyed villain who had sworn to kill me.

I swear I gave a small cry as I stared at him. Then I saw that the scar was different, and both his eyes were staring at me in surprise.

I squeezed my horse's sides and caught up with Marcus.

"What ails?" he asked. "I heard you cry out."

"That man was scarred down his face," I said. "I thought it was Jacob Cruddon of Ipswich – a man I fought in the forest in Suffolk after he did me foul." I felt sick in my belly as I recalled Cruddon's evil face with its long scar and dead white eye. "I bested him with my sword, but would not do him to death, for I would ne'er kill a man in cold blood. For all that, I later heard how he would take his revenge on me if he ever saw me again." I shuddered. "I thought it was him we just passed."

Marcus paused, as if considering his response carefully. "Well, 'tis good fortune it was not," was all he said.

Eventually we came to the Lud Gate with its forbidding gaol; passing out of the city and into the area to the west. Here the air was a little clearer and the streets somewhat easier to ride through.

"Nearly there," said Marcus with a grin as we turned into a lane that led down to the river. "The King has granted his son a dwelling on the Strand. Durham House."

"Is that the place from where the lad went missing?" I asked.

He nodded. "It was nigh-on a week ago. The King had allowed the boy to stay a while in his mother's care, so she held a masked ball in his honour, where there was much drinking and revelry. Young Prince Henry was said to be enjoying the wine and the dancing with the others. He took himself to bed at the end of the night. But the next morning his chambers were found empty, and he has not been seen since. His mother is most distraught. Not only does she have the gravest concern for her son, but she also fears the wrath of his father if the abduction is discovered. She would have failed in her care of the boy."

"I see," I said. "And she has no clear knowledge as to who has taken him?"

"Nay," Marcus answered. We rode side by side a little further. Then he added, "There were many men at the masked ball – it could have been any of them.

"There is no-one that she suspects?" If I was risking my neck on this venture, I felt justified in asking for as much information as possible.

"Indeed not."

We continued along the lane in silence. My thoughts turned from the fourteen-year-old boy taken from his house to my part in replacing him.

"At least we can help with the King's visit," I said. I envisaged bowing low before the King; a tall, noble figure. I would rise from my bow and look up at the man who was 'my' distant father.

At least I had some knowledge of such a parent – for although my own stepfather was well known to me, he was indeed a distant, unloving figure.

He had been first cousin to my true father Thomas Fox, and I am told, had bitterly begrudged that my mother loved my father, not him. So when my father died in a tragic hunting accident some six months before I was born, cousin Sir Andrew was quick to step in and marry my mother. But she then died in childbirth – mine – and he blamed me thereafter for his loss.

From that day on, he seemed to make it his mission to vent his anger on me in any way he could. And there is no doubt I did little to help my cause. Maybe if I had been the dutiful daughter, meek and mild, he would have found some sort of acceptance in his heart. But nay – I was a rebellious child, wearing boy's clothes, learning to fight with a sword – and finally refusing his arranged marriage with the odious de Courtney. And he had never found another bride for himself, so I was by default, the lady of the house from a small girl.

Not a role I had accepted, either.

I returned to the subject of King Henry. "And you say the father knows not his son's face?" I asked.

There was a brief hesitation from Marcus. "Not well enough to see the substitution," he muttered. "Although it may be safer to keep the lights dim, withal."

I was about to ask why this level of caution was necessary, when he exclaimed brightly, "Here we are!" The question passed from my mind as we clattered under an archway into a small courtyard. Two liveried servants ran out and took hold of the horses as we dismounted.

"Come," Marcus said, striding towards an oaken door set into a brick wall, "in here."

I followed him inside, and found myself in a wood-panelled passageway with a fine plaster ceiling. I barely had time to appreciate the quality of the mouldings or the panels, before he opened a door at the far end and stood back to let me through.

The door led into an imposing hallway, with two thick columns supporting the roof. Beyond them was a magnificent stairway leading up to a central landing, which branched off left and right under a fine window with coloured glasswork. This showed a quartered coat of arms in the shape of a shield.

"The insignia of Prince Henry, Duke of Richmond," observed Marcus.

A woman in an elegant pale grey silk gown appeared from the right. She paused on the landing, her face almost invisible due to the bright light of the window behind her. "Master Kytson," she said, in a soft, almost musical voice, but one seeming tinged with sadness, "you are indeed well met."

"Lady Kyme," he replied, making a deep bow.

I stepped forward from the shadow of one of the columns and bowed also, as would a boy.

The woman's face lit up and she gave a small joyous cry. "Henry!" she exclaimed. "Oh, Henry! You found him!" She lifted her skirts and almost fell down the stairs in her haste to get to me. She held out her arms. "Henry, oh God be praised! But look at the state of you…"

Then she stopped and stood back with a frown. There was a moment's silence as her eyes narrowed and she stared hard at me. Then she gave another little cry, but there was no joy in this one. "Nay, as the Lord is my witness, I was mistaken – you have longer hair." She looked at Marcus. "Nay, 'tis not my Henry!" She sank down, as if the air had been pulled out of her body, and gave a small sob. "Nay, nay! Not my Henry! He is still lost!"

Then her sorrow seemed to turn into anger. "Master Kytson, you rode at great haste to Ipswich on hearing of a possible sighting of my son, and you return with this…" she glanced back at me, "…this… this dishevelled lad." She frowned. "I understand you not, so pray, explain yourself."

"Indeed, Lady Kyme," Marcus replied. "There was talk of a boy being seen in Ipswich, in a tavern called the Green Dragon. One who answered to the description of your son."

"Oh!" I exclaimed. "I was at the Green Dragon in Ipswich! I spent a night there."

Now it was Marcus's turn to stare at me. "You were in that tavern?" he asked. "Then it was you that was seen and mistaken for Fitzroy?"

I nodded. "So it appears."

"But I discovered no trace of the Prince in Ipswich, so I turned back to London. While you had gone to the Sun Inn at Dedham?"

"Not by my own choice." I agreed, "But, yes I was perhaps but a day ahead of you."

Marcus turned back to Lady Kyme. "So you see, my Lady, the word I heard of a fellow answering your son's description was based on this uncanny resemblance. One that even had you believing it for a moment. So when I found myself in the Sun at Dedham, and saw how close was the similarity, I concocted a plan – to bring the Prince's double here to London to be his stand-in, so we might at least avoid having his father know of the kidnap before we have a chance to find the real boy.

Lady Kyme looked me up and down. "And who is this young man?" she asked, with a small sidelong glance at Marcus. "Does he have a name?"

I was conscious that I presented a sorry figure of a boy. I was still wearing the same doublet, nether-stocks, hose and boots that I had removed from a lad called Tobias Whyte at the Sun Inn. They were now sadly torn, burned and covered in much filth. And smelling most foul – as was no doubt my hair, pulled back and tied behind my head. For all I hated being clothed as a girl, I could see that this was indeed a most sorry state to be presented to such a gracious lady.

Then her eyes narrowed, and she took a pace back, studying me carefully. "Nay, Marcus, I was mistaken. For sure, 'tis no lad. I warrant 'tis a girl?" I said nothing as she walked all round me. "I had thought he spoke with an unbroken voice, but I was mistaken – you have brought me a girl?" Her eyebrows raised. "A girl to play my son for his father? You are fond of being the joker, Marcus, this I know, but a girl? Seriously? To pretend that he has not been taken?"

"I came upon Mary Fox masquerading as a boy in an inn full of rough men, and none saw through her deception until it was pointed out," Marcus said, his tone one of sensibility. "She then proceeded to take on several men with her sword, and better them all." He put a hand on my arm, and I was surprised to feel the heat of it. "I believe she has the courage and the wit needed for this challenge, not just the look of the young prince himself."

Lady Kyme said nothing, so Marcus continued. "She also saved my life these three days past, pulling me from a fire while I slept, moments before the whole building fell in." He nodded briefly and removed his hand. "She saved me from being burned. This is the reason why we are late. We needed three days to recover from breathing in much smoke."

"I see." She looked back at me, and seemed to have recovered her poise. "So pray tell," she said to Marcus, "your plan is to substitute Mary Fox here for my missing son? Do I have that correct?"

Marcus nodded. "With her hair cut, bathed and wearing the Prince's clothing, she will be a perfect stand-in for him."

Lady Kyme stepped up close to me, studying my face. I maintained my gaze into her eyes with some difficulty, for I was not used to being so deeply inspected. Particularly by such a lovely woman, while I was most unclean and no doubt, foul-smelling. She went to my side and peered at my hair, before coming round to my front again.

"I will admit, Marcus, the likeness is uncanny, for all she is a girl and he is a boy. How old are you, girl?"

"I am seventeen," I answered.

"And he is but fourteen," Marcus said.

"Hmm." She stood back, her eyes still on mine. I shifted from one foot to the other, feeling like a prize horse being assessed for soundness. Then Lady Kyme nodded to Marcus.

"It is as if they are twins born of the same womb."

"Then you agree?" Marcus asked.

She nodded slowly "I do," she said. "We will go ahead with this plan.

---0---

Lady Kyme led us into the Great Hall, and we sat.

She looked at me with a small twinkle of amusement in her eye. "Tell me, Mistress Fox, I am fascinated by this tale of a fire, and your rescue of Master Kytson. I have known him this many a year. Why was he so deeply asleep that you must save him? Why had not the heat, or the noise, or even the smoke, already woken him up?" She glanced back at Marcus. "Unless, of course, he had been drinking?" She gave a small chuckle. "For all he is a fine fellow, well-built and possessed of a ready wit, it is well known that even the smallest amount of wine will render him quite senseless. It has oft been remarked."

"We were both weary from riding through the night, Lady Kyme," I replied, not wanting to gainsay her, but also recognising my loyalty to Marcus.

"I see you take his part – that is most admirable," she said. "If somewhat misplaced, now you are in my house."

"Yes, Lady Kyme," I said.

"Good." She gave me a smile, and I felt I had gained her approval. "I am sure you and I will get on famously." She nodded, as if to confirm her decision. "So tell me more of your plan, Marcus."

"It is one born of simplicity, my lady. We clothe Mary as the Prince, so if the King calls to see his son, as he has said he might, we can secure ourselves more time to find the boy."

She frowned. "But…" she began.

Marcus quickly continued, "We need also to school Mary in the ways of the Prince, so she can carry off the deception more effectively."

"Yes, but…"

He raised an eyebrow. "Is there a problem?"

She paused a moment, and I fancied a look of warning had passed between them. "No problem. We will proceed with this plan, Mistress Mary Fox." Her voice then took on a more business-like tone. "So, we have work to do. It is fortunate that the King has not yet paid us a visit; belike it is because his new Queen, Anne Boleyn, takes all his attention. She is with child and has only recently gone into confinement." She smiled. "But if the King legitimises my Henry, as he has said he will, then this new child, assuming it is a boy, will be second in line." She took my hand. "Come girl, we must have you prepared and ready for the King." She glanced at Marcus, and again, I fancied another look passed between them. "We have much to do if you are to convince the King as to who you are."

3

BECOMING PRINCE HENRY

Lady Kyme's face creased into a frown.

"Nay," she said, "Henry holds himself with more confidence than that. Come again into the room, and this time look straight before you with your head held higher."

I went out as instructed, then stepped back through the door, this time making greater effort to carry myself as I had been shown – more like a true Tudor prince. This was better received by Lady Kyme and Marcus, who were seated at the high table and watching my every move.

It was two days after our arrival, and my every waking hour had been under instruction in the fine art of becoming Henry Fitzroy.

But before that could start, I had to have a bath. I was thoroughly immersed in a magnificent copper tub by a servant and scrubbed until raw. The servant was a girl of around my own age, introduced to me as Hannah. I tried to engage her in some conversation, but she studiously avoided my eye and kept quiet throughout, for all I sensed she had many questions she would ask of me.

After she had dried me and gone, Lady Kyme came back. I asked why the girl had been so silent.

"The servants know the Prince has been taken. He is their master, so they are most concerned," she explained, holding out a strip of cloth for me to bind my chest. "But our plan to put you in his place has not yet been shared with them."

"Will they not be confused by my sudden appearance as the Prince?" I asked. "I am sure that serving girl Hannah is no fool, and will quickly conclude the nature of the substitution."

"We will wait until you have had your hair cut and been clothed to an acceptable level, then I will reveal the plan to them. It will be part of their duties to treat you exactly as the true Prince," she said, handing me a man's shift to put on.

Next, the barber had been called. He was an obsequious little man, who removed his cap to reveal he had not a single hair on his own head. This did not fill me with confidence. However, he seemed up to his task, and cut away almost all my locks, then trimmed and shaved what was left. On instruction from Lady Kyme, he coloured my hair to the exact shade of red required, rubbing in a smelly mixture which he told me was of henna, ground walnut shells and vinegar. Finally, there was a nod of approval from Lady Kyme, and we were able to move on to the clothing.

This involved a series of nether-stocks, doublets, sleeves, over-gowns, pairs of hose and shoes being brought out and tried on me. Lady Kyme placed those that fitted and looked correct in one pile. Those that were ill-fitting or received a shake of her head were put in another.

Eventually we had a workable selection of clothing. These were carefully folded and committed to a single chest for future use, apart from the ones I now wore. This was a pale cream embroidered doublet with grey puffed sleeves; a burgundy over-gown with brown fur trim, embroidered nether-stocks, white hose and a pair of duckbill shoes. Across my chest lay the fine gold-link chain that signified the Prince's Dukedom of Richmond, and on my head a black jewelled cap. I must confess the weight of all these items was much greater than expected, and I yearned for the simple garb I had been wearing for so many days before.

But these clothes seemed to achieve the required effect, and Lady Kyme noted several times how uncannily like her son I now looked.

We had then moved to the more detailed instruction. I was shown how Henry Fitzroy held himself; how he walked, how he put his shoulders back and how he would look slightly to the side of any person talking to him. Lady Kyme expressed her surprise at how, after my first few false starts, I settled into the role.

"I grew up with three older brothers, Lady Kyme," I said. "And spent much of my time dressed as a boy, practicing swordplay."

She paused a moment before replying, her head on one side. "You must call me 'Lady Mother', as does Henry," she said.

"Lady Mother," I said slowly, as if the words were another garment to be tried on. Did they fit? I will admit that they sounded false in my mouth. Never having had a mother of my own, I had scarce cause to use such words – something I felt with deep pain each and every day.

"Yes, Lady Mother," I tried again, and maybe this time it sat just a little easier.

I thought this would elicit a smile from her, but instead she frowned. "Henry has started to talk with the deeper voice of a man," she observed. "I would you try and do the same."

But no matter how hard we tried, I could not find the gravelly depths in my voice that the fourteen-year-old prince would have had, without it sounding like a parody of a man. Eventually we agreed to let this part of the role go, and suggest instead to the King that the Prince's voice had not yet broken.

Once this was agreed, I got the smile from Lady Kyme, and even a little tinkle of laughter at the suggestion from Marcus that the Prince was reverting back into his boyhood, now he was being played by a girl.

It all seemed very agreeable, as if a piece of simple playacting by mummers on a stage, and I felt myself being swept along by the conceit. Indeed, I was even starting to think of myself as a fourteen-year-old boy.

Except… Except I could not dismiss the unspoken concern of Lady Kyme when we first met, and which Marcus had seemed to warn her from expressing.

They were hiding something from me, and I needed to know what it was.

Perhaps Lady Kyme's concern had been to do with the King's recognition of his son? I had tried a couple of times over the past days to ask about this, especially when I had been alone with Lady Kyme, but each time she had seemed to sense I was about to broach the subject, and found some reason to lead the conversation elsewhere.

I knew I needed to try a different approach.

Sitting between them at the high table, I poured some wine into a goblet, "How does the Prince take his wine?" I asked. I took an almost lady-like sip. "In small parts like so?" Then I emptied the rest of the goblet in a single gulp, and crashed it back onto the table. "Or does he do it like that, in one?" I looked at them both in turn. "Or does it matter not, for in truth, the King does not know the boy well?"

There was a chilled silence.

"You must tell her, Marcus," Lady Kyme muttered. "She does have a right to know."

My ruse had worked – for all I felt like a rope was now being twisted around my gut.

Marcus cleared his throat as he poured himself some wine and drank it down.

Before he could speak, Lady Kyme said, "The King knows my Henry very well. They have spent much time together – indeed, many more hours than I have enjoyed in the company of my son." She shot a look at Marcus. "I am sorry if you have been told otherwise."

Marcus seemed unusually lost for words, and instead seemed to find the bottom of his goblet most fascinating.

I had a sudden picture of the moment two days earlier as we rode through London towards the Strand, when I had asked him if the King knew his son's face. I had not thought of it at the time, but now I recalled how he had hesitated, muttered something about keeping the lights low, then quickly changed the subject.

And then, of course, how he had stopped Lady Kyme saying anything when I first met her.

This made everything different.

"Then I will be unmasked in an instant!" I exclaimed, my voice coming out like a tortured mouse. "You said the King knew not his son! This whole venture is set to fail!"

Marcus looked up.

"Why did you not tell me this, in Heaven's name?" I demanded.

He glanced at me, and I could see the guilt in his face, like a small boy caught stealing apples.

"I thought it better if you initially believed the King was unfamiliar with the Prince." He cleared his throat again. "Or you would never agree."

"By the Lord," I squeaked, "that is not the point here! The point is that you lied to me, Master Marcus Kytson! When were you planning to tell me?"

"In good time, withal. Once you were settled in the role. But we were delayed by our enforced rest after the fire, so the time to prepare you has been greatly shortened."

I stared at him, and it seemed as if the breath had been knocked from my body. "I saved your life, and you knew all along you had lied to me?" I whispered.

"A small bend of the truth is all," he said, with a cheeky grin.

"This is not supposed to be funny, Marcus," I growled.

The grin disappeared. "I' faith Mary, would you have agreed to this scheme otherwise?"

For once I found myself unable find the words to reply, such was the rage boiling inside me. Marcus had stopped me in the lane that night in Dedham and made me take part in his venture on a wholly false basis. He had assured me the deception would be simple and brief, and even offered me coins for my trouble. How far did his lies extend?

"And the hundred sovereigns you promised," I asked, trying hard to keep my voice calm, "I presume that was also untrue?"

Lady Kyme interjected, "No. Master Kytson was fully authorised to offer that sum for information leading to the return of my son. I consider your participation in his scheme to meet that condition."

Then my anger boiled over. I stood, then snatched off the cap and flung it down. "I refuse it!" I snarled.

"Oh come now, Mary," Marcus exclaimed, putting a hand out, as if to take hold of me. "This is but a minor misunderstanding! In a moment we will all laugh heartily…" I shook his hand away, stepped around the table and marched towards the door.

"This is not a moment for your levity!" I said over my shoulder.

I felt a hand on my arm, then Lady Kyme spun me round.

"Mistress Fox," she said quietly, her blue eyes ice cold. "I understand you have been told a falsehood. That is unfortunate. But it does not change our need. A boy has gone missing – my own son – and I fear he may be in the gravest danger of his life."

"It is more than unfortunate," I answered. "It is dishonest. This venture has enough danger for me too." I rubbed my neck. "And now I hear the King knows his son well, I fear that danger has increased tenfold."

"It is not insurmountable," she answered. "We will say you are unwell, and present you in your chamber, with low light."

That was what Marcus had said. It must be how the crafty chancer had planned it all along. Once he had hooked me like a fish into the scheme he had constructed.

"Then why all this play-acting as to how the Prince walks and talks?" I asked. "Why does that matter?"

"Even in low light it is good for you to have my Henry's manner," she answered. "It is less likely the King will suspect aught."

"There is still danger," I said.

"I know, but we will do all we can to reduce it." She gave me a small smile. "I need you, Mary Fox. I need you to help me. If the King thinks his son is gone, he may well not legitimise him. I cannot have that, and nor can my Henry. So it is not just for me, it is for my Henry as well. We look to you to help us." She nodded. "Once I have my son back, you can leave us and go on your way, knowing you have done a good thing. And, you will have the freedom of a hundred sovereigns in your purse." She gave me a hopeful-looking tilt of her head. "Do you say 'aye', Mary Fox?"

This woman, for all her beauty, was trying to trap me in her awful plot. Should I refuse, cast off these clothes and leave now? I would be no worse than I had been before meeting Marcus. Except that I was now in London, a place where both my stepfather and de Courtney had properties and came often. A place I had vowed not to visit for that very reason.

At least with a hundred sovereigns I could clothe myself well, live well, and have more choices for my life.

And in truth, had I ever shied from danger?

Reluctantly I made a small nod of my head.

I felt Marcus come up behind me, and I turned to see him holding out the jewelled cap. With a scowl at him, I snatched it and put it back on.

"Good show, Mary," he said. "You know it makes sense."

"I do not do this for you, Master Kytson," I muttered, "I do it despite you." I looked up at him. "And if one more untruth crosses your lips, I will abandon this venture in an instant, whatever the consequence."

He put on an air of wounded innocence. "You will henceforth have naught from me but the truth."

"I would that were so," I replied. "I would that were in your nature."

He was about to reply, when there was a knock at the door. Lady Kyme stood back and it opened. A middle-aged man stepped in, dressed in the garb of a house steward.

His face was impassive, as befits a practiced servant – until he caught sight of me, dressed in the Duke of Richmond's clothing. Then his eyes opened wide as he looked at me, then back at Lady Kyme, then me again.

"The master has been found, my lady?" he asked. Then he studied me more closely, and frowned, his eyes searching across my face. Lady Kyme cut in before he could say any more. "Sadly no, Christopher, we have secured the services of Mistress Mary Fox to stand in until such times as the master is returned safely to us." He raised his eyebrows at my name, as if to question how a girl could undertake this task, but then seemed to let his unquestioning duty take over. He took one more look at me, then stood back with a small nod. His face became impassive again.

"I have come to tell you, my lady," Christopher continued, "that the royal barge has just docked. His Majesty the King awaits your welcome."

4

THE MAGNIFICENT KING

Then everything happened very fast.

While Lady Kyme hurried out to greet the King, Marcus rushed me up the stairs to the Prince's chamber. There he helped me strip down to my chemise, put on a man's coif, before I leapt into the bed. There was a moment when I felt the chemise ride up as I clambered up between the drapes, and I am sure he was treated to the sight of my bare bottom, but such was our haste that it seemed to draw no comment from him.

Once I was in the bed and propped up on the bolsters, he closed the heavy curtains at the window and stoked the fire. Then he lit one candle and placed it on a side table some distance from the bed. The room was now so dim that I could scare see much myself.

"There," he said. "Lady Kyme and I have agreed that your illness is to be a severe cold. This has resulted in tiredness and an inability to speak. Too bad we lost time on the journey. It was time that could have been used in teaching you all the shared memories that the Prince has with his father. Without such learning it is better if there is a reason why you cannot talk."

"You will stay to speak on my behalf?" I asked, my voice a panicked squeak. "Do not leave me alone with the King."

"I will not," he answered.

Just then there was a deep growl from outside the room. "Where is my boy?" came a gruff voice. "Suffering a malady? A cold, you say?"

There was a pause, and Lady Kyme could just be heard replying, although it was not possible to make out her words.

"Lost his power of speech, eh?" came the voice.

Marcus and I shot each other wide-eyed looks. I took a deep breath and tried to let it out slowly, to calm my racing heart.

The door opened, and the tallest, broadest man I had ever seen stood silhouetted in the opening.

"Henry, my boy!" he barked. "They tell me you have a contracted a cough and a cold. And lost your power of speech." He advanced a few paces into the room, then stopped. "I will not come closer," he said, "lest it is a contagion."

Lady Kyme came in behind him, and he moved slightly to one side. This meant the candle on the table now illuminated him better and allowed me to see him more clearly.

King Henry VIII was a magnificent man, and it was no playacting that robbed me of the power of speech now I was in his presence. He stood easily, with his gartered legs apart, casual power coming from him like heat from a fire. His fine-shaped legs were clad in silken hose, while his gold and white nether stocks were split by an enormous, jewelled codpiece. I had to tear my gaze from it, lest he realise he was being stared at by a wide-eyed girl, not his fourteen-year-old son. Desperately I forced my eyes upward, past the heavily embroidered doublet, to his face.

The King was possessed of a gingery beard, a small round mouth and dark eyes that were closely positioned either side of his strong, hawk-like nose.

I had never been in such a presence before, and felt as if I should hide away beneath the blankets, lest his piercing gaze see into the heart of my deception.

But I managed to keep myself still, and even raise a small smile.

He seemed to notice Marcus. "You there. Master Kytson, is it not?" he said. "Has a doctor been called?"

Marcus bowed low, then replied, "Indeed, Your Grace. A barber surgeon was called only yesterday."

I refrained from pointing out that the little bald man had been there in his capacity as a barber, not as a surgeon.

"What did he prescribe?" the King asked. "Some balm for the chest and the throat? I am told wormwood is a good remedy. And mint. And honey." He paused, staring at me most disconcertingly. "Shift the phlegm, that is the thing." I smiled back weakly. "I want you better, my boy, for I would have you join me at Whitehall in a week, for a reception. You hear?"

I nodded, but my heart was starting to race again. Join him in a week? That was not part of our plan – for I was expecting to be on my way long before then with a hundred sovereigns in my purse. Not continuing this awful deception.

"Well, I will not tarry here longer while my boy is in his sickbed," the King said. "A week is all, you hear? I want you at Whitehall, hale and hearty as usual. I will see you then." He turned to go, then paused. "I have an announcement to make about your future, my boy, and I would have you there to hear it." Then he marched out, followed by Lady Kyme.

There was a long pause, as I considered what had just passed. I am sure Marcus was doing the same.

"Hmm. This is a pretty pass," he muttered. "You will be fortunate to continue the deception if he sees you in daylight."

"Indeed, Marcus," I replied, unable to stop myself sounding caustic. "Thank you for stating aloud what we both know full well."

"It was supposed to be but a quick deception, 'tis all."

"It is a mess, Marcus," I snapped, allowing my annoyance to show. "In truth, I should have realised that your plan was so thin." I glanced at him in the dim light. "And now we have to work out how the King is to have his son join him, without both of us stretching our necks."

—0—

It was a half hour later, and I was once more fully dressed as Fitzroy. We were sitting in the hall at the high table and supper was being served.

"I think we are being over-cautious," Marcus stated, once Christopher and a servant had withdrawn and we were alone. "We will school you more in the ways of the Prince, such that you can carry off the deception. You will be 'Your Grace' in no time."

"Marcus, we have said it before; the King knows his son too well. He will see it as quickly as did Christopher earlier today," Lady Kyme replied, gesturing towards the door where the man had just left, in a voice that betrayed just how weary she was. "That is no answer."

"I can see only one way out of this," I said. I had been giving it much thought as the conversation had run round in ever smaller circles. "We simply have to find the Prince himself. It is the only solution."

"I would we do that, for sure," said Lady Kyme. "It is my dearest wish, as you know. But we have given this much thought already. We have little or nothing to give us direction in the matter."

"We are not thinking this through properly," I said slowly, as an idea started to take shape. "Why are we not asking the necessary question? Who it is that benefits by the Prince's disappearance?"

Lady Kyme's face fell even further.

"You have a good point, Mistress Fox," she said. "And one I have pondered myself many a time since Henry was taken."

Something that the King had said came to mind. "Next week, the King has some plan for his son that affects his future," I said slowly. "And you have told me that his Majesty plans to make the Prince his legitimate heir." She nodded. "So, belike the event next week is the announcement of the King's plan?"

"Now you say so, that does seem likely."

"So, I say again, who benefits from your son's disappearance?"

They both stared at me, and I could see that they were thinking the same thing as I.

"Exactly," I said, "it is…"

Just then the door swung open and Christopher appeared, carrying some puddings. My words hung in the air like circling hawks while he put the plates down with agonising slowness. Then he crept at seemingly the speed of a snail over to the door, eased himself out and closed it behind him.

We all let out a sigh of relief, as if our collective breaths had been held while the name of the perpetrator could not be said.

It was Marcus who gave voice to what we were all thinking.

"…the Boleyn woman. The Queen," he whispered.

There was a moment's silence, as we all tried to come to terms with this.

Yet it did make sense.

"For sure," I replied. "Queen Anne is about to be delivered of a child, and as you said yourself, Lady Kyme, if it is a boy, her son will become second in line to yours."

"And my boy Henry still cleaves to the true Catholic faith, as does his father in his heart," Lady Kyme said. "While that Boleyn person holds to the heretical Protestant views." She looked at me and shook her head as if in sorrow at this revelation. "So it interests not just the Queen, but all her Protestant acolytes, to keep my son from his birthright."

"And who would have knowledge of the King's plan, such that they could arrange the kidnap?" I asked.

"Again, it is the Queen," answered Lady Kyme. "His Majesty would no doubt have shared his thoughts with her before she went into confinement."

"Exactly," I agreed. "So the King's aim is to make sure he has a legitimate male heir, even if his queen produces a girl, or a stillborn. And if she has a boy, then he will only inherit after my son."

"This is nonsense," said Marcus. "This is the King going against his own Queen?"

Lady Kyme sniffed and shook her head. "The King wants to continue the Tudor line, so he needs at least two sons, if not more, to be certain. And he is the second son himself, becoming king only after his brother Arthur died young. So he knows what it is for that to happen, and would see it as natural to have both an heir and a spare."

"Yet the Queen must see it as an insult?" Marcus said.

"Indeed so," replied Lady Kyme. "So she has taken action."

There was another moment of silence as we considered the full magnitude of this. Could it indeed be true; that the Queen herself was our enemy in this?

"She would not have done this alone," mused Lady Kyme. "She will have had men to carry out her will." She paused, then said, "Like that man who…"

Marcus cut her off swiftly. "We need not dwell on the past, my lady. Let us now look forward."

Lady Kyme looked as if she was a small child reprimanded for stealing comfits. I shot an accusing look at Marcus. Was he lying to me again, and so soon after his promise only to tell the truth? Or, at least, was he keeping the truth from me?

I swallowed hard. I would choose to ignore it – for now. While we had the more weighty matter of finding the boy to discuss.

"We must follow the trail from the Queen," I said. "Find such men – and we find your son." Then I added, "And we have but a week to do it."

5

A PLAN TO FIND THE PRINCE

After much discussion, Marcus, Lady Kyme and I decided the best – indeed the only – way to test our theory that it was the Queen behind the kidnapping, was to try and provoke some reaction to prove it.

Our plan was simple, if rather bold and certainly highly risky.

It was for Marcus and me to find a tavern at Greenwich, near the Palace of Placentia where Queen Anne Boleyn was in her confinement. We hoped to find a place that might be frequented by some of the Queen's men. I would then allow myself to be seen openly as Henry Fitzroy.

The Queen, who no doubt had people able to get messages into her confinement chamber, would hear talk of the boy being seen. This would raise the gravest suspicions in her. If she had otherwise arranged his kidnap, how could the Prince be seen in a tavern?

We would then see whatever reaction this would cause – and maybe gain some further intelligence on the boy's whereabouts.

Marcus and I set off the following morning and arrived in Greenwich later in the day. It was a small town situated beyond the parkland that surrounded the Palace of Placentia. There were but a few streets, some of which had rough tenements and tumbledowns; streets that seemed too poor for their taverns to be frequented by such grand men as Palace servants. After walking the streets further, we came across an area where the houses were larger and kept in better condition. There we found a single tavern by the name of The Feathers that was soundly built and freshly whitewashed.

"This is the most likely," I said.

"As you wish, Your Grace," Marcus replied. He had now taken to addressing me only this way when I was clothed as the Prince, which seemed to amuse him.

It did not have the same effect on me.

We found a table by the fire, ordered some beer, and took in our surroundings.

A number of men came and went as we sat, and a few directed glances our way. But these were mostly merchants or yeomen and not of interest to us. And to be sure, none of their looks in our direction were anything more than normal curiosity.

I glanced idly up at the roof. It was formed of some blackened beams set into the plasterwork in a 'star' pattern, radiating out from a central boss. I drummed my fingers on the table; it reminded me of a similar roof I had seen not so long ago…

Then I recalled it. The Green Dragon in Ipswich. It also had just such a roof construction.

The Green Dragon! Why did that seem to beg a question? Why was that important?

I took a swig of beer to help me think.

Then it came to me.

I observed Marcus over the rim of my cup, forming the question in my head.

"When you heard of the sighting of the Prince at the Green Dragon in Ipswich," I asked, "which we now know was me, why did you give it credence? It could have been any lad with even a passing resemblance to the Prince."

He stared at me blankly. "I gave it credence, Your Grace," was all he would say.

"Oh come now, Marcus," I snapped. "I have said I will brook no more of your evasions and half-truths. Tell me, or I leave this very moment and you will not see me again." He was silent a little longer. "I mean it," I added. "If you truly believe we are in this together, then why must you hold information from me?"

He gave a deep sigh.

"Very well, Your Grace," he said, avoiding my eye. "I will say."

"And no more secrets?"

"Nay. No more."

I waved a hand to signal he should continue.

"You will not like it," he warned.

"Let me be the judge of that.

"Very well. A man was seen a few times outside Durham House in the days before the Prince was taken – so we believe he was most likely involved in the abduction, working with whoever was at the masked ball. A man we understood had connection to Ipswich."

"The man Lady Kyme was going to tell me about?" I asked. "Before you stopped her?"

He raised an eyebrow. "You noted that, Your Grace?"

"I am not a fool, Master Kytson," I said softly. "So do not treat me as one."

"Very well, Your Grace."

"And stop calling me that when we talk alone."

"But you are Prince Henry, Duke of Richmond and Somerset," he said blandly. "Knight of the Garter. I would lack respect if I called you aught else." He regarded me a moment, then added, "Your Grace."

I sighed. "Tell me of the man."

He nodded. "He was an older fellow with grey hair, standing in the street and looking up at the building." He paused. "And he has not been seen since." He gave me a curiously appraising look. "A man you thought you saw selling bread that day we rode into London. A man with a scar down the side of his face, and but one eye."

I flinched, as the full implication of his words hit me like a punch to the belly.

"Jacob Cruddon," I whispered. "And now I think on it, Cruddon was from Ipswich."

"I said you would not like it," he said. "Your Grace."

I stared at Marcus, unable even to reprimand him for his insolence.

In truth I was seeing that awful old scarfaced man standing in the Suffolk forest, but a few weeks before, snarling at me that I was the cause of his son's death. And vowing to kill me on the spot. Then that same man lying prone by a tree after I had bettered him in a sword fight, with my travelling companion Robert Fitzwilliam preparing to run him through. But I had forbidden it – saying we were not going to kill a helpless man in cold blood.

I shook my head slightly. Would I had let him!

And now here was Cruddon once again involved in an evil plot. One that I must stop.

I realised that I would have to tread carefully. Very carefully. For if I ever found myself at Cruddon's mercy, it would not be hard to imagine how he would deal with me.

Then I must ensure I never found myself at his mercy.

Another thought hit me. "You would not tell me of this," I said to Marcus, "for you already knew that Cruddon and I were adversaries. I told you that as we came into London."

He nodded.

I needed to make something clear. Very clear.

"Listen, Marcus Kytson," I said, putting a little steel in my voice. "I am not some simple lubberwort who cannot think, but one who has faced many challenges and has succeeded. I even rescued you from a blazing inferno, by all the Heavens. So stop treating me as a small child who must be cosseted from the truth, but as a grown person who recognises danger and is able to meet it in the face."

"As you say, Your Gr…"

"I mean it, Marcus."

He was about to reply, when something caught his eye. I looked round, and saw three men had entered. As they sat at a table a few away from ours, I noted that the quality and cut of their clothing suggested they were from the Palace.

I glanced back at Marcus, our previous conversation put aside. For now.

I nodded, to signify that I thought them of interest, and he nodded back.

Their conversation was not loud enough for me to hear, but it was intense, and they all leaned in to each other as they spoke. When a serving girl came over with a pitcher and poured their drinks, their conversation stopped, and only resumed once she had moved away. That was enough to raise my suspicions, but then something happened which confirmed them for sure.

There was a pause in their talk, and one of them, a sturdy looking fellow, took a drink. He looked round the room as he did so, and happened to catch my eye.

If I had hoped for a reaction, it could not have been a better one.

The man's whole body jerked as if he had been punched in the belly. Drink sprayed out from his mouth, covering his fellows.

The man's companions followed his wide-eyed gaze and they too, reacted with horror at the sight of me. Immediately they pushed back their chairs and almost fell over each other in their haste to get out.

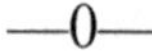

A stout oak tree stood close to the servant's entrance to the Royal Palace of Placentia, Greenwich.

Marcus and I were in the shadows behind the trunk. I had changed into a plain doublet and cap, matching Marcus's attire, so we looked to be two men of no particular note.

But we were two men who had their eyes firmly fixed on the wooden door across the way. We were watching like hawks to see if anyone came out who seemed to be about the Queen's business. Our thinking was that the three fellows we had alerted in The Feathers would have got a message to the Queen, saying that the Prince had been seen.

We hoped she would send them, or possibly some other of her men, to check on the real Prince. Which meant we could follow them to see where they went.

"They may go to the right and down to the river," Marcus suggested, "or left towards the town. What if men go in both directions?"

"Then we must separate as well, and each follow alone," I replied, touching the hilt of the knife I had in my belt. I peered towards the busy river, teeming with so many boats plying back and forth that the opposite bank could scarcely be seen. "There are several wherries tied up," I said, "with their boatmen aboard. So whoever follows them by river will have a wherry available."

"Hmm," he replied. I was not sure if he was agreeing with me or not, but after the revelation about Cruddon I had neither the time nor the energy to ask the question.

There were a few minutes of silence as we both watched the door.

I wondered if we had guessed correctly. Was Queen Anne truly behind the disappearance of the young prince? If the child she carried was a boy – and we must assume it was – then King Henry's plan to legitimise his first-born son would disinherit the baby she carried. And a woman who could entrap a king had proved she was devious enough for anything.

The door opened.

We shrunk back into the shadows, watching closely. Two men came rushing out. I recognised them as the sturdy fellow from the Feathers and one of his companions, for all they were now dressed in drab black.

The companion turned left, and started walking briskly towards the town, while the sturdy man turned right and made his way towards the river.

"To the town," I hissed at Marcus. He nodded, and started after the companion.

I pulled my cap down, then set off towards the river, trying to keep at least one tree away as I followed.

The man was already on the slipway as I rounded the corner of a small hut at the top. He paused halfway down and looked back. I shrank into the shadows, trusting that he had not seen me. When I looked out again, he was walking quickly down the slipway. He jumped into the back seat of the first wherry. The boatman untied his craft, settled in his place and started rowing into the flow of other boats proceeding up the river.

I ran down after him, and jumped into the next wherry.

"Upriver, boatman," I snapped, in my best growling voice. It must have sounded convincing, for he muttered, "Aye, master", before untying and pushing away into the stream.

I kept my eyes firmly on my quarry, concerned not to lose him among the multitude of other wherries plying their trade on the Thames.

The light was becoming flat, with grey clouds scudding in from the west.

"Storm coming," observed the boatman between strokes.

"Aye," I muttered, glancing briefly up again at the clouds, before resuming my observation of the wherry ahead.

"Where do you want to go, master?" the boatman asked. "Queenhythe? Southwark? Blackfriars?"

"I know not for now," I replied. "I will say when necessary." He did not answer.

As we made our way upriver, I began to think my quarry was drawing away. "Faster, please," I said. "If you are able." I glanced at the man's red face. "I will pay double the fare."

From the corner of my eye I saw his eyebrows raise, but it had the required effect, and he increased his pace. Soon we were gaining on the other wherry, and were now but four or five lengths behind it.

The boatman glanced back over his shoulder, no doubt to help him steer his way through the traffic, then he said, "I warrant you are giving chase, young master?" He took a few more strokes, before adding, "The fellow who took the wherry moments before you?" I said nothing, so he continued, "I know him. He oft hires one of us to go upriver, or return him to the Palace." He made some more strokes, then added, "Robson. Noah Robson." Despite my concern to keep my attention fixed, I glanced at him in enquiry. "I know the man," he explained. "Why do you chase him?"

I thought fast. "I know not," I said. "I am ordered by my master."

He nodded, as this was as expected. "Ours not to ask questions," he agreed.

"Where does he go?" I asked. "This Noah Robson?"

"Many places," he answered. "He goes mostly on the Queen's business."

"And lately? In the last few days?"

"Blackfriars, mostly."

I glanced at the man again. "You are free with your information fellow," I observed. "Yet he is a regular passenger and perhaps more deserving of your loyalty. Why so?"

He gave a small chuckle. "I like him not. He has a sharp tongue, and pays the fare with bad grace. While you, young master, have an honest face, for all you growl at me like a small dog. And you have offered double fare."

6

THE OLD HOUSE IN BLACKFRIARS

Noah Robson's wherry pulled up to a small jetty at Blackfriars.

He jumped ashore and was already walking briskly between two large buildings just beyond the riverbank as we landed. I thanked the boatman and leapt ashore myself, leaving him smiling and admiring the two penny coins I had pressed into his hand in payment. Double the usual fare.

Keeping a close eye on Robson, I scuttled from one shadow to the next. I had to stop still in a doorway at one point as he turned round to look behind, but was able to continue once he went forward again.

After a few minutes he came to an old house at the end of a row. It was poorly built from daub and wattle, and covered with a dirty render that was cracked and broken in many places to reveal the straw inside. It was a foot or two apart from the slightly less decrepit house beside it, leaning away like an elderly drunk.

I watched from my hiding place in an alleyway across the street as Robson went up the four or five steps to the front door and knocked. The door creaked open and he slipped inside.

I studied the building. Could the Prince be held inside? I desperately needed to see what was in that house. I kicked a stone in the dirt at my feet in my frustration.

Should I try and gain entry unseen so I could explore? The door looked poorly fitted, and could easily be pushed in. Would it open directly into the parlour, where Robson and his host could still be sitting? This would make my discovery inevitable.

I looked up and down the street. The houses all looked poorly maintained. The men and women who walked along were dressed in the basest of garb. My doublet, although plain and unadorned, was clearly well cut. My shoes were finely made and reasonably new. They were quite out of place in this basest of streets. If I were to explore around the house dressed as I was, it would cause curiosity in anyone passing by, for sure.

I kicked the stone again, taking my anger out on this inanimate object. A cloud of dust blew up and settled on my toe.

Dust!

Quickly I kicked my shoes into the dirt, and even found a small muddy puddle to make them even more filthy. Then I whipped off my cap and worked some of the mud into it with my hands, pausing only to smile weakly at a goodwife who was walking by. She smiled back, but with concern, as if she thought me soft in the head. After she had hurried off, I ducked into the shadows between two buildings and quickly smeared a few more handfuls of mud on my doublet and on my legs, then a goodly amount onto my face. It made a rough approximation of a few days' stubble.

I took a breath as I emerged into the daylight. As the house was at the end of the row, all three sides were easily accessible, and even the narrow passageway between it and the next house could be passed by one as slight as me.

I made my way across the street, slouching with my shoulders forward and my head down. To any observer, I would have been just another fellow down on his luck and wandering about without aim or purpose. I even gave the stone a final kick for good measure.

A small blackened iron grating was set into the wall a little way along the passageway. It was a half-circle in shape, and had a few tendrils of ivy growing up the bars. Possibly the window of a cellar?

Noting this as of interest for later exploration, I carried on around the rest of the house.

The side facing the far street had but one ground floor window and no door. I slouched further as I passed the window and gave the briefest glance within, but it was too dark to see anything.

As I came to the corner, a swarthy looking fellow suddenly appeared and strode towards me from the other side. I turned immediately and started walking away, as if this had been my intent all along. But I kept my hand close to the hilt of my knife, in case he was one of Cruddon's men.

His steps echoed behind me as I carried on up the street.

With luck he was just a man going about his business, which happened to be in the same direction as me.

With luck.

I walked faster, anyway.

His steps sped up as well. With my heart starting to pound, I increased my pace again.

So did he.

An alleyway came up on my right. At the last moment I ducked in and stopped, standing in the shadow facing the street. My knife was now held ready, hidden behind my back.

Almost immediately he turned into the alley. He stopped, facing me with the grey light behind him. I could just make out that he was a thick-set man in a leather jerkin and breeches.

"What is your business, fellow?" he snarled.

"None of yours," I growled back, assuming my best air of defiance.

"Nay," he replied. "I think it is. You were hanging around somewhere you had no right to be."

He took a step towards me. I took one back, deeper into the shadows.

"I can be any place," I said. "I have no need of your permission to be on a street."

He looked me up and down. "You have the voice of a youth," he said. "Art naught but a runt. Yet for all you are dirty, your clothes look well-cut." He took another step forward. "Who sent you?"

I gripped the hilt of my knife. "I know not what you mean," I said, taking two more steps back.

"You lie," he snarled.

His body seemed to tense, and I knew he was about to make a move.

I snapped round so my back was to the wall and whipped my knife out, just as he came at me. There was a glint of his blade above. I tried to raise my own, but he put a hand to my wrist and pushed it away with strength that made me cry out.

"Aye, squeal if you may, spying little runt," he snarled. "It will be the last sound you make."

His blade swept down towards my chest.

It would have pierced my heart if I had not bent my knees and twisted away at the last moment. Instead his arm crashed onto my shoulder, causing me to cry out again.

He grunted in seeming annoyance and stepped back, still holding me tightly.

His blade raised again.

Before he could strike, I twisted my whole body round, using his hold on my wrist as a pivot and kicking out my legs as I spun.

My foot caught him on the shin, causing him to overbalance and fall forward.

This left me free of his grip as he crashed to the ground like a felled oak.

I leapt onto his back and pressed my knife point to his neck.

"Now it is my turn to ask the questions," I said. "Who do you work for?" He was silent. "Is it Jacob Cruddon?" He did not answer, so I pushed my point into the flesh behind his ear, just enough to draw a little blood. "Is it Cruddon?" I repeated.

He gave a small gasp. "Aye."

"And who does that one-eyed man serve?" He shook his head very slightly. "Tell me," I insisted. "Who?" He shook his head again, so I pushed a little harder. I wanted information from this man, but not necessarily to harm him. "Tell me," I repeated.

Then suddenly he rose up, as fast as a bolt fired from a crossbow. It was so swift and unexpected that I was thrown through the air like a piece of chaff.

I landed with a jarring crunch on my back.

"Think to better me, runt?" he said triumphantly.

He dropped down on top of me. All the air left my body in the instant his weight landed, and there was a sharp pain in my ribs. I thought they must surely be broken.

With another yell, he raised his knife, and this time I could not roll away.

I was trapped beneath him.

I closed my eyes, expecting to feel the bite of the steel, and know that my life would soon be ebbing away.

But the blow did not come.

I looked up.

There was a deep frown on his coarse features. Then he gave a cough, and a bright gobbet of blood ran into his beard.

"Runt!" he exclaimed. "What have you done?"

With a sigh, he sank down on top of me, pinning me to the ground.

With another cry, this time of disgust at the weight and the rotten smell of him, I pushed with all my strength until he rolled away enough that I could get out from under.

I lay still to catch my breath a moment, then made a cautious prod of my ribs. Thankfully they seemed sore, but not broken.

I struggled to my feet, and looked over at the man.

He was on his side, and now I saw why he had not been able to kill me.

The handle of my own knife stuck out between his ribs.

The metallic smell of hot blood filled the alleyway. I looked at my hand. It was covered in his gore.

I must have had my blade held up as he came down, and it had buried itself in the man's chest with the force of his own descent.

My stomach clenched and I thought I would spew.

There was a groan. His eyes fluttered open.

I crouched down beside him. Maybe there was the smallest chance I could still get the answer I so desperately sought.

His eyes seemed to focus on me.

"Who does Cruddon work for?" I whispered. "Tell me." He was silent, staring with a pinprick gaze. "Is it the Queen?"

But he made no answer, as he drew one laboured breath after another.

Then his eyes went distant again and rolled up into his head.

With a final rasp, his breathing stopped.

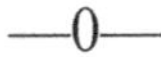

I took a time to restore my own breath, and to assure myself that my ribs were definitely bruised not broken, before struggling to my feet.

But my pain was nothing compared to that of the man beside me, gone to meet his maker – or more likely, Satan – because of me.

Thou shalt not kill.

I offered a small prayer to Jesus, asking for forgiveness.

Meanwhile, I needed to conceal the body. No doubt a local constable would be less forgiving than the Lord.

There were some old hessian sacks in the alleyway, so I used them to cover the body as best I could. I tucked it deeper into the shadows, then wiped some more of the blood from my hand on the sacking. I also relieved the body of the knife and scabbard, which I added to my belt alongside my own.

I peered cautiously out of the alleyway, but there was no-one looking in my direction. Indeed, with the clouds coming in, it seemed as though rain would be coming soon. People appeared more concerned to get inside than bothering about a strange young man emerging from an alleyway. I stepped out and made my way back to the old house.

I judged it to be around half an hour since I was last there, so it was unlikely that the man I had killed would yet be missed. My guess was that he was a guard, and had been hiding somewhere around the house to see off any threat.

Such as me.

It was galling that I was not able to confirm our assumption that it was Queen Anne Boleyn herself behind the kidnap. But for sure, the man chosen to carry it out was none other than my old enemy Jacob Cruddon! When I had left Cruddon unconscious in the Suffolk forest, I never believed I would see the evil one-eyed villain again. Sir Reginald de Courtney had told me that he had thrown Cruddon's unfeeling carcass across a horse and taken him back home to Ipswich, by which time the old man was awake, and vowing to get his vengeance on me.

I stopped in the street. Could Cruddon have recovered soon enough to make his way to London, be recruited to the scheme, then kidnap young Fitzroy?

Or more likely, he had already been recruited as a known rogue, probably on recommendation as a man who would do evil if required, and all that remained was to travel to London and execute the plan. Meantime, had he happened to be in Suffolk looking for extra mischief when our paths crossed?

Once a thief, always a thief.

And an opportunistic one at that.

Either way, it seemed that it was Cruddon once again standing in my way with evil intent.

I arrived back at the house, and looked carefully about. There were still a few people in the street, but none appeared to be looking my way, so I slipped into the dark narrow passageway between the two buildings.

The iron grating was close by, so I crouched beside it, listening intently.

There was no sound. After a few minutes, I slowly put my face to the edge of the aperture, and looked in.

At first it was hard to make anything out in the darkness, but after a few moments my eye grew accustomed. It was a bare cellar, with a person sitting on a bench by a damp-streaked wall. I shifted slightly to get a better view. It was not possible to discern anything, other than it was a male figure with a hose-covered leg and a heavy man's shoe.

A small dark shape moved across the floor, and the foot made a desultory kick at it, but it seemed not to respond. It stopped by a pool of black water and seemed to be drinking. From its size and shape, I took it to be a rat. Another joined it at the pool, then they both scuttled away.

There did not seem to be anyone else in the cellar, so I prepared to make a soft call to get the occupant's attention. But just as I was about to do so, there was a creaking sound and light flooded into the room as the door opened and a man entered carrying a tray and a candle.

"Some cheese and ale, young master," the man said, his voice dark and coarse.

"How long must you keep me here?" said the boy in a wheezing, just-manly voice.

Henry Fitzroy?

The boy broke into a fit of thin coughing. "This place is damp and cold, and fit only for the rats," he said eventually. "I feel it has gone to my chest. My father the King shall know of this, and he will hang, draw and quarter you for sure."

My father the King? Then this was Prince Henry, Duke of Richmond for sure.

I had found him!

"Do you want these victuals, boy?" asked the man. "I am minded to take them away. I have told you before to hold your tongue, lest I gag you again."

The Prince broke into a further fit of coughing. Then he took a couple of laboured breaths and said quietly, "I apologise, Master. Pray leave them."

There was the sound of a tray being placed on a table. The gaoler said. "I know not how long you are to be held, but for sure at least another week. I am under strict instruction to keep you until then."

"Why? Under whose instruction?"

"I have said before, I am not at liberty to tell you that. Now eat your food and keep your tongue still. Or perhaps I might cut it out." There was a moment's silence, then the door closed and a key turned in the lock. I listened hard for the sound of it being withdrawn, but felt sure that did not occur.

I waited a short while longer, then put my face to the grille.

"Your Grace?" I called softly. "Prince Henry Fitzroy, Duke of Richmond?"

There was an immediate sound of him getting up off his bench and coming towards the grille. There was also the sound of a chain clinking as he moved.

"Who is there?" he called, a rising sound of hope in his voice.

"My name is Mary Fox," I replied. "And I have come to get you out."

7

STORM SENT BY GOD

The first few drops of rain fell as I studied the iron grating in the little moonlight that filtered down into the alleyway.

Assuming it was set into the rough daub and wattle of the building, then surely it would be easy to pull out?

I positioned my feet on either side to give purchase, grasped the bars and settled back to pull.

But even with the most strength I could find, it was not enough to move the bars. I tried to pull harder, gritting my teeth with the effort, feeling as if the sinews across my back would tear apart, but it was still not sufficient.

I must soon abandon the attempt, lest I break open my shoulders.

"I am sorry, Your Grace," I whispered down, "but I need to find a different way to get these bars off."

"Is there no other way out?" he asked. "By the door?"

"I fear the key is still in the other side," I answered. "No, it has to be this window. I must get these bars out of their place. Then I can come in, and help you escape."

"You have all night, Mary Fox," he hissed back. "The man who holds me is unlikely to come again before first light."

I looked at the bars once more, and in my mind, compared their place in the house to the position of the front door – and presumably, therefore, to the level of the parlour.

"I warrant I could use my knife to work them free," I observed, "but I will be but a few inches from the other side of the wall just below the parlour. It would be impossible not to be heard by those in the house."

Just then there was a flash of lightning, and a few seconds later, a crash of thunder. Then there was a pause, and it was as if the heavens opened. A solid curtain of rain started to fall from the sky.

A sign from God?

Any sound of my knife in the wall would easily be masked by the thunder and rain. Feverishly I started digging into the wall around the bars, using the guard's knife. It was thicker than my own blade, and no doubt better for the task.

Making sure to time each gouge into the wall with a rumble of thunder or a heavy fall of rain, I soon exposed more and more of the bars higher inside the wall. They ran up half as far again inside the wall as their visible length, but it took me another hour of carving before I reached their top edge. By this time I was thoroughly soaked through, as much as if I had been thrown into the river.

But I had the bars exposed, so again I put my feet either side and waited for a flash of lightning. Then there was the thunder. As it crashed and rolled across the sky, I took the strain and pulled for all I was worth.

The bars moved.

I waited for the next roll of thunder, and pulled again.

This time they moved further.

One final blast of thunder. One final pull. With a creak and the cracking of the plaster at the base, they came away completely from the wall above.

Now the bars were lying down away from the opening. Cautiously I put my head in and addressed the Prince. "I will drop down, Your Grace," I said, "then we will get you away from this place."

"I am chained," he called back, rattling it with his hand.

"One thing at a time," I muttered, as I turned and put my legs into the aperture, then wriggled past the bars, eased myself over the edge and dropped down beside him.

There was a moment as I observed this boy, that I had been schooled so comprehensively to impersonate. It was hard to see his face in the near darkness, but we were of a similar height, and I could tell that his hair was cut the same as mine, if a little longer.

He, too, stared at me, as a flash of lightning gave a brief and sudden light to the room. "You remind me of someone," he whispered.

"Aye," I muttered. "But let us discuss this when we are away from here."

"Indeed." He held up his hand, with a heavy cuff on his wrist and a chain hanging from it. "This will need to be cut away." The chain went to a ring attached to the wall, securing him to the room.

I picked up one of the links and studied it closely in the dim light. As I hoped, it was simply bent into shape, with an unfinished join; one that could possibly be prised apart.

"Move to the bench," I said. He nodded and went over as instructed. "Sit," I said, "and put your hand out." I took out the knife and held it over his hand.

"What are you going to do?" he gulped, staring at the blade. "Not cut off my hand?"

"Nay," I answered. I gave him a grim smile. "Unless, of course, that becomes absolutely necessary."

I selected a link that lay on the bench, and carefully placed the tip of the blade inside, with one edge against the join. "Your shoe," I ordered.

Wordlessly he removed it and handed it over. It was a fine piece of manufacture, with a solid wooden heel. I held it above the knife hilt and waited. Eventually there was a flash of lightning. A few moments later came the thunder, and under its cover I managed two solid blows on the hilt.

Each one caused the knife to go deep into the bench, and with it, the link to open up. But only by a hair's breadth.

The next clap of thunder allowed me to open it up more, and finally, on the fourth, I had it opened enough to work the blade right in.

I gave a twist, and the blade snapped in half.

"What now?" he asked, staring at the broken blade.

"Again," I said, putting the remaining tip again into the gap and twisting until it was open wide enough to allow the next link to pass through.

I threw the knife to one side and pulled the next link out. Now he was free.

"Come, Your Grace," I snapped, grabbing his wrist after he had replaced his shoe. "Let us be away."

We ran to the window, and I made a cradle of my hands. He stepped in, and I lifted him up. He grasped the bars and slipped through. Then he turned round and leaned back in, extending his hands down. I grabbed them, and walked myself up the wall, until I could grasp the bars and pull myself out.

As the rain continued to fall in a torrent, we ran together out of the alleyway and into the night.

—0—

We found a wherry at Blackfriars, and I commanded the boatman to take us to the Strand.

It was a different fellow to the one who had brought me earlier from Greenwich, and he held his silence as he pulled into the fast-flowing stream, not commenting on the two bedraggled and soaking boys in the back of his craft. I caught him looking from me to the Prince and back with a slightly puzzled expression. No doubt he thought us to be twin brothers. Certainly with our haircuts we could easily be mistaken as such.

The only difference was that the Prince was clearly suffering after his confinement in the damp cellar, and could not take more than a few breaths without coughing. It was a deep, chesty cough, and he wiped his mouth with his sleeve a few times after, as if there had been a little phlegm brought up.

"Art well enough to get home, Your Grace?" I said in his ear, against the noise of the rain.

He nodded wide-eyed at me and I wanted at that moment to put my arm about this suffering boy and draw his head to my chest, giving him comfort and reassurance that all would now be well. He was so young and vulnerable; and so cruelly used through no fault of his own. But one glance at the boatman, who was now frowning at me, convinced

81

me that he would see this not as an older girl giving solace to a younger boy, but as two boys possibly displaying an affection that went against the bible's teachings. So I resisted, and stared ahead at the lights of the other wherries, merchant vessels, carracks and small ships plying their trade up and down the Thames. There were many of them, even at this late hour.

Eventually we came to a small jetty at the end of the Strand. The boatman jumped onto it and secured his craft as I scrambled out and held my hand to the Prince. He took hold and I pulled him up, as the boatman raised his lamp above us to light the slippery planks of the jetty.

My heart sank as I caught sight of red streaks on the Prince's sleeve, but I said nothing. The sooner we could get him into bed and seen by a doctor, the better.

But then and there I vowed to get even with the man who had captured and imprisoned him, Jacob Cruddon.

It was bad enough he had kidnapped the King's only son, but to have the boy held in such a cold, unfitting place that it had rendered him deeply unwell – that was something I would like to have out with the one-eyed old villain.

With that resolution hardening in my heart, I led the Prince stumbling along the muddy street to the door of Durham House.

After ringing the bell pull and beating on the door with my fist a few minutes, it opened. Christopher stood there with a lamp, wearing a nightshirt.

At first he looked as if he was about to admonish me for beating on the door so late at night, but then he seemed to recognise me and put his hand to his chest. "Mistress Fox!" he exclaimed. Then the Prince coughed, and stepped out from behind me. The man's eyes looked as if they might jump from his head. "Master!" he squeaked. "Your Grace! Oh Heavens be praised! You are come back to us!" He turned and shouted back into the house, "Mistress! Lady Kyme! Come quick, by the Lord, come quick!"

Lady Kyme must have also been wakened by my banging, as she appeared almost immediately, floating towards us in a pale housecoat like a dishevelled spectre.

Then she gave a most un-ghostly cry. "Henry!" She pushed past Christopher, holding up her lamp, "Oh my Henry!"

She thrust the lamp into my hands so she could sweep her son up into her arms. She held him to her chest and swayed back and forth as she stroked his hair. "Henry, oh my Henry!" she crooned. "I have you back!"

After a few moments, he once again gave a harsh cough, one that seemed to come from deep in his chest. She held him away from her, the relief at his return seeming now to turn into concern. I raised the lamp so she could see him, and she frowned. "Art unwell, Henry?" she asked.

"He was held in a damp cellar," I explained. "I fear the cold has gone to his chest."

I feared it could be worse still. There was a large streak of blood down the front of Lady Kyme's housecoat.

"We must get you into bed, Henry," she said. "Come, let us first get you out of these wet clothes."

I put my arm around the boy's waist. There was a clink as he moved his wrist, which still had the metal cuff and remains of the chain attached.

Lady Kyme gave a little cry and her hand flew to her mouth as she stared at his hand. "Oh Heavens!" she breathed, "Oh my Henry, you were chained!"

"Mary Fox broke the link so I could get away," he whispered. "After she had worked the bars off the window with her knife during the storm." He coughed again.

We followed Lady Kyme up to her son's chamber, which until that morning had been mine. The Prince was hardly able to walk and it took all my strength to keep him on his feet as we ascended the stair.

"Some hot honey and milk," she ordered Christopher over her shoulder.

While Christopher went to fetch this, she said to me, "Mary, you, too must change into dry clothing. I will see you in the parlour shortly."

I nodded, grabbed a few clothes from one of the chests, and went down to the parlour.

The fire there was still smouldering, so I fed it with some small logs to get it going again, then pulled off the wet clothes and struggled into the dry ones.

I was just fastening the doublet when she came back in, carrying a tray with two goblets and a carafe. She put them down, then stood back and looked me up and down a moment.

"Mary, I… I…" she began, then she faltered to a stop. "Mary…" she tried again, before taking a deep breath. "Mary, I do not think I have the words in my head to thank you enough for what you have done."

Suddenly it was me in her arms; being pulled against her chest as she held me so tight that I could scarcely breathe. "You are the bravest, most amazing girl in the whole of

God's Kingdom," she said in my ear. "Thank you, thank you, thank you!"

After a few moments she let me go and stood back, a tear glistening in her eye.

"That you found my son, and you brought him back to me – that should be enough," she said, "but I would know more. Pray tell me, how you found him and how you secured his release. Was anyone hurt in the rescue?"

I thought of the man in the alleyway and decided that news of him was best kept out of my tale. But I told her of the success of our stratagem in The Feathers tavern, and my pursuit of Noah Robson to the house in Blackfriars.

"And you are certain this man works for the Queen?"

I nodded. "I was told by the boatman, who is oft hired by this Noah Robson, that he is employed on the Queen's business. So when he saw me in the tavern and thought me the Prince, he went straight to the Palace at Greenwich where the Queen is in confinement, and from thence I followed him to check on the real Duke in his imprisonment."

I explained how I had managed to release the Prince from captivity.

"The storm was truly a gift from God," she observed. "The Lord is for sure on our side in this matter."

"Indeed," I said, then paused a moment. Something else needed to be told. Something that perhaps made some sense of the kidnap. "I overhead the gaoler telling the Prince that he must stay a prisoner for at least another week." I looked her in the eye. "That must be to keep him away from the King at Whitehall declaring him his legal heir."

She gave a thin smile. "Which is as the Queen wants." The smile became a frown and she rubbed her temple a moment. "But now we have Henry back, will he be fit to attend? It is less than a week away, and he coughs greatly from the chill he has developed from being in that awful cellar these past days. As his mother, I would not have him leave his bed in such a short time."

I glanced at the streak of blood still on the front of her housecoat. I feared it was not just an ordinary chill, so I pointed at it. She looked down, and gasped as she lifted the cloth to see it better.

"A doctor is needed with the greatest urgency," I said quietly. "As well as a locksmith to remove that awful cuff."

8

THE KING'S ORDER

It was the following morning.

The doctor had thankfully come as soon as he was called, and hurried straight up to see the Prince. He was the same little bald man who had cut my hair, only this time he had a red cap on, to signify he was here on the business of health.

Christopher and I stayed in the hall with a pitcher of wine and some cold meats. We hardly conversed; both of us too concerned for the sickly boy upstairs.

Around half an hour later we both jumped up as the doctor and Lady Kyme came down. I glanced at Christopher, and it seemed that we had the same thought – that this was bad news. Lady Kyme looked almost white, as if all the blood had been drained from her face.

"The doctor is of the opinion that Henry has contracted the consumption," she whispered.

The doctor nodded, twisting his cap in his hands. "I am most sorry, but he shows all the signs. He has a persistent cough that brings up bloody phlegm. It seems he is thinner than before, even more than would be expected from his imprisonment, and he sweats uncontrollably. I have put my hand to his head and he burns hot."

"And he has little appetite," added Lady Kyme.

"That as well," added the doctor.

"What do you propose to do for him?" I asked.

"I have prescribed garlic steeped in hot water, with hot milk and honey for his cough," he replied. "Those can help keep the fever down so his body might recover." He looked Lady Kyme. "Otherwise we are in God's hands." He bowed at each of us, replaced his cap. "Please be assured a full recovery is possible, and I would hope for it in one as young and strong as this boy. I shall return on the morrow to check, and daily thereafter."

After he had left us, there was a long silence, with each of us lost in our own thoughts.

Mine were that the boy being so sick seemed deeply unfair. We had managed to release him from captivity, but at what cost? Cruddon had kept him in such poor conditions that his health had suffered. Again, I cursed Cruddon for being so foul a knave; a double-crossing, thoughtless cruel villain. In truth the man was more like a maddened cur, and that was how he must be treated.

"The doctor said recovery is possible?" Lady Kyme whispered, breaking into my thoughts.

"We are in God's hands, madam," Christopher said. "With God's good grace, then yes, perhaps."

She looked at me. "And God sent the storm to enable you to get my Henry out," she said. "That must mean God favours Henry in this?"

I nodded slowly. "That would seem to be so, my lady." If it gave her hope, how could I take it away?

"Then we must pray to God for his recovery," she said, sounding a little brighter. "And I am sure He will hear our prayers." She looked at us both, hope written across her face.

"We will do so, madam," agreed Christopher. "I shall instruct the household to pray for the master daily, and we will pray for him in church at every attendance."

"And not forget the cures prescribed by the doctor," I added, and they both nodded.

There was another silence, and I decided it was time I could ask a question that had been on my mind since we had returned to Durham House.

"At the Palace, Marcus and I saw two men coming out," I said. "I followed Robson and was fortunate that he led me to the Prince's prison, but Marcus followed the other man towards Greenwich." I poured some wine for Lady Kyme. "Has Marcus returned?" I asked, handing it to her.

She shook her head before taking a drink. "Nay, he has not been seen since you both went off yesterday morning." She gave me a slight smile. "I am sure he can take care of himself, and we will see him back here soon."

Privately, I was not so sure of this. His natural assurance and cynicism could make Marcus easy to spot. But I did not feel it was the right time to mention this. Instead I nodded in agreement. "I am sure."

Another silence.

Suddenly Lady Kyme asked, "What if that man comes back here, to try and recapture Henry?" She was studying the bottom of her wine goblet. "What then?"

"Just let the mangy cur try," I said. "I will give the one-eyed old bastard what he deserves."

She glanced up. "You say that with feeling, Mary Fox." She frowned. "I understand you know this fellow already? Marcus said something to that effect."

"Aye, I do know Cruddon," I replied. "He and I have fought once before. I bested him then, and he vowed to get his vengeance on me."

"Oh my Lord!" she exclaimed. "Why did you fight?"

I tapped my finger on the table a moment. Should I share with her what I had done? She was looking at me curiously, and I decided she should know the truth.

"I caused the death of his son," I said simply.

"By the Heavens, Mary!" she gasped. "You killed a man? A mortal sin! How?"

"It was not my intent; he ran onto my sword," I replied. "After robbing some friends of an object most precious to them. Which I was then able to restore to its rightful place."

"Then he was a brigand, like his father?"

"That he was," I agreed.

She frowned. "Then he deserved his fate? In the name of justice?"

I nodded, not totally sure if she was approving of my actions or otherwise.

She chewed her lip as she stared at me. "You have a remarkable power to do good," she said eventually, and I let out a small breath of relief. "You were doing God's work. Were your friends grateful for your help?"

"They were," I said. "I was offered a hand in marriage."

"Oh," she frowned. "And you refused?"

I nodded. "It did not suit me."

"Oh," she repeated. "Then their loss was our gain."

I was about to reply, when the door opened with a loud crash.

We all looked round as a man marched in, with the royal standard on his tunic. Two more liveried men entered behind him.

"My lady Kyme, His Majesty the King is here," the man announced. "To see his son."

—0—

Seen in the light, the King seemed even taller and wider than I remembered from previously. His presence was so commanding, that I could imagine very few men could – or would – say him nay.

We were in the hall, and the King had come down after looking in on the Prince. I was lurking at the back of the room, taking shelter behind a fire screen, lest my appearance cause complications. I could still imagine being led to the gibbet if the King found out how I had deceived him before.

"By Heavens, Bessie," he boomed at Lady Kyme, "The boy was sick last time I came, but now he is in a very bad way. Please tell me a doctor has now been called?"

"Aye, sire," she replied, "and has prescribed remedies to stabilise the Prince's fever, so God can help his body to recover."

"I hope he does, for as you know I want the boy at the Palace of Whitehall this coming Wednesday. Five days! For the announcement."

She shook her head. "I am sorry, sire, but I cannot be sure he will be well enough in such a short time."

The King paced across to the fire, then turned back. "I want him there, Bessie. I have planned this, and I will not

91

have my plans changed." He strode over to where Lady Kyme was standing. "I need him as my heir. I simply cannot make such an announcement in his absence – or must I look a fool?" He continued his pacing, with a tread so heavy I could see the candlesticks shaking and the tapestries flapping as they hung on the walls. "If the Queen gives birth to a stillborn, or a girl even, I need to know he is ready to take my place if, and when, he must." He came back to her and put his face close to hers. "And if she gives birth to a son, I need to know I have two boys in line." Then he added darkly, "Just in case."

"Indeed sire," she whispered.

"My father had Arthur and me. Good thing, too, for when my brother sadly died, I was there, ready to take his place." He waggled a ring-encrusted finger at her. "Can you imagine what will happen if I do not have a son, eh? Carnage! The Cousin's War could start all over again! No. I must have him declared legitimate, and I must have him there. That is all to be said on the matter."

"I am sorry, sire, but I cannot confirm he will be well enough." I admired Lady Kyme's bravery, and the King stopped pacing and stared at her.

"But he will recover?" he asked after a moment's pause. "In time?"

"I believe he will," she answered. "God takes his side."

"Then do something, for pity's sake!" he roared. "Have him there on Wednesday!"

"And if I cannot?"

"Then find a double! There must be a lad who looks like Fitzroy somewhere in my realm! Find one and send him instead!"

Lady Kyme nodded. "As you wish sire."

My heart sank as I saw the half smile on her face.

It went without saying exactly who that 'lad' was going to be…

The King held out his hand, and Lady Kyme curtsied down to kiss it. "See to it, Bessie," he said as she stood. "You see to it."

9

INTO THE PRINCE'S SHOES

The next few days passed in a blur of preparation, as my instruction in the role of Prince Henry, Duke of Richmond and Somerset, proceeded with renewed vigour.

It seemed most bizarre, that the boy himself was abed in the upstairs chamber, while each day in the hall below, I was wearing his clothing and perfecting his manner.

The doctor came daily, and professed himself reasonably satisfied with the Prince's progress, for although there was still some blood in his phlegm, he was coughing less, and eating a little more. Lady Kyme was delighted, and confided in the doctor that it was all God's doing. I happened to be behind her as she said this, and caught a look on the doctor's face which suggested that some of the credit should also come to him. But he nodded wisely and muttered something about God moving in ways 'most mysterious'.

The Prince's recovery was good news for us all, but it was clear he was not going to be well enough to attend the King's announcement himself, so my calling as his double was not in question. This was something that the Prince was made aware of, on a grey afternoon as he sat up in bed with many bolsters to support him.

Lady Kyme had informed me that he felt well enough to thank 'the brave and resourceful Mary Fox', so I agreed to see him.

I entered the room cautiously. "Your Grace," I said, with a small bow.

A look of surprise crossed his paper-grey face. "You are Mary Fox?" I nodded as I stood straight. "The girl who effected my rescue from that awful place? Yet you remain dressed as a boy, as you were that night…" He took a breath, and thankfully it did not end in a cough. "I thought you were in some form of disguise, and would have resumed your normal garb by now." He studied me some more, then his eyes widened. "By Heavens, Mary Fox, that is my doublet! My chain! I warrant you are dressed… you are dressed as me!"

I smiled. "You said I reminded you of someone when we were in that cellar, Your Grace," I said. "Perhaps it was your own reflection?"

"Belike it was," he answered, nodding like an old man rather than a young boy. "Belike it was." He took a few breaths, then asked, "Which must beg the question; why?"

"I have stood in for you once before, Your Grace, when you were taken," I said. "So will do so again, while you recover."

"At the ceremony hosted by my father? At Whitehall? My Lady Mother has told me of this."

"Yes," I replied.

He frowned, staring up at the corner of his bed canopy as if all the answers resided there. "Yet my mother told me not that she was planning for you to take my place."

"I am sure she was thinking not to burden you as you recover, Your Grace," I said.

He looked back at me and said, "But my father the King knows me well. He will see through this conceit for sure. How do you plan to manage this?"

I told him that it was the King himself who had suggested a double should stand in. "He will understand that your recovery is more important," I said. "My presence will enable you to assume your rightful place once you are sufficiently recovered."

He nodded. "That is understandable." A weak smile appeared, showing a hint of the young boy so cruelly masked by his illness. "There has been talk before that my father would legitimise me and make me his heir."

"Is that something you desire, Your Grace?" I asked.

The smile broadened, and I could see it was something that pleased him greatly. He nodded. "It is my dearest wish," he whispered.

"Then I will do all I can to ensure it can happen," I said.

"And I am truly grateful," he replied, making my heart swell. It was good to think I could be of more help to this boy, so he could achieve his ambition.

He was thoughtfully silent again. "Did you know the King has a double himself?" I shook my head. "A fellow called Nathan Rose. He sometimes appears in my father's place, when the King is too tired or has not the inclination to come before his people. So my father is well used to such a deception."

"I am pleased to hear this," I said.

He gave a small grin. "I do not doubt it has been much on your mind," he observed. "My father not only has the means – but also indeed the willingness – to dispose of those who cross him. You are fortunate if he is already expecting a double to take my place. It will not come as a surprise to him.”

“Then I must be sure not to disappoint him – or you – with my performance in your place.”

He nodded, then gave a few coughs. “For sure, ‘tis strange,” he said eventually, “to see myself standing there. As if I were one of a pair of twins.”

“I will do as I must, then I will be away, Your Grace,” I said. “We will be twins no more. You will no longer have to concern yourself with me.”

“But I do concern myself with you, Mary Fox,” he replied. “Because you have shown such bravery and resource in my rescue. My mother has told me how you made it your mission to find me.” He regarded me with a half-smile a moment. “So I must say ‘thank you’ from deep in my heart for all you have done, and continue to do for me.”

“I am sure ‘tis naught,” I muttered. “As much as any person would do.”

“But it was you who did these things, and I give you my most profound thanks.”

“Then I have your blessing to stand in for you?” I asked.

I could see he was tiring; his face again turning spectral grey, so I understood the audience was over.

“Indeed you do, Mary Fox,” he whispered. “Indeed you do.”

—0—

The sun sparkled off the tips of the waves like a thousand flickering candle flames.

It was the following Wednesday morning, and Lady Kyme and I were taking the Prince's fine barge up from the Strand to the Palace of Whitehall for the ceremony. We were sitting on luxurious cushions in the stern, while six boatmen in the Prince's livery pulled us smoothly along and a coxswain called the strokes.

Was every pull on the blades taking me closer to mortal danger?

What if I said or did something out of keeping with the Prince's manner? What if someone other than the King exposed me, so he had no option but to have me arrested?

I could only breathe deeply and trust to my wits to keep me safe.

The wind blew gently across the river, ruffling the edges of the fringed canopy that shielded us from the sun and bringing with it the heavy, salty smell of the mud flats at the river's edge. An occasional waft of smoke blew across from cooking fires, and with it came the smell of meats and breads being prepared.

Ordinary people going about their ordinary lives.

Not planning to deceive the King's court.

Carracks and small gaff-rigged scows made way for us; their sails flapping and cracking as they turned out of our path. There was even a large coastal vessel making its stately progress upriver, with several smaller craft riding its wake; for all the world like little ducklings following their mother. The ship reminded me of the *Curlewe* – a vessel I had been aboard a few weeks previously. I shuddered slightly; her superstitious crew had been less than pleased when they found they had a girl amongst them. They thought such a thing brought bad luck. It was only by good fortune and a quick tongue I was able to stop them throwing me over the side to my death.

There were also many wherries passing us in all directions. One came close by; the boatman straining to pull on his oars to get out of our way as his passenger clung tightly to the sides with white knuckles. I settled in my seat and crossed my silken ankles. "How unlike my last experience of the river this is," I observed with a thin smile, hoping some conversation would take my mind off the dread in the pit of my belly. I had barely nibbled at the bread and cheese I had to break my fast before we left, yet it felt like I had eaten the heaviest of meals.

"I have no doubt," Lady Kyme replied. "And are you feeling confident in your role as my son?"

How like a real parent – that she instinctively sensed my fears. Would that I had known such a thing for myself, rather than having to find it in this play-act.

"In part, Lady Mother," I replied slowly. "My head is so full of the instructions you have given me over the last few days that walking, talking and holding myself as the Prince has become second nature to me now."

"But?" she enquired. "I feel there is a 'but…' to come."

"But… I am to meet the King as if I am his son. Only a fool would not be nervous."

She nodded. "The King is expecting a double. So he will know immediately you are not the Prince."

If this was meant to reassure me, I fear it failed.

A carrack came close to fouling our oars, but managed to turn aside at the very last moment. "There are bound to be others who have their doubts, but few know the Prince as well as his father, and anyway, if the King treats you as genuine, no man will dare to expose you."

I was not sure that this allayed my fears completely, but I did my best to put them to one side. There was something else that was troubling me.

"We spoke of Marcus Kytson a few days ago," I said. "And you thought he could take care of himself. But now time has passed, and we still have no word. I am greatly concerned." I leaned in towards her. "Has there been any news of him?"

She shook her head. "None that I have heard." She glanced at me. "He is a man of strength and character. I still warrant he can look to his own safety."

"I wish I shared your confidence," I said. "For all he puts on an air of capability, I fear he often needs help."

She raised an enquiring eyebrow, but I was seeing Marcus on all fours after the fire, groaning as he threw up the copious amount of wine that had kept him asleep while the flames raged around him. And recalling how he had been so impulsive in recruiting me to this role with little or no thought as to how it could be carried through. I shook my head. "If Marcus has managed to get himself taken captive, then not only is he likely to threaten our safety if details of the deception are extracted under duress, but he is also in the gravest danger himself."

She stared ahead a moment as the oarsmen carried us rhythmically along. "You are right as ever, Mary Fox," she said. "I will see if I can find any information on his situation."

We settled into a cautious silence for the remainder of the journey, until the barge was brought to a gentle stop alongside the jetty at the Palace of Whitehall.

IO

THE BROKEN PROMISE

The King towered above me, like a solid statue clothed in red, white and gold. He put his hand on my shoulder.

"Our son Prince Henry Fitzroy, Duke of Richmond and Somerset, Earl of Nottingham and Lord High Admiral of England," he boomed at the nobles, courtiers and ladies assembled in the Receiving Chamber behind me. I bowed my head, studying his black leather bear-paw shoes with their gold buckles, together with the white silk hose on his legs. Lady Kyme had told me that the King always used 'we' not 'I'. She said it was because in formal speech he spoke not as an individual, but as a representative of himself and the realm together as one.

"Your Grace," I acknowledged. Then I felt his hand move to my chin; lifting it so I was staring up at him.

"By heavens, we are pleased to see you," he said loudly, then leaned down and hissed quietly in my ear, "whoever you are in truth."

It was as if my blood had turned to ice. There was no sense in denying it. I mumbled some garbled thing about only wanting to help.

"No doubt," he whispered. "Then let us carry this play-act through." He studied my face a moment, the small dark eyes working into mine, as if he would pull the very soul out of my body. "'Tis a good likeness," he murmured eventually. "An excellent one. Lady Kyme has done well to find you. Has she briefed you in full?" I nodded. "Good. Of course, I can see the deception, but I warrant no others will." He smiled at me, then looked over my shoulder at the crowd. "We shall dine in style!" he boomed, then glanced down at me again. "Come, young fellow," he said more quietly. "You shall sit by my side as we eat."

With that we processed into the dining hall, where the King sat at the head of the table and I was placed on his right.

I looked past the King and saw Lady Kyme had been seated a few places further along. She gave me a smile, much as a mother would to her son, and I gave the same back. It was reassuring to have her so close; someone on my side now I was in the King's company. I raised an eyebrow and glanced at His Majesty, as if to say the King knew of my deception, and she gave a small nod, as if to confirm that she was already aware.

Once again I wondered why God had so cruelly decided to deny me a mother's love in my own life. And how He was showing me what I was missing in Lady Kyme.

"Of course, were she here, that seat would be for the Queen, our Lady Anne," the King said, throwing his napkin across his shoulder and washing his fingers in a silver dish held by a servant. "It will soon be announced officially, but I will tell you now. The Queen has this past day been delivered of a child and is recovering from the birth."

"Indeed, Your Grace?" I replied, also putting my napkin in place and washing my fingers, "and I trust both mother and babe are well?"

"They are, they are," he said, then tailed off with a sad look in his eye.

"Is aught wrong, Your Grace?" I asked.

"Nay, nay." He looked down at me with a thin smile. "Both Anne and my, um, daughter…" he paused and swallowed hard, "…my daughter are in fine health. I am told the babe has the loudest cry, and is sure to make her presence felt in life. We will christen her Elizabeth."

"That is good news indeed, sire," I observed, although from the look on his face, it was clear he thought it was anything but. It was hard not to be sad for this man; one who had so clearly yearned for a son, yet whom God had chosen to bless with a second daughter instead. And whose only real son was lying ill in bed while an imposter took his place.

"Yes, yes," he muttered, then he turned those hard, dark eyes on me. "Tell me, young fellow," he said quietly, "how fares my true son, whose face and manner you share? Do you have news of him? Does he get better or worse?"

I thought back to the Prince, sitting up in bed like a pale grey spectre, and was tempted to say how badly he was doing. But then I recalled that he had finally been able to hold a lengthy conversation without coughing. And how the physician had expressed a positive view of his progress. So instead I murmured, "He makes steady improvement, Your Grace. He coughs less, and without blood in the phlegm. I am also told he eats more, and is gaining weight."

This seemed to lighten his mood. He gave a small barking laugh that made me jump, then he said, "I am pleased to hear it. God has given him my strong constitution. He recovered from an illness but a year ago. I am certain that God will let him enjoy a full recovery from this one as well."

I was just thinking of a suitable reply, when a dark-haired man with a long nose and a face like an undertaker came up to the table and bowed low, sweeping off his cap. As he stood, I saw he had a chain of office across his chest that featured the red and white Tudor rose, surrounded by the words 'Honi soit qui mal y pense' (*shame to him who thinks evil of it*). I knew from the chain I also wore, that these were the words of the Most Noble Order of the Garter. His ermine-trimmed overgown and purple doublet also confirmed him to be one of the highest in the land.

"My Lord of Norfolk," the King greeted him.

Norfolk! Lady Kyme had given me a thorough brief on this man.

"He is highly influential," she had told me. "He was Lord High Admiral until removed from the position a few years ago, and you – by which I mean the Prince – took over the role."

"So he has cause to wish me ill?" I asked.

She shook her head slowly. "Nay, I think not. For a while he has actually been in charge of your welfare, and his son Henry has been your firm companion."

"Then he must know the Prince well by sight?" I asked, aware there was an edge of panic in my voice.

"Nay, he has not spent any real time with you," she gave a brief smile, "and certainly not since you were away in France. I think you need have no fear there. Boys of your – my son's – age grow and change quickly." I gave no reply. However confident she might be, I resolved to be on my guard with this nobleman.

Norfolk took a step forward towards the King. "Your Majesty," he said, and his voice had a chill to it that set my teeth on edge, "I would ask if our plans regarding the nuptials are in place?"

"Ah, yes," said the King. Then he turned to me. "Your marriage to Mary Howard, daughter of my lord of Norfolk here, is set for this coming November."

"I thank you, Your Grace," Norfolk said, then bowed again and returned to his seat.

He had not looked at me once during this whole exchange.

I stared ahead, seeing not the comings and goings of the dining hall, but instead something that Lady Kyme had, either by carelessness or design, completely omitted to mention.

My marriage – to, of all people, a girl called Mary.

"I have decided that our plans have changed," the King said in my ear, and it took a moment for me to re-adjust my thoughts back to him. "I will no longer declare my son – you – as my heir. Or not immediately, anyway." He said this in a quiet, but seemingly conversational manner, as if it were something of very little consequence. But in truth his words made my stomach tighten in surprise and anger. If not for me, then for the Prince, who had made it so clear how much he wanted this outcome.

The King continued. "It will look as if I do it to spite my wife for delivering me a daughter. She is clearly able to carry a babe to term, so I will give her the chance to bear me many sons in future. Meanwhile, this gives my existing son a chance to recover fully." He smiled, a thin grimace. "And certainly before the wedding." His eyes narrowed.

"For it would not be seemly in God's eyes for such a marriage to take place by proxy. No," he shook his head, "not seemly at all." He nodded, as if to confirm his decision. "You have done me good service, boy, by standing in for my son this day, but I will not have you do this again. From now on, I will expect Richmond himself to be by my side."

—0—

Lady Kyme paced away from me, then turned back with an angry swish of her skirts.

"The King said he would not have you legitimised?" she asked for the third time.

"Not now," I replied. "Belike sometime in the future."

"But by Heavens," she snapped, "this whole event, this banquet, was to make that announcement!" She stamped her foot with a small cry. "The King should have told me this when we arrived! He said naught when I informed him you were here while my true son stays abed. Naught! He merely nodded, that is all! He could have said something!"

"To be fair, I think he made the decision later, when we spoke at dinner," I suggested. I told her of the King's words; how he felt it would look as if he was being spiteful to his new wife following the birth of their daughter.

"I care not for the feelings of that conniving bitch!" she retorted.

"Lady Mother!" I hissed, looking at the door of the small chamber where we stood. We had found it empty and slipped inside so we could talk freely after the banquet. "Someone might hear your words and think them treason!"

"Let them," she snarled. "If that woman gives him not a son, it will be no time before she is sent away to rot like Queen Katherine. He will cast her aside, and a sight more easily than he did with the first one." She rubbed her chin as if in thought. "Of course," she said slowly, "he would be rid of her much sooner if he were aware of her plotting," She paced away, then rounded back on me, "Do we not have clear proof that the Queen was behind my Henry's kidnapping and ill-health? What if we were to make this known to the King?"

I bit my lip. This was true, but even the thought of repeating such accusations to the King could hardly be countenanced. He would be as likely to turn on the accuser. Even on short personal acquaintance, I had developed a healthy respect for the King's unpredictable temper. "I fear that might end up being to our detriment, rather than hers."

Lady Kyme nodded, frowning in thought. "You are right, of course, Mary Fox," she said after a while. "We will keep this to ourselves." She paused again. "For the moment."

"In the meantime," I observed, wanting to change the subject and remove the calculating look on her face, "the King has made it clear he does not want to see me again, but insists the true Prince must be restored to his duties as soon as his health allows."

"My Henry is certainly better than he was," she said. "Belike it was only a chill brought on from being held in that damp place? Not the consumption that the physician talked of."

"He has two months to be restored to full health," I observed, pleased that we were no longer on such a dangerous topic. "Which is when he weds Mary Howard."

"Oh!" She seemed genuinely surprised. "Mary Howard? Is that now to take place? I had thought that notion was long since dropped."

I decided to give her the benefit of the doubt that this was why she had not mentioned it.

"Indeed not, Lady Mother," I said. "And the King was most insistent that it is the true Prince that is wed, not me in his place." An awful thought occurred to me. "And it is not as if I could consummate the marriage on his behalf, is it?"

She gave a small laugh. "Nay indeed." She looked me up and down. "So what are your plans, Mary?"

"I have been giving this some consideration," I said. "And my concern is Marcus Kytson. Not just for his safety, which I believe is under the gravest threat, but also for our own security if he is made to reveal to the Queen's men what we have done."

"You make a good point," Lady Kyme observed. "So what are you going to do?"

"I am going to find him," I said. "And I am going to set him free."

II

THE BROKEN STAIR

I stepped ashore at Blackfriars and hurried towards the old house where the Prince had been held.

My cap was pulled low, and I kept my shoulders hunched as I walked, in keeping with the poor state of clothing I now wore. Gone were the fine silks and embroidery of the Duke of Richmond, and in their place a dirty jerkin and rough woollen breeches. I had insisted on a stout pair of boots, to keep my feet in best condition in case I must do a lot of walking, but that was my only indulgence when I had taken my leave of Lady Kyme.

She had overseen my transformation back at Durham House.

"And you would travel as a boy still?" she asked as I adjusted the cap in the mirror.

"Aye," I replied. "Not just because I have this cut of hair, but also because it stops many questions as to why a girl would travel alone." She nodded, and I added, "And I can run and fight a sight more easily than in a gown, believe me."

"Where will you go?" she asked.

"To Blackfriars."

"Why so?"

"In case Marcus is there, held in the same conditions as the Prince." I replied. Then I added, "And it is the only clue I have."

The old house looked much as it had when I left it a few days previously; most rickety and seeming in danger of falling down on the slightest breath of wind. Was there anyone inside? Cruddon even? I slipped into the shadows opposite and watched for what seemed like an hour. In all that time there was no movement in or out, and nothing that seemed to indicate someone was within. I decided to take a closer look.

The narrow passage between the house and its neighbour seemed eerily familiar as I slipped inside, and headed to where the barred window had been.

Nothing had changed from when I had helped the Prince to get out; the bars were still bent down to the ground, and the plaster all around the window was cracked and broken.

It was disconcerting to see it in the daylight, as the depth of wall that I had been forced to remove was much greater than I recalled. I could not help but think that if I had known just how hard it was going to be to prise the bars away, I would perhaps not have tried to do so. But then I thought of that young boy being held prisoner, and knew I would have done all I could to get him out.

A quick look down into the empty cellar showed me that sadly, Marcus was not being held inside. Nay – that would have been too easy. If I knew one thing of Jacob Cruddon, this was not going to be easy. For I was convinced that Cruddon was behind Marcus's disappearance, just as he had been of the Prince.

How soon before I came up against the evil old man again?

I swallowed hard. This was deeply concerning. I had bested him twice now; once in the forest in Suffolk, and again in this very house, by removing the Prince from under the nose of his gaoler. But would my luck hold a third time? I took a deep breath as I sat back on my haunches and stared down into the blackness of the cellar.

My luck must hold. For Cruddon had vowed that if he ever saw me again, he would not hesitate to get his revenge.

He would kill me.

So I must get ahead of him. Be ready. And for that I needed to know if Marcus still lived – and if so, where he had been taken.

I felt myself clenching my fists. I must hang on to the hope that Marcus was still alive, for it had been my instruction to send him after the other man while I followed Noah Robson – so it would be my fault if he had been taken.

If Cruddon had done Marcus to death – then I could never again rest easy.

There had to be some clue in the house, if only I could find it.

Taking another deep breath, I turned onto my belly, then eased my feet down into the room. Gripping hard on the bars, I slithered down their length like a snake, until I was able to drop down inside.

The door that I had seen the gaoler using that night was slightly open. I could only imagine his shout of anger as he unlocked it to find the Prince was gone. On this somewhat uplifting thought, I took out my knife and held it before me as I pushed the door fully open and crept slowly up the stairs.

In the darkness at the top, I could just make out another door.

I opened it as slowly as possible, praying that it would not creak. It did. Loudly to my ears, like the cracking of several whips. I stopped immediately and waited for a shout or some noise of movement.

There was only a slight scratching sound.

I waited until it stopped, then pushed again, even more slowly, until, by the grace of God I had the door narrowly open.

I waited again, my breathing held, straining to hear if there were any further sounds from within.

More scratching. After a moment it stopped again. Then nothing.

Were there men behind the door, weapons poised, alerted by the sound? Was Cruddon there, an evil smile as he prepared to attack the intruder?

I waited.

Still nothing.

Now or never...

Holding my knife in a slightly shaking fist, I gave the door a sudden, violent push and ran into the room with a fearsome yell, ready to slash at any man coming for me.

There was a scurry of movement, some heavy thumping sounds then the clatter of claws on the floor.

I spun round, my knife ready, but there was no man there.

The room was empty.

Feeling something of a fool, I lowered my knife and looked about me. The light came from the two small windows. I turned back to the room itself, which seemed hurriedly abandoned. There was a table with two chairs in the centre. On the table were some trencher plates with the remains of bread and cheese. All these were liberally covered in blue and grey mould, while the rest of the table was scattered with rat droppings.

It must have been rats that I heard – running off the table, jumping down with a thud and scurrying away.

There was a grate to one side, with ashes that looked cold. There was no glow to indicate anyone had been keeping it alight. I pushed my blade into the ashes to check, and it came out cold. Wiping it on my jerkin, I looked around the rest of the room. It was remarkably bare, with few clues to the lives of the occupants – no trinkets or papers that could give me some insight into the people who lived here, and had abandoned it in such haste.

And no clue as to where Marcus had been taken.

An archway opposite the fire led to some narrow stairs going up. There was a small open window at the top, illuminating the stairs in a bright beam of light. I considered the steps carefully; seen in the light they looked the most rickety thing in this shabby house. Each stair had cracks and splits.

One even had a board that appeared to be broken right through the middle.

Should I try them, and risk falling through? And maybe sustain an injury?

If this house was truly abandoned, then no-one would come to my aid, and I might be unable to move. And then the rats would come to investigate. Maybe they would find the courage to take a small bite into my flesh. And when I could not resist, maybe they would grow bolder?

How many bites before I would stop screaming?

Before merciful death gave me release?

No! I must not think like this! I must be positive. It is but a stairway…

With maybe a vital clue at its summit…

With a slow, careful breath, I tried the first stair, keeping my weight to the outer edges where it was fixed to the wall.

It creaked badly, but held.

The next creaked even louder, but again, it held.

The following three were reasonably solid and held my weight without protest.

Then I came to the one with the broken board. I paused a moment to ready myself, then stepped carefully up to the stair above, missing it completely.

Only a few more to go…

With even greater care I managed to ease myself up from stair to stair. Eventually, with my heart thumping fit to burst, I made it to the top.

I crept into the first room, my knife held at the ready, while the floorboards gave a series of creaks as I moved.

There was a small window with no glass; just a thin piece of oiled linen flapping gently in the breeze. I ripped it away and looked down. I could just see the bars I had removed lying in the passageway below.

Now there was more light, the room appeared to be an empty bedchamber. There was only a straw mattress on the floor, covered in a few wool blankets. An open door led to another room, so I went through.

And struck gold.

It was a small, dark, windowless chamber, with only a single desk and a shelf above. I suspected it had been Cruddon's office. Unsurprisingly, there were few papers to be seen, as no doubt he had cleared out anything incriminating. But the remaining ones might yield some form of clue.

I gathered every single paper I could find and took them into the bedroom so I could see them by the light of the window.

Mostly they were poorly written notes that were hard to decipher, as if Cruddon needed to make reminders of conversations or things to be done, but in a hand that only he could read. But one paper was different – it had a crude drawing instead of notes and had a torn edge as if it had been ripped from a larger sheet.

The image might have been roughly drawn, but there was no mistaking that it was the frontage of a fine house. And one that seemed familiar. I held it by the window to see it more clearly, then gasped. There were some letters in the corner; 'DH'.

Durham House?

Was this part of the planning for the kidnapping of the Prince?

I held it even closer to the window, looking over every inch to ensure I had not missed anything. Then I saw there was a line of writing along the bottom. I squinted to make it out clearly, and was able to read, 'If all discovered, hie back to Ipswich forthwith.'

Ipswich – Cruddon's hometown.

Then I noticed some other faint writing showing along the tear. Quickly I flipped it over. The words were cut almost in half, as if the person who had torn the paper from a larger piece had not realised there was writing on the reverse. It was not particularly clear or easy to read, as every word was horizontally split and only the tops of the letters were visible. After a few minutes careful study, I felt I had defined the letters, revealing the words, *'The Queen has ordered it, but will deny.'*

Queen Anne Boleyn?

Of course! She would have good cause to claim there was no connection between her, confined to the birthing chamber, and a desperate plot to remove the King's son and hold him captive.

Except that I now held possible evidence that proved what I had already worked out – that she *was* involved. Evidence that could be most damaging to her.

I folded the paper carefully and slipped it into the purse at my belt.

So it looked as though I must now get back to Ipswich. If Cruddon had gone there, it was most likely he had taken Marcus with him as a useful captive and bargaining counter.

Assuming he had not killed Marcus already.

I crept back to the top of the stairs, and had just taken my first step down, when there was the sound of a door opening below.

I froze, with my heart in my mouth.

I kept as still as possible, while whoever was down there moved around. I listened out for any talking. That might suggest there were more than one man. Whoever it was remained silent.

Most likely he was alone.

Very slowly I lifted my foot off the first step. Then I stepped back towards the bed chamber, thinking maybe to get into the dark office and hide.

The floor gave a loud creak.

Again I froze.

"Who is there?" came a voice.

I let out a small breath. It was not Cruddon's rough tone.

I moved to the top of the stairs with my back to the light. The man must have heard me, and came to the foot of the stairs. It was not easy from above to see more than the top of his head.

"Who are you?" he called.

"One who seeks Master Marcus Kytson," I replied.

"Then you are gravely mistaken," he said, drawing his sword. "For he is not here."

"What are you doing?" I demanded.

"You have no business here, whoever you are," he said. "You trespass. And that means I will remove you at the point of my blade."

He ran up the stairs towards me, without, it seems, looking where he was going. There was a loud crash and the sound of splintering wood as he put his weight onto the broken stair. Then the sickening crack of his bone breaking. He gave a scream and sprawled up the stairs. His sword fell from his hand and clattered down to the room below.

He looked up at me with a white face, whimpering like a wounded dog.

I frowned. I knew the man, but could not place him… Then it came to me – the Feathers in Greenwich! He was the sturdy looking fellow who had reacted so strongly when he saw me dressed as the Prince. And who I then chased up the Thames to Blackfriars and this very house!

"Master Noah Robson," I said.

"Yes," he winced. "Who are you that knows my name?"

"That is not something I wish to share," I said.

"Well get me out of this," he gasped, "and I will forget you were ever here."

I looked at the man, sweat covering his face like he had been in a heavy fall of rain. "Tell me first what I need to know," I said, trying to keep my voice calm.

"Just get me out!" he snarled.

There was a scraping of claws, and a large brown shape appeared by his free ankle, sniffing curiously. He looked down, then back up at me with wide eyes. "A rat," he whispered. "Oh, by all the Heavens, a rat! I will be eaten alive!" He struggled to free his leg, but it was stuck fast, and the movement brought a yelp of pain.

Then another rat appeared, and scrambled up onto his exposed ankle. He shook his leg and the rat jumped off, but stayed close, watching him with unmoving black eyes. "Get me out!" he screamed. "Lest they start to devour my flesh!"

"Tell me first what I wish to know," I insisted.

He kicked his foot again as one of the rats came closer. "Very well," he muttered. "What is it?"

"Marcus Kytson," I said. "You knew of him just now. Does he live?" To my relief Robson nodded. "Then that is welcome news indeed," I continued. "And is he held by Cruddon?"

"He is."

"In Ipswich?" Again he nodded. "More good news. I will need an address."

He hesitated. "Cruddon will kill me."

"If I do not help you out, the rats will do it first."

He looked down. The first two rats had been joined by several more, presumably drawn by the smell of blood and sweat, and, I warrant, fear. They were gathering around his free leg, all watching intently with their little black eyes.

"You will free me?" he asked, biting his lip. "For sure?"

"I will," I said, "and splint your leg, but then you are on your own."

"It is house number ten in Vernon Street," he muttered. "Now get me out."

I did not move. "Thank you." I said. "But I do have one more thing,"

He groaned, making another kick at a couple of emboldened rats that had crept closer. "What now?"

"I must know," I said, "of the plot to kidnap the Duke of Richmond." I paused, choosing my words with care. "Was it at the behest of the Queen?"

He stared at me in silence a moment. "Who are you?" he whispered. "Who are you really? With the clothing of a man, but the voice of a woman? You, who knows of my business and that of my mistress?"

I was unable to stop myself from making a grim smile. So this confirmed for certain that I was correct! The Queen was in truth the master planner behind the plot! Which made the folded paper in my purse of even greater value.

"I will take that as an admission that Queen Anne is indeed behind the Prince's disappearance and incarceration," I stood up. "My business with you is concluded. I have all the information I need. Let us get you free before the rats develop a taste for your flesh."

I climbed down to where he lay and held my hands out. For a moment he gave me a baleful stare, then took them. They felt sweaty, and I was concerned they might slip from my grasp, but he managed to keep a tight hold as I took a stance on the step above and began to pull him upright. It was not easy as he was a heavy man, but I succeeded after a few heaves and many curses from us both, until he was able to lift his free leg up and place it beside mine on the solid step.

"Now put your weight on the good leg," I panted, "and push upward."

He grunted his agreement. Slowly the trapped leg came free, with a few cracking sounds and even louder yells directly into my ear.

"Now turn round," I said, my ears ringing. He did not smell too fresh, either.

He shuffled round so he faced down the stair. I kept hold of one hand.

He looked up. "How do I have faith you will not push me to my death?" he whispered.

"I could have left you to the rats," I observed. "But instead I spent much effort to pull you upright. Is that not faith enough?" He nodded briefly. "And besides," I added, "how do I know you will not try to play me false?"

"For precisely the same reason," he muttered. "Do not let me go, lest I fall again."

"I will not."

He prepared himself, like a horse that steadies to jump a fence, and hopped down one stair. I waited until he hopped another, then I stepped across the broken tread, still supporting him by the hand.

By this method of hops from him and steps down from me, we made it to the foot of the stairs.

I steered him to one of the chairs, and he collapsed onto it, clearly spent of all energy. I could see he was becoming so distracted by the pain, that he was unable to focus. He began staring into the distance as if he had lost all wit. He might even faint at any moment.

The rats appeared to decide that their amusement was now over. They scattered away into dark corners, their claws scratching and scrabbling as they went. A few gave voice with the most unnerving screeching. I will admit their presence sickened me; not just for what they might have done to Noah Robson, but because I could not help but imagine that they may have done the same to me, had I found myself in such a situation.

I gave Robson slap on the cheek that brought his head round to stare at me.

"You must extend the injured leg," I said.

He did so, and I could now see the true nature of the break. The shin made a most unnatural angle – as if he had grown a new knee below his own, but this one facing the opposite way.

"I will have to straighten this," I told him, and he nodded at me, his face now a pasty white, and his eyes mere pinpricks. I took off his leather belt and made him put it between his teeth, then told him to bite down on it. It was something I had seen a physician do when resetting a servant's leg at Marchington Manor after a fall.

"Are you ready?" I asked, and he nodded again. Taking hold of his foot I braced myself, then pulled hard.

Noah Robson spat away the belt and screamed like he was at the very gates of Hell.

Unfortunately the ends of the bone remained no closer, so I muttered, "Need to try again."

After three more attempts, and progressively louder screams, I managed to get the ends of the bone to mesh together, into an (almost) straight shin.

Robson's cries subsided into a few whimpers as I broke off one of the legs from the other chair. I held it against the shin, then strapped the belt tightly around to make a splint.

"There," I said, "at least the bone is straightened. I wonder half the local populace have not come to see what the noise is about."

But Noah Robson made no answer. I looked up, to see that he had finally fainted; his head lolling back as he slumped in the chair.

I stood up. While he slept I could make a crutch. I looked at the table. It was formed of a series of planks, each one around the right length. Using my knife I prised one of them away. I tested it under my own armpit, and by holding tight to its edge with my hand, it seemed to work. A careful journey up and down the stairs secured me one of the blankets from the bed, and I tore a long strip off it. I then rolled this to make a bolster for the top of the plank, which I secured with a thinner length of the blanket.

I slapped Robson a few times across the face. His eyes fluttered, then opened and focused on me with a distant look, as if he was unsure where he was.

"You need to be away," I said. "Or your rodent friends will be back to take their supper. I have made you a crutch."

"Why do you do this, strange one?" he whispered. "You could have left me to die. I would have done as much for you."

"Well, there is the difference between us," I replied. "You have helped me with information, so I am helping you."

He nodded. "So be it," he said. I got him up from the chair, then positioned the plank under his arm. He took a few stumbling steps towards the door, then stopped and turned. "My sword," he said. "Give me my sword."

"I may have offered to help," I said, retrieving the weapon and securing it through my own belt, "but I am not stupid." I patted the hilt. "I shall think of it as an additional keepsake for all my troubles."

12

HIE BACK TO IPSWICH

Robson stumped out of the door and I followed him into the daylight. He made a slow clumping descent of the stairs to the street. Each step was accompanied by a gasp of pain, and I could see that as I had suspected, the bone was not fully straight. Even if it healed completely, he would have a permanent limp in that leg. And if it did not, a barber surgeon would no doubt have to remove it.

He reached the street level, and stopped to catch his breath.

Seen outside the dim confines of the house, he looked even more grey and drawn.

"Wither now?" I asked.

"I will make my way back to Greenwich," Robson muttered, then twisted on his crutch to look at me. There was a pause as he studied my face. Then I could see the exact moment when he realised where he had seen me before. It was as if a candle was lit and flared into life.

"By Heavens," he gasped, "It is you! The one who assumed the face and the manner of the Duke of Richmond! That we saw in the Feathers!" I gave the smallest nod. "Yet you are… you are a woman," he exclaimed, "as is clear by your speech, if not by your clothing and hair."

Then there was a further silence, during which I could see him working out the next piece of the puzzle. It was not long before he drew a great breath and staggered slightly on his crutch. "Fox!" he said. "Mary Fox! That was the name that Marcus Kytson told us, when we put him under some pressure."

Again, I gave the smallest nod, waiting to see if I would gain further information from him.

While trying not to ask what was the 'pressure' they had applied to Marcus.

"And 'twas a name that sent Master Cruddon into such a fit of rage," he continued, "as I thought he would drop dead on the spot!"

For all that I wished he had, I suspected I was not to be so fortunate. "Jacob Cruddon and I have crossed swords already," I observed. "He blames me for the death of his son."

Robson gave me a sideways look, as if he did not believe me. "Do you say you were not responsible?" he asked. "Master Cruddon was most clear that it was you that ran his son through with your sword."

"It was rather the other way about," I said.

He frowned. "Yet you did kill the lad?"

"I mean that I merely held a sword out," I said, "and he saw it too late. I stopped him in the act of trying to kill another, and he turned his ire on me. When he came at me, he ran onto the sword by his own force." I saw again the scene in the Essex forest, as the brigand I now knew as Cruddon's son ran forward and impaled himself on my blade. I grimaced as I saw once more his contorted face, and the moment his life left him like doused flame. "I had no intent to kill him," I said, "But had I not, he would have done me the same service."

"That is not how Master Cruddon tells it," he said.

"Yet he was not there," I replied. "And I was."

Robson nodded, and was again silent, looking me up and down. After a few moments he appeared to come to a decision. "You have helped me, Mary Fox," he said, "when you could have left me to perish." He tapped his crutch with his hand. "And as you say, Cruddon was not there when his son died. So his assessment of the event is clouded by grief."

Again I was silent, waiting to see if he would give me more.

"You found the note upstairs, leading you to Ipswich?" he asked.

"Yes I did." I frowned. "Was that not genuine?"

"Nay, it was specially written and placed there deliberately for you to find."

Now it was my turn to be surprised. "Cruddon is setting me a false trail?" I decided to omit what I had found on the reverse of the paper, which may actually show the truth. I could imagine Cruddon's smile as he tore it out to make his false trail, not realising he had left part of some incriminating words on the other side.

"Indeed so," Robson continued. "Cruddon is holding Kytson hostage in Ipswich in order to draw you out. He means to let you find the man, and says you will attempt a rescue, as you did with the boy. Then he will spring a trap, that will ensnare you as well." As I stared at him in amazement, he continued. "Cruddon means to submit you to death by torture."

I drew a sharp breath and felt my belly tighten as if a noose had been placed around it.

"For revenge?" I whispered.

"Yes. He says he has much to lay at your door." Robson held up his fist and opened up each finger as he listed his points. "The first, that you killed his son. The second, it seems you took the lad's purse." He looked at me for a response, but I held my peace. "I see. This you do not deny. The third, that you masqueraded as the Duke of Richmond when the real duke was held here. The fourth," he gestured towards the side of the house. "That you did strip out yonder bars from the wall, and remove the boy. And the fifth," he waggled his little finger, "you appeared as the Duke alongside his father at the Palace of Whitehall, thus putting Cruddon in dire trouble from his mistress in this matter, who has berated him roundly for his failure."

"The Queen?" I asked.

Robson nodded. "She needed to have the Prince under her charge, so she could have options in the different situations pertaining to the birth of her own child." He shifted a little, putting his hand back on the crutch. "If her child was a boy, then she would have had Cruddon kill the Duke of Richmond, for she could not risk there being a Catholic male claimant to the throne, in case it started another civil war. If it were a girl, as indeed it was, then she would also have the Duke disposed of, for again, she would not want a stronger Catholic claim against her Protestant daughter, were anything to happen to the Princess Mary." As I struggled to take in the full import of his words, he added, "The only situation where she would have released the boy unharmed, was if she had another stillbirth, for then there would have been no change to the status quo."

"So is the Prince still in danger?" I asked.

"Not while Cruddon is in Ipswich," he replied. "But once he returns to London, then, yes." He looked me in the eye. "His orders are to take the boy once more, and this time, to make sure there is no failure. His orders are to kill the boy."

"And if I do not seek him out in Ipswich?"

"Then he will return to London and kill the boy anyway." He pursed his lip. "After he has tidied up the loose ends, of course."

"Loose ends?" I asked, although I fear I knew the answer.

"He will dispose of Kytson."

I nodded slowly as I thought through my options.

Abandon Marcus to his fate, and stay in London to protect the Prince?

Or attempt a rescue of Marcus, and possibly fall into Cruddon's trap and be killed myself?

Unless, of course, I could defeat Cruddon in the process.

I could see there was no contest. For all Marcus's cynical wit, bluster, and inability to hold his drink, I could not now abandon him. I had saved his life once before, and now it must be my duty – not just as a Christian, but as a decent person, to do so once again.

I must proceed to Ipswich, and put an end to Jacob Cruddon's plans.

13

THE TRUE JACOB CRUDDON

Should I have believed Noah Robson? This was my uppermost thought as I walked up from Blackfriars, turned onto the Fleet Street and made my way towards the Moor Gate out of the city.

The man had seemed genuine enough; grateful for my help with splinting his bone and providing him with a crutch. Yet he could have been feeding me with false information on the orders of Cruddon. It would not have surprised me if the one-eyed old villain had envisioned just such an exchange.

But then it seemed unlikely that Robson would have been so forthcoming about the Queen's plans if he were trying to play me false, as the options he set out accorded closely with our own assessment of Her Majesty's motivations.

Noah Robson was a small part of the plot, caught up between the political machinations of his mistress and the ruthless scheming of Jacob Cruddon. A pawn in the chess game being played by those considerably more powerful than himself.

So I decided to believe him, and act accordingly.

Which led to the question; how would I find Marcus and get him away, without falling into precisely the trap set by Cruddon?

Such thoughts weighed heavily on my mind as I bought an unassuming old mare from a horse trader in the Moorfields outside the city gate, and plodded her eastwards in the direction of Ipswich.

By the time I had stopped for the night in a coaching inn at Ingatestone, I fancied I had devised a plan. It had some rough edges, but it was essentially sound. If it worked, I might be able to get Marcus away before Cruddon had a chance to imprison me as well.

And if it did not?

Well, that did not bear thought.

I set off in the morning, deciding to go north of Chelmsford and take the road through the little town of Witham. This was in order to keep well away from Maldon and the nearby house, Marchington Manor, home of my stepfather Sir Andrew Fox.

Even though I was many miles from Maldon, I could not help but be nervous as I rode. Just being in the same county again as Marchington made the pit of my belly feel as if it were full of lead. Every time I came to a corner I would slow the horse and peer round with caution, lest there were riders coming the other way who might be my stepfather or men that might know him.

I understood that it would be an uncommonly bad stroke of luck were such a thing to happen, but still I looked.

On one occasion some riders did come past. I kept my head low and my cap pulled down over my eyes until the noise of their hooves and the creak of leather had faded, before I dared to look up again. For all I was disguised as a boy, and a common one at that, it was in just such a guise that my stepfather would be looking for me.

"Do not flatter yourself, Mary Fox," I muttered as I stared at the lane over the mare's ears, "your stepfather is most likely relieved that you are no longer there to challenge him. He probably gives you little or no thought at all by now."

But I could not help thinking of his words the last time I had seen him, snarling at me through the bars of the Marchington gates like a wild animal; "I will punish you for your disobedience and your dishonour to my name. Do you know what I will do? I will kill you."

So no, I could not believe he would ignore me. If he truly believed I had dishonoured him, then he would never give up his hunt for revenge.

On that happy thought, the mare and I plodded on through the countryside.

We reached a little hamlet a few miles from Ipswich later that evening. A welcome coaching inn provided a hot meal and a bed for me, while the mare was contented by being stabled with some water and a nosebag full of mash.

I slept fully clothed on the hard bed; my fitful sleep disturbed by dreams of my stepfather and Cruddon. They both appeared as terrible demons who would pull me to the depths of hell, while Marcus and the Prince watched on with worrying indifference. I awoke at the break of dawn to find my blankets were wet with my sweat, and my hair stuck to my forehead as if with wax.

For a moment I lay on my back looking up at the cracked plaster ceiling, trying to dispel the feeling of sick dread revealed in my dreams.

"Now then, Mary," I whispered aloud, "you have a plan, and it is a good one. Do not be held back by such fears, but lift your head up, and ride into Ipswich with confidence. You have bettered Cruddon before and rescued his captive; you can do the same again."

But I knew this time it was different. When I got the Prince out of the house in Blackfriars, Cruddon had been unaware of my presence.

This time he knew full well that I was coming, and would be waiting for me.

This time he had his own plan in place, and I knew not what it was.

I must be one step ahead and be prepared.

I rolled off the bed, picked up my cap and stuck it squarely on my head.

Come now, Mary Fox, I told myself. *Now is not the time for doubts. Now is the time for action.*

—0—

Number 10 was a substantial building of three storeys halfway along Vernon Street. Like all the houses, the upper floor was built out as a jetty so it was but a few feet from its opposite neighbour. A thin strip of grey sky shone weakly down onto the cobbles below, leaving the street itself and all the ground-level storeys in a state of almost night-time darkness.

I assumed it was Cruddon's own residence, while the rickety old place in London had been used only as a base for his activities there. This house was constructed of a timber frame with white plastered walls and diamond lead-paned windows. No doubt Cruddon had amassed enough money to buy such a place, and I could not help but think it was by the proceeds of his evil activities, rather than by honest Christian toil.

I rode slowly along the street, my cap pulled low and my head down. The mare's hooves sounded unnaturally loud on the cobbles, and I was aware this might draw attention, but I had two reasons for not being on foot. The first was that I could be away more quickly if spotted. The second was so I might get even the briefest of glances up into the first-floor windows of the house.

As we approached, it suddenly struck me just how close I had come to the murderous Cruddon, and my heart began to pound. It seemed so loud to me that it was impossible no other person would hear. Indeed it was the mare who seemed to notice, whether by hearing or that strange sense of understanding that horses seem to have. She tossed her head and slowed her pace almost to a stop. For all it was heartening that she was sensitive to my fears, I needed her to keep moving. So I took some calming breaths, and urged her to walk on.

The windows were set a little higher than I sat in the saddle, but as I went past, I rose and gave a momentary look in then sat quickly back, leaving the image captured in my memory for review as the mare moved me past.

The room had seemed empty. All I could see were a few plain green wall hangings, and the slight flickering orange glow of a fire.

In truth this told me very little; only that Cruddon, or some other person, was in residence and had lit a fire. It also told me that Cruddon had not spent money on fripperies for such a room – the wall hangings had looked to be made of unadorned wool – so this was part of the house where visitors were not invited. Maybe a bed chamber or family parlour.

I had to admit, it did not tell me anything I really needed to know, such as where Marcus might be held. But while there had been nothing of real value to see, it did help in my plan.

I kept riding until I came to a tavern a few streets further on. After stabling the mare and securing a room, I sat in the parlour with a tankard of ale, planning my next move.

An hour or so – and a fine pigeon pie – later, I set out to find two things that I needed.

The first was a watchman in his sentry box. Every town has one; to ensure order in the streets at night, or to raise the alarm in the event of a fire, lest it spread. I found the sentry box for Ipswich in a corner of the market square, with a scrawny, thin-faced, officious looking fellow seated inside. He was leaning out and conversing with passers-by. I noted his position, then set off in search of the second thing, a particular sort of shop.

I found one in a street just off the other side of the market square; a small place that specialised in wooden toys and playthings for children. I selected a finely carved horse, which I purchased, then asked for it to be delivered to the house in Vernon Street as a gift for the owner. The shopkeeper wrapped the horse in a linen packet, agreeing readily to my request.

I walked confidently out of the shop, then scurried across the street and waited. After some quarter of an hour, a woman in a simple linen dress and coif walked out, with the toy under her arm.

I followed her at a discreet distance as she walked unhurriedly over to Vernon Street. At one point I had to duck into a doorway and bide my time while she stopped to exchange some tittle-tattle with another woman. But finally she arrived at number 10 and knocked on the door. I watched her from a dark recess a few houses further back, biting my lip in anticipation of what was going to happen next.

My plan hinged on it not being Cruddon who answered.

Thankfully, I was in luck, as it was a woman who came to the door. There was a brief conversation, which mainly involved the woman from the shop gesticulating with her hand then holding out the package, while the one on the doorstep shook her head and folded her arms. Eventually, however, the woman from the house tossed her head in a dismissive gesture, took the package and went inside.

I let out a long breath, and allowed myself a small grin.

So far, so good.

I settled back against the wall and waited.

I did not need to tarry long, for soon Jacob Cruddon himself came storming out of the house with the package under his arm. I could just make out that his one working eyebrow was lowered in an angry-looking frown.

It was as I had planned; it would be Cruddon who returned the apparently wrongful delivery. I had judged that he would want to have it out with the shopkeeper himself.

But I will admit I drew a sharp breath when I saw him, for I had not set eyes on the man since we had fought in a forest clearing a few weeks earlier. Then he had been dressed in the simple tunic and breeches of a yeoman farmer, with unruly hair and a dirty cap. But now he was well-scrubbed, his beard and hair trimmed, and wearing a fine scarlet doublet and russet hose. On his head was a black cap set with a jaunty peacock feather, and on his feet were some fine leather shoes.

Was I now seeing the true Jacob Cruddon; a man of means and substance, who lived in a fine provincial town house and who presented himself as a worthy citizen? Someone who had wealth and was prepared to show it, however he might have come by such money?

Perhaps I was – for would Queen Anne and her servant Noah Robson have deigned to do business with the dirty ruffian I had first met all those weeks ago? Most likely not; Queens do not do business with such base men, even for such an evil venture as the kidnap of a young boy.

As soon as Cruddon had stormed around the corner, I pushed off the wall and hurried across the road for the next part of my plan.

Keeping well behind him, I retraced my steps to the watchman's sentry box.

The watchman was sitting on his stool, gazing at the crowds with a vacant smile.

I scurried up to the box, for all the world a small boy with some most important news to impart.

"Please Master," I said, tugging on his sleeve, "Please! You have to come quick! There is a house I saw with smoke coming from a first-floor room. I think it might be a fire!"

"A fire, lad?" He jumped to his feet, the smile disappearing from his face in an instant.

"I think so, Master!" I looked up at him. "You had best come now!"

"That I will, by Heavens!" He straightened his cap. "You have done the right thing to tell me, lad. Now lead me to this place, double quick!"

I grabbed his sleeve again, and started dragging him across the Market Square. He pulled his arm back, and snapped, "You lead on, lad. You lead on, and I will follow."

I ran across the square in the direction of Vernon Street, glancing back over my shoulder every few yards to make sure he was still behind me. Our hurried passage was causing much attention, and I heard the watchman informing the people we passed that "this lad thinks he has seen a fire!"

By the time we reached Cruddon's house, there were some twenty or thirty concerned citizens in our party, all crowding up behind the watchman as we came to the door.

He gave a few sharp raps on the knocker, and the door opened to reveal the enquiring face of same woman I had seen earlier.

She glanced at the crowd, all chattering excitedly, and visibly paled.

"What is it?" she asked.

"We have had a report of a possible fire at this property, so I demand we are allowed entry to check it over," the watchman said, his tone sufficiently official that the woman should have no option but to obey.

She did try to resist. "There is no fire here," she said, crossing her arms, "other than the ones safely contained in their grates."

"A report is a report," the watchman barked, "and everyone in the house must leave now. I will then check all the rooms."

"I am sorry, but that is just not possible…" the woman began, but the watchman snapped. "Enough of this nonsense!" and grabbed her collar. He forcibly pulled her out of the door. I was impressed that for such a thin man, he seemed to have enormous strength. As the woman staggered past, he stepped inside and called, "All out! All out! Report of fire!"

Within a few seconds three wide-eyed female servants and one male appeared in the hallway, and were quickly shepherded out by the watchman. I rather hoped one of them might have freed Marcus so he too could escape the supposed fire, but there was no sign of him.

With my heart in my mouth, I followed the watchman inside. He stopped in the hallway and turned to me with an enquiring look. "Now tell me, lad," he said, "where do you think you saw the fire?"

"From a front room window, sir," I replied eagerly, recalling the chamber I had seen earlier. "On the first floor."

"Good, then that is where I will start," he said. "You can wait outside with the other people."

I nodded, as he made his way to the stairs and leapt up them two at a time.

Of course, I had no intention of waiting outside, but instead I headed further into the house, looking for a room, a cellar or perhaps an outside store where Marcus might be held. I was aware that it would not be long before Cruddon returned, so the time for my search was most limited.

The hallway led into the dining hall, which seemed to be at the centre of the house. It was a fine room with walls painted in a geometric diamond pattern in red and white. There was a long table up the centre, set with fine silverware dominated by a large soup tureen and well-crafted candlesticks on either side. Again, this seemed to confirm that Cruddon was a man of considerable means.

How many honest men had toiled, only for this one-eyed crook to take their wealth by dishonest means?

I ran through the hall, and found myself in the pantry. There were wooden shelves groaning with jars, packets and cheeses, while several joints of meat hung from hooks. Beyond the pantry was a small buttery, then a door to a cobbled yard outside.

There was a rendered cob wall enclosing the yard. A small wooden hut leaned against it, with its door secured by a large black bolt. A pile of fire logs was stacked to one side.

The bolt slid open easily, and I peered inside.

In the dim light from the doorway, I could just make out a small pallet bed, with the shape of a man curled up.

I touched the man's shoulder. He grunted, then turned onto his back and looked up.

For all his hair was unkempt and his beard was long, I recognised him immediately.

Marcus.

He stared up at me. "Who are you, boy?" Then his eyes widened in surprise. "Mary Fox?" he exclaimed. "This is no dream? Truly, art Mary?"

I nodded. "Hello Marcus. It has been a while."

"By Heavens, have you been taken as well?"

"Nay," I said, crouching down and putting my hand on his shoulder. "I have come to set you free."

He took a deep breath and struggled up to a seated position. "Are you mad, Mary?" he hissed. "Jacob Cruddon will kill you."

"I know," I replied. "And it will not be the first time he has tried."

"Then how will you do this?"

"I will think of something," I began, but was interrupted by a loud shout echoing from the house.

A shout in the gravelly voice of Jacob Cruddon.

"What in the name of all that is holy is going on here?" he yelled.

For a moment I stared at Marcus, then leaped to my feet. "I cannot be found," I said. "Wait here."

He gave a hollow laugh. "I am tied up, sweet Mary. I am going nowhere."

I slipped out of the hut, slid the bolt back in place, then scrambled around the pile of logs. There was a tiny space between them and the wall, which I managed to wriggle into. I crouched down low and held my breath.

It was not a moment too soon, as I heard the sound of leather shoes on the cobbles, and again Cruddon's voice.

"Where is this boy, then, that reported a fire in my house when there was none?"

"I know not, most likely gone away with the townsfolk," came the voice of the watchman. "I bid him wait outside with them."

"Well, should I find him, I will string the little runt up for causing so much nuisance to an honest man," snapped Cruddon. "You may go now. Thank you for doing your work, but I fear it was wasted time. My wife will see you out."

"Good day, Master Cruddon," said the watchman. There was the sound of feet walking away, the closing of a door, then silence.

I kept my breath as still as I could, and tried to ensure I did not make even the smallest movement.

The silence continued, and I envisioned Cruddon standing not two yards away, his single eye roving suspiciously across the yard.

A cramp started in my calf.

I tried to ignore it, in the hope it would quickly subside. But it did not.

Within a few short moments, it had flared into the worst pain imaginable; pain that would normally have had me yelling aloud, jumping to my feet and stamping my leg to try and end it.

I nearly bit through my lip as I fought the urge to move.

The door opened again and a woman spoke.

"They have all gone."

"Good."

"Is the hostage secure?"

"Let us see."

There was the sound of the bolt being withdrawn and the hut door opening.

The cramp in my calf started to reduce, leaving a dull, but blessed ache. I took a couple of deep breaths and welcomed the end of the pain.

The hut door closed and the bolt was drawn.

"Yes. He is still there."

"So this was not an attempt by that woman to extract him?"

"Perhaps. But if so, it has failed." I imagined Cruddon shrugging. "I will keep a watch out for her, but if all this was her doing, I warrant she has run off like the cur she is, with her tail between her legs."

The cur in question maintained her silence just a few feet from them, wishing she could stand up and rub the ache from her calf.

A small movement caught my attention. It was a woodlouse crawling across the nearest log. It stopped immediately before me, waving two tiny hairs on its head. For a moment I feared it would try to crawl up my nose. I blew gently on it, and it ambled off again.

There was a silence form the other side of the logs.

Had they heard me?

Were they exchanging glances, or even pointing wordlessly at the logs?

Would a hand soon be reaching over and pulling me to my feet?

I felt I could hardly breathe.

I kept still.

Eventually there was a grunt from the woman and the scrape of a shoe. "Come, then, we should go inside and see if that officious fopdoodle of a watchman has broken anything, or worse, pilfered from us," she said.

"Indeed," Cruddon replied. "Come then."

There was the sound of the far door opening, then closing.

Then silence.

Very, very slowly, I raised my head a few inches above the logs.

The yard was empty.

I glanced up. One single window on the top floor overlooked the courtyard. Could I risk someone being in that room, and looking out?

I must, or I feared I would be stuck in my hiding place until nightfall.

I raised myself higher, until I was fully standing – at which point my aching calf gave way. I put my hand on the top log to stop myself falling, and it shifted with the loudest scraping noise.

Immediately I dropped back out of sight and waited, almost unable to breathe.

After a few minutes I cautiously raised my head.

The yard was still empty.

I stood again, and this time my leg held. In one movement I slid round the logs, withdrew the bolt and slipped into the hut, leaving the door very slightly open to give some light. I crouched down.

"Marcus," I hissed. "We do not have much time. We have to get away."

14

THE PRISONER

It was clear that Marcus was in a weakened condition, and in truth, no fit state to make an escape.

He told me that Cruddon's wife would come to the shed in the morning and the evening, bringing some plain vittles like rye bread, old cheese and small beer. Occasionally she brought some meat, which Marcus thought might be the scraps from their own table.

"She is quite the shrew, that one," he said. "On one occasion she even appeared to take great pleasure in kicking me."

Considering all the foods I had seen in the pantry, and the fine furnishings on the dining table, I felt great anger on his behalf that he had been used so badly; I had read many stories of hostages held in the past, and it seemed usual that they were treated as honoured guests by the gentleman who were holding them.

But then, Cruddon was no gentleman, for all he presented himself as such. And, it seemed, his wife was just as bad. Treating Marcus no better than a dog in a kennel was inexcusable behaviour, and I vowed that Cruddon should pay for it.

And, of course, there was the matter of how Marcus had been 'questioned'. I resolved to find this out later, as and when he was prepared to tell me.

But first I needed to get Marcus away, and particularly before the vile Mistress Cruddon came with his evening meal. There was no place in the hut where I could hide, so she would be bound to see me. Much better that when she opened the door, he was already gone.

"Can you stand,?" I asked.

"I can try," he whispered.

I stood up myself. There was only just enough room for me, but Marcus was much taller, so I said, "Get to your knees only, lest you hit your head."

As he struggled up, I asked, "Where are you bound?"

Wordlessly he held up his wrists, which were tied together with a rope. I looked up. The rope looped through a ring secured to the roof beam, then returned to his wrists, where it was tied further.

"Did you not try and untie this with your teeth?" I asked.

"Early on, yes I did," he replied. "But I fear I just made it tighter, so I gave that up."

"Hmm." I lifted his arms so the rope could be seen more clearly in the light from the doorway. I cut it through with my knife, then had him hold his hands in the light, so I could slice away the knot.

He rubbed his wrists slowly while I put my knife back in my belt.

"How are we to get away?" he asked. "We can hardly stroll through the house and out of the front door."

"I know," I replied. "So we need to go over the wall behind us."

He was silent a while. Then he whispered, "I am not sure if I have enough strength for that, Mary." I could just make out his pale face in the darkness. "I feel as if I have no more than a newborn kitten."

"I will help you," I said, "As I did in the fire."

I explained how we were to get over the wall.

He gave a small chuckle. "You seem to make a habit of coming to my rescue, Mary Fox," he said.

I gave him a small, playful punch on the shoulder. "Well, you should stop getting yourself into such desperate situations, Marcus Kytson," I muttered. "For then I would not need to do so."

He made an attempt at one of his boyish grins. "I will try."

"Let us start now, by you getting you over that wall," I said. I did not mean to sound like a scold, but time was pressing.

He got to his feet, crouching over to avoid hitting his head, while I peered cautiously round the open door.

The yard was empty.

"Come," I said, "follow my lead."

I slipped out of the hut and slid backwards into the space behind the logs, crouching with my hands cupped together and held before me. "Now!" I hissed, and Marcus emerged, scrambled round, then put his foot onto my hands.

The little forward movement he had was changed into an upward one as I stood up sharply and lifted my hands with as much strength as I could muster. This gave him enough lift to get his hands on the top of the wall. With another heave, I managed to get him further up, so he was able to swing his legs over.

With a little grunt of relief, I heard him drop to the ground on the other side.

Now it was my turn.

Suddenly the wall seemed enormous; its summit stretching away into the far distance, and I had a moment of doubt that I could ever get over it on my own.

But I knew there was no other option.

I put my foot on the highest log on the pile, then clambered up using the roof of the hut as my support. Once I was standing on the logs, I was able to get my hands onto the top of the wall. I took a breath to steady myself, then prepared to pull my body up.

Just then I felt a movement in the log pile.

With a sickening lurch, and a sound like a momentous thunderclap, the logs, loosened by my earlier movement, finally gave way and fell to the ground. This left me hanging from the wall like a sheep carcass on a hook.

From behind me I heard the sound of a window opening, and Cruddon's voice calling out.

"Hey! What is happening?" I said nothing, but started trying to pull my weight up the wall. "Mary Fox! Is that you?" he called. "By all the angels, it is! It is Mary Fox! Ha! My plan has worked! So it was you who called the fire, and you were here all along!"

Then I heard a sound that made me sick with fear.

A crossbow string being pulled back.

"Oh, by the Heavens, I have waited many weeks for this moment, Mary Fox!" Cruddon said. "It will be a pleasure to send you to hell! It is where you belong, woman. But not too fast! I would not want a quick, easy death for you!"

That would mean a shot to the arm or leg.

Not fatal immediately.

Desperately I started to swing my legs left and right as I hung.

There was a cracking sound and I looked down. A bolt had snapped into the wall, burying itself exactly where my left knee had just been.

There was but a few seconds until he reloaded.

I lifted my left foot, putting it on the shaft of the bolt. Praying it would hold, I put my weight to it and lifted myself up.

It held.

I was able to get my belly across the top of the wall. Then I swung my legs up to the side.

For a split second I was lying along the wall, and in that moment, I glanced back.

Cruddon was at the upper storey window, aiming his crossbow directly at me.

I rolled off, just as there was another crack and the swish of a bolt flying over the wall.

I dropped down the other side like a felled tree, yelling with the sick realisation that I was now about to break my back, leg or shoulder when I crashed to the ground.

But instead I landed in Marcus's arms.

The weight of my fall carried him to the ground also, but it was the softest of landings for us both.

"Are you whole?" he asked, as we staggered to our feet.

"I am," I said, "thanks to you."

"That was close." He pointed at the crossbow bolt that was embedded in the base of a nearby tree trunk. A sudden dizziness came over me, as I imagined what it would have been like to have taken that shot myself, in the head or perhaps the chest.

"Mary?" Marcus asked with a concerned-looking frown.

"It is not over yet," I muttered, forcing myself back to the task in hand. "Come, stay low and close to the wall, so he has no clear shot from that infernal bow."

Together we ran to the end of the lane that went behind the houses. Beyond was the main thoroughfare that led past the end of Vernon Street, so I turned and went in the other direction.

"We cannot go to the tavern where I am lodged," I said as we ran, "for he will try all such places first."

"Then where?" Marcus answered.

"I thought the docks," I said. "Maybe a boat to London."

I glanced back every few yards as we ran on, seeking sight of Cruddon's scarlet doublet.

By God's good grace I saw it not, and after a few shouted requests for directions, we eventually arrived at the docks. I was tired from the run, but Marcus was almost in a faint from the exertion.

"Let us get you fed and tidied up," I said. "Then we can get a boat out of here."

15

A BURNING ISSUE

There were plenty of taverns along the dockside, but we chose the one furthest from the entrance, on the basis that Cruddon would probably start searching the nearest first.

If he had indeed followed us.

In truth, I thought it unlikely. We would have had quite a start on him by the time he had come down from the top floor and out onto the street. And if he had not actually seen Marcus going over the wall, he would most probably have wanted to check the hut as well.

So, while I knew we could never be truly confident, I was of the opinion that we had time to eat and make Marcus presentable, before finding our passage to London.

He certainly ate well, having two mutton pies with vegetables, washed down with a large ale.

"You had a hunger," I observed, as he sat back with a slightly glazed look in his eye.

"In all the days since I was taken, I have not eaten in total more than this one plate," he replied, pushing it away.

"And how exactly were you taken?" I asked. "I followed one of the Queen's servants up the Thames to Blackfriars, but you followed the other across the park and into Greenwich."

"Ah, yes," he said. "When we left the Palace, I followed the serving fellow in black into the town of Greenwich. I kept him in sight, as I hurried along, with my cap low. On a couple of occasions he stopped and looked round, but each time I managed to hide in a doorway or an alley." He gave a hollow chuckle. "It reminded me of games I used to play with my older brother and sisters; they would try to get away from me within our house, and I had to follow them without being seen."

"And were you able to catch them?"

He shook his head. "Not often. But it was fun."

I nodded. "And you think you were not seen by the Queen's man in Greenwich?"

"Nay, I think not."

I thought it unlikely – as a grown man, Marcus's broad shoulders would probably have made him an obvious follower. His next comment made me certain.

"Then the man slowed down, almost to a stop, so I must hang back myself, lest I walk past him."

An obvious ruse to confirm if one is being followed, as a genuine walker will continue on past.

"Then he sped up again, and went towards a tavern. I entered as well, and took a seat on the other side of the room. After a few minutes, a well-dressed man in red came in. He was most fearsome looking, with a scar that ran down one side of his face, and an eye that was quite white and milky."

"Jacob Cruddon," I observed.

"Aye." Marcus took a draught of ale. "He was the one we saw lurking outside Durham House, before the Prince was taken. Although not as well-dressed."

"And you saw all this from across the tavern?" I asked.

"Ah. No. At first all I saw was a gentleman in red sitting down with the man I was following. It was a few minutes later when the gentleman arose from his seat and came straight over to my table."

I raised my eyebrows in surprise. "That must have been unnerving," I said.

"Indeed it was. He sat down, gave me a lop-sided smile and said he knew I was following his companion. I denied it, but he was not to be deterred." He looked hard at me a moment. "By Heavens, the man sets a new low in ugliness. He has a most unpleasant voice and manner."

"Agreed," I said. "Most unpleasant."

"You say he has also tried to kill you earlier, before today?"

"Yes, he has," I said. "But this is your tale not mine. What did he say after accusing you of following his companion?" I wanted to know as much of Cruddon's intent as possible.

"He said he would call a constable and have me arraigned for theft."

"Theft?" I asked, staring at him. "How can that be so?"

"He said I had stolen his purse, and held it up before my eyes. He told me he was not without influence, and if he made such an accusation, his tale would be believed over my denial. I blustered a bit, and gave him some 'do you not know who I am?' flummery, but it was to no avail."

I could imagine not. The Kytson cheek and charm would no doubt rebound off Cruddon like a blade glances off an armoured breastplate.

"What did he want?"

"To ask some questions."

"Such as?"

"He wanted to know how we found a double for the Prince," he said.

"But you did not say?"

"No, of course not."

"Then what?" I demanded.

"He seemed to lose interest and said I should leave. I recall stepping out of the door, and starting to walk back towards the Palace… Then I think there were steps behind me…" he frowned and rubbed at the back of his head. "I am not sure what happened next, but I know nothing more, until I awoke in the back of a hay cart with my hands tied and straw all round me, as the cart swayed along country lanes."

"You were cudgelled," I said. "Hit over the head."

He nodded. "That certainly seems so," he replied. "Then, after maybe a day's journey, I was brought to that house and tied up in the hut."

"And did you see Cruddon at all, or just his wife with the food?"

"Nay, just the men who took me off the hay cart and tied me in the hut, then the wife. I did not see Cruddon himself for several days."

He must have returned to the house in Blackfriars to clear it out and plant his false trail.

"What happened when you did finally confront him?" I asked, dreading to hear how he had been forced to talk.

Marcus swallowed hard, his usual cheek and bluster quite gone. "The men carried me into the house and tied me to a chair by the fire with my arms bared. Then Cruddon put a poker to the flames. He held it close to my arm, so I could feel the heat, and I knew he had only to drop it an inch or two, and I would be scarred. Then he asked me the same question as he had in Greenwich – how we had found a double for the Prince.”

I nodded. “So naturally, you told him.”

“Only as much as needed to stop him branding me like a hog.” His mouth worked and I could see this was hard for him. “All I told him was that it was at a tavern in Dedham.”

“But he wanted more?” I asked. As an answer he silently pulled up his sleeve, his eyes holding mine.

I felt deeply sickened as I stared down at the angry red marks running up his forearm.

I was unable to speak.

“In the end I told him all,” he whispered. “That it was a woman. That she was named Mary Fox.” Our eyes met, and I am sure mine were just as troubled as his. “I am deeply sorry,” he added.

I traced a feather-light finger across one of the wheals, feeling the pain he must have gone through for me. “’Tis no matter that you told,” I replied in the same soft whisper. “But why not before he inflicted any of… these?.” The sheer number of wounds suggested Marcus had held out for far too long.

“I knew he would come for you, Mary,” he replied. “When I said your name it was if he would explode like gunpowder. He kept repeating it over and again, and there was murder in his eye. I wished I could have remained silent to protect you, but the damage was done.”

“Protect me? Why, at such a cost?”

“You saved me from burning, Mary,” he said simply. “So I took burns to try and save you.”

16

A STORM OF ILL LUCK

We found a barber working in a room above a small chandlery, cutting the hair of men who had been at sea a while and who no doubt wanted to present themselves well to their wives and sweethearts.

Marcus had his hair and beard trimmed back to their usual length. It made him look much as he had before the ordeal, but for a loss of some weight and a certain hollowness to his cheek – and perhaps a little older, as well.

I asked the barber for news of a boat sailing soon for London, and he paused as he settled the next man into his chair.

"You will be wanting *The Margarita*," he said, "but you had best not tarry, for I believe she sails within the hour."

I thanked him, and we made our way down the stairs. I kept Marcus behind me in the shadows while I looked both left and right for some minutes, but saw neither Cruddon, nor any man who seemed to be searching for us.

We were then directed by a harbour master to where *The Margarita* was berthed. Again, I proceeded with the utmost caution, checking at all times that no man was watching.

Reassured that we were unobserved, we walked up the gangplank. At the top we stepped aboard, and I asked a sailor if I might speak with the captain.

The man nodded and scurried away. As we waited, I looked around *The Margarita,* comparing her in my mind with *The Curliewe*; the boat that had taken me and my then travelling companions, Sir John Fitzwilliam and his son Robert, up from Maldon to Harwich a few weeks before. I shuddered slightly, for the thought of Maldon and its proximity to my hated stepfather at Marchington Manor, was not a happy one at all.

I thanked the Heavens that we were keeping well away from that place.

The Margarita was perhaps a little smaller than *The Curliewe.* She had two masts, each bearing an upper and a lower crossed spar, all four hung with furled sails. As we watched, men scrambled up the rigging, balancing with seeming ease at heights that would have scared me to death, then undid the ties that kept the canvas secured.

The sails fell open and started flapping and cracking in the breeze. Indeed, now we were well above the shelter of the dock and out on an open deck, it was apparent that there was a strong wind. Even as we waited, it seemed to strengthen. Marcus tapped my shoulder and pointed to the west, where some dark grey clouds were building.

"It looks like there is some bad weather coming," he said.

I recalled how we had ridden some very big waves in *The Curliewe.* "Maybe a little rough," I agreed. "Will you be sick with the movement of the ship?"

He shook his head. "I think not; I have been to sea before." He looked up at the sailors sliding feet-first down the rigging. "And these men seem to know what they are doing."

Just then a small, well-dressed man appeared, with a grey-peppered beard and bright blue eyes.

"Can I help you, sirs?" he asked, his head to one side. "I am the captain."

"We seek passage to London, sir," I said. "Are you taking passengers?"

"Aye, but there is a charge," he replied. I nodded and he looked at me curiously, then up at Marcus. "The boy answers for you sir," he observed. "Does he always take the lead?"

Marcus smiled. "My, er, nephew… has a sound mind and makes good judgment, Master Captain. I trust him in matters such as these."

The captain studied me a moment, his eyes narrowed. He appeared to be about to say something, when a blast of wind howled across the rigging, making the sails whip and crack like canon-fire. "So be it," he said, once the noise had subsided.

"And how much is the passage?" I asked.

Once we had agreed a sum, Marcus and I were shown to a small cabin with a single bunk. A lantern cast a dim orange light, making Marcus seem even more drawn than on deck.

"It should be a swift voyage with this wind," I observed. "So I will sit on the floor if you want to lie on the bunk."

He laughed. "They know not that you are a girl, or they would not have put us in here together."

"They would not have allowed me on board at all," I said, shaking my head.

"We should ensure your secret remains hidden," he replied.

"Indeed we must; so you must not think of me as Mary, lest you let slip that name."

He appeared to ponder on this a moment. "Then I shall think of you as Henry, after the Prince." He managed a small grin. "That is easy for me, after all the training we did at Durham House."

—0—

The ship was making great progress as we came up on deck, proceeding swiftly along the Orwell river towards the open seas. A great foaming trail from the stern pointed back towards the Ipswich docks, that were now just a distant black mark behind us.

The air in the cabin had become thick and hard to breathe, so the fresh winds above deck were a welcome change.

I leaned next to Marcus on the rail, and we watched the flat, muddy banks of the river slipping past, taking us ever closer to London.

The captain came up to us. "We are making good speed," he observed, "but once we come out to sea and away from the protection of the riverbanks, the wind will pick up greatly. I still fear a storm."

I glanced back over my shoulder. The dark cloud was still off to the west, but now much closer. And if anything, darker. "What then?" I asked.

"I will ask you both to go below," he said. "It will not be safe for you above decks if we have strong winds to deal with."

I nodded, and he strolled away, his hands behind his back. He climbed the steps to the stern platform, then stood beside another well-dressed man at the rail. They conversed with each other, both keeping watch on where the ship was headed.

A fresh-faced sailor came past, coiling a rope in his arms. Like the other men, he wore a heavy linen singlet and cut-off breeches. These were a dark blue colour, while most others seemed to wear grey or brown.

"You two are passengers?" he asked, making casual conversation.

"We are," Marcus said. "We have business to attend in London."

"London is such a big city," he observed, settling the rope across his shoulder. "I have oft been to the docks there, but never ventured further."

"There is much to see," I said. "You should explore when we get there."

He laughed. "Nay, these coastal sailings are quick affairs; the ship is reloaded with new merchandise and we set sail again in two or three tides. No time to see aught but a dockside tavern, a pie and a yard of ale."

"Then back to Ipswich?" I asked.

"Aye." He leaned against the rail, clearly happy to talk a while. "But after this voyage I have decided to stay at home in Maldon and take work on the land. My lovely wife has not long been delivered of a baby boy. She is the bonniest lass in all of Essex and the babe is one who laughs at anything. I value every moment with them both and would be there with him as he grows."

"You have good fortune…" I said, raising an eyebrow to seek a name.

"Job," he said. "Job Carver."

"Then you have good fortune, Job Carver, to be blessed with a loving wife and babe."

"My wife is loving, to be sure," he said with a broad grin. "But I will tell you," he leaned forward with a conspiratorial smile, "she is a strong-willed woman. One with a fiery temper who brooks no nonsense."

For a moment I forgot myself, and was about to reply to the effect that all women should be strong-willed, but then I remembered I was not Mary Fox, but a lad by the name of Henry. "She sounds an interesting person," I said. "And would tell her so if we were to meet."

Job glanced at Marcus, whose clothes, while dirty, were clearly well cut and new enough to have been made for him. "Aye, but she likes not those of high birth."

"Why so?" I was curious. This was unusual.

"She was in service as a girl to a noble family, and they did not treat her well. She was cast out when the son of the family tried to lie with her unbidden. She has never forgotten such treatment and sees all of high birth as tainted the same."

Marcus gave a small whistle through his teeth. "A sad event."

Job nodded, then gave a bright smile. "But all is in the past. Now she is a loving wife and has given me a bonny babe."

"Then I wish you God's blessings, Job Carver." I smiled at this man.

And God forgive me, I did feel a small pang of jealousy at his happy family life ahead.

"I wish you all the best, and God's blessings as well," Job replied. "I trust you have good fortune in London."

He gave a friendly smile and wave as he went back to his duties.

The Margarita's easy progress continued for another two hours or more, until the riverbanks fell away sharply, and we came past Harwich and out to the sea.

There was a shout from the captain, and the steersman, who seemed to have arms bigger than both my legs together, pulled the whipstaff to turn the ship towards the southwest.

The sails began to flap as they lost wind, while the sailors, who seemed well prepared for this, pulled on ropes and scurried about the rigging like squirrels on a branch. The sails came in tighter, and once again were moving forward. But now we were in the open sea, and suddenly there were waves that were as high as the decks. The whole ship lurched as each trough opened up before her. She buried her bow into a wave, then came up and shook herself like a dog emerging from a stream.

Marcus had knuckles that were white as he gripped the rail to stop himself being thrown along the deck, and I looked at my own and saw they were the same. The ship was leaning away from the wind, as she rose and fell to meet each wave.

The dark cloud was now very much overhead; blocking out all but the flattest grey light. Suddenly there was a bright flash from within it, lighting up the ship as if by a hundred thousand candles, then immediately the deepest roar of thunder.

One of the sailors came past, and yelled "Captain says you are to go below!"

We made our way slowly back towards the door down to the cabins, keeping our hands on the rail and sliding them from one grip to the next.

The door was in the middle of the deck, away from the rail. So we had to judge when to let go of the rail and run to the door, at a point when the ship was level. I went first, and made it just as the ship lurched forward. I grasped onto the door frame to stop myself pitching back down the steps into the blackness of the passageway beyond.

Marcus was still at the rail. His face was white, and twice he seemed about to let go, but each time his nerve seemed to fail him, so he stayed where he was.

"Come on!" I yelled.

His jaw lifted and a determined look came into his eye. As the boat crested a rise and dropped down he let himself lean back, and as it rose to meet the next wave, he let go.

He shot across the deck as if he were a ball from a canon. Straight into me.

The force of it ripped my hand from the door frame, and we tumbled together down the steps. As we fell, his greater weight carried him past me, twisting him so he landed on his back on the deck below. He made a loud grunt as the air was pushed from his chest. Then he grunted again as my full weight crashed down on top of him.

For a moment we lay in the semi darkness, lit only by the open doorway and a small hanging lamp in the passageway. My face was but an inch from his and our eyes locked as the boat continued to rock and roll.

"Are you whole?" I asked, unsure of whether he could possibly be so, after such a fall.

To my relief he nodded. "I think so. You?"

"I had a good landing," I said, finding myself starting to laugh. "I came down upon the softest thing in all of Christendom."

He laughed also. "You mock me."

"Do you blame me?"

"Nay."

He looked up at me, and seemed about to say something more. But at that moment the ship made its most violent lurch so far, falling to one side and throwing us both across the deck. As I struggled to find something to hold on to, we started to lean so far to one side that we were forced to roll together, until we were lying more on the wall than on the floor.

Then there was a deafening sound, as if the thunder was now inside the ship, rather than in the sky.

I looked up as a solid fall of water burst through the doorway. It plummeted down onto us, covering us from head to toe, dousing the lamp and plunging us into greater darkness.

As I struggled to take in a breath, the ship lurched once again. Now it was leaning so far over that it must capsize completely.

The Margarita seemed about to sink.

We would be trapped in this passageway. Pulled down to our watery graves.

I tried to stand, but there was no solid floor – only the wall and a torrent of water rushing past.

Another breath. More water than air.

I flopped away from Marcus, retching and choking.

I heard him shout, as another wave crashed through the doorway. Again the passage was flooded. This time I held my breath, pushing up from the wall until my head was clear of the water. As I drew in welcome air, there was another bright flash from the skies, then the loudest crash I had ever heard, accompanied by screams and shouts from the men above. I felt the whole ship shake and twist, as if she was tearing herself apart.

Then she righted. I found level floor and cautiously stood, as the water cleared from the passage. I felt Marcus rise up beside me.

"What in Heaven's name..?" he began. But he did not finish, as we were flung sideways onto the wall, then back again to the other side of the passage. This continued for several more movements; each one becoming less than the one before. *The Margarita* was wallowing; simply riding the waves. She finally settled with a permanent lean to one side.

I found my way to the steps and cautiously climbed up.

As my head came up into the air, I was greeted by a sight of total carnage.

The main mast had broken apart, around a third of the way up. The stump remained upright, but most of the mast was leaning down over the ship's rail, its sails part in the water and part flapping in the wind.

The ropes that held it secure had parted – and were flicking like angry serpents around the deck.

A body lay by the mast, a pool of red spreading about it.

A body with blue breeches.

I gave a small scream and put my hand to my mouth. Job Carver! I felt a desperate pang of pity for his lovely wife and new babe. How could God take one so well-meaning?

As I stared in horror, two men ran to the mast with a large saw. They started cutting through the splintered break, while other men moved Job Carver away.

"Quickly!" a voice yelled, "before it drags us over!"

In minutes the men had cut through the remaining part of the mast. The bottom of the fallen section dropped down onto the deck, causing the ship to lean even further over.

"Cut the ropes!" screamed the voice, but men were already using knives to sever them.

As each rope came apart, the end whipped away like a horse's tail.

One poor fellow lost his hand in an instant, staggering away clutching at the stump with a fearsome scream.

"More!" yelled the voice. "Cut them all!"

As the last ropes were cut, the mast slid into the sea and *The Margarita* righted herself again.

Now there was only the fore mast with sails intact, all flapping heavily in the wind.

"We make for port!" shouted the voice, which I now took to be the captain. "Where is nearest?"

A different voice shouted back, "Maldon, Captain."

"Very good," replied the captain. "Make way under fore sails only. We head for Maldon."

17

HESTIA AND THE BLUE BOAR

The evening sun was low in the sky as *The Margarita* limped into the Hythe Quay at Maldon, like the last battle survivor crawling in, bloodied and broken.

As we slid onto a berth, our battered appearance was made all the more obvious by contrast with our new neighbour: a magnificent three-masted merchant vessel. It even had a row of wooden shutters along the side, which I took to be gun ports, presumably to defend it against pirates. Whereas we had needed only to defend ourselves against a thunderstorm, and in this, *The Margarita* had very nearly failed.

"You and your nephew must continue your journey by land, unless you find another vessel sailing to London," the captain said to Marcus as we stood by the gangplank down to the quay. "It will take days, or even weeks before *The Margarita* is ready to set sail once more."

"Thank you, Captain, we will find a way," said Marcus. "Our thoughts and prayers are with you and your crew after such dreadful ill-fortune."

"Ill-fortune indeed," the captain agreed, "to be hit by a bolt of lightning at sea and to have lost a good man. I cannot help but think how we must have offended God for Him to give us such a punishment."

I declined to mention that there had been a girl on board, even if they had not known it.

Bad luck indeed.

Marcus put his hand on my shoulder. "Come, Henry, we must depart the ship."

I had been dreading stepping ashore in Maldon, but that had been as we made our way in from the open sea and up the Blackwater estuary. Again, the thought of being so close to my stepfather near paralysed me with fear. So when it was time to walk down the gangplank, I found myself frozen to the spot. I was unable to move anything but my eyes, desperately looking over every man on the quay below. Might one of them be my murderous stepfather? I felt ready to spew up the bile that was rising in my throat at the thought.

"Come on, Henry," Marcus repeated, now pushing me forward. "We have to go."

I stumbled forward, and the gangplank seemed to suddenly shrink, as if the quay was but a few inches away. I put a hand to the rail and stopped.

"What ails you, Henry?" asked Marcus. "This is not like you at all."

I took a deep breath.

No, it was not like me. What kind of fool I was for thinking my stepfather would just happen to be at the quay on this very day? A day when by the merest chance, I was coming ashore? How could such nonsense be given any credence? Indeed, I could hardly recall when he would ever have come to this place, unless to conduct business with the merchants whose ships he owned.

I stepped onto the gangplank, took another deep breath and strode briskly down.

Immediately Marcus and I were in the midst of a crowd of men that swarmed about us like bees by a hive. There were sailors of every age; from young lads scampering about in cut-off breeches, to hoary old men with plaited beards and skin like darkened leather. Few of these seemed to have escaped their life at sea without some form of mutilation; several stumped along on wooden legs, many had an eye-patch, and a few even had their teeth filed down to points. I saw a man with a hook for a hand, and could not help but pity the fate of the poor fellow who had suffered just such an injury in the storm. The captain had told me that the man would likewise be fitted with a hook before returning to his duties.

And of course, there was poor Job Carver, who had lost his life when the mast first came down. It had been a sombre moment amongst the crew when prayers were said for his soul, and his body committed to the sea.

As we pushed through the crowds, I still could not help but search the face of every man, lest my stepfather was indeed here.

Once again, my fears were taking over.

Perhaps that merchant vessel in the next berth was one of my stepfather's? I flinched at the thought. He might even now be striding across the quay to meet with the captain. We could cross his path at any moment.

As I had that very thought, I spotted a wide-brimmed hat with an ostrich feather coming towards us.

My stepfather had just such a hat!

I gave the squeak of a timid mouse, and ducked behind Marcus, as a stout fellow in a well-cut doublet emerged from behind two sailors and strode towards us.

"What ails?" Marcus asked.

I stole a brief look at the man in the hat as he passed.

A stranger.

"Naught," I muttered.

"You have been quiet and withdrawn ever since the storm," Marcus observed. "Not your usual self at all." He stopped and looked down at me. "Henry… Mary… I would have thought that our survival and passage to a safe port like this should have pleased you greatly. Yet you have been as cold to me as the snows in winter."

Safe port? Maldon?

How little he knew.

"What more must I do to gain the return of your good humour?" he continued.

"Get me away from this place," I muttered. "A ship. A horse. A cart. Anything."

"I see." Marcus scratched his beard with his eyes wide. "You wish for me to make the decisions?"

"If you get me out of here."

He shrugged and smiled. "As you wish. But the night will soon be upon us, and we need to rest." He glanced around. "There are several taverns, but I warrant they will be full. Belike we should go up into the town."

"No!" I snapped. "Not there."

"Whyever not?"

"Because…" I began, then stopped. Maybe Maldon for one evening was not such a bad idea? My stepfather had little reason to go into the town at night, nor at any time, really. So maybe my fears were ill-founded? And there was a good reason to go to an inn called the Blue Boar – it was where I had said goodbye to my faithful and much-loved mare Hestia before setting off by sea to Harwich all those weeks ago. I had asked the landlord to sell her for me. At very least I might collect the sale money, and at best I might find out where she was now so I could buy her back. I gave a small smile as I remembered her kindly brown eyes, and how she would nuzzle me for her oat mash. The thought of how I might once again to be with her, made me realise just how big was the Hestia-shaped hole in my life.

"The Blue Boar in Maldon," I said. "That is where we will stay." I started walking towards the end of the dock with renewed purpose, and heard Marcus trotting along behind.

He came up beside me. "I see my tenure as leader of this venture has lasted but a minute," he muttered.

—0—

Samuel, the landlord of the Blue Boar, did not recognise me at first.

I gave him a hard, but enquiring, stare; the kind that indicated he should know me. He frowned, then gave a hearty laugh.

"Mary Fox! As I live and breathe!"

"Indeed, Samuel," I replied with a grin.

"You dress as a boy, Mary, this much I know," he chuckled. "But now you cut your hair as well? I knew you not at first." He looked from me to Marcus, then back to me again with a raised eyebrow. "Last I saw, you were

177

breaking into Marchington Manor with some young lad. Is this…?"

"Nay," I replied. "Different."

"Good," he said. "As I recall, that fellow was blind drunk when you returned in the middle of the night."

"He recovered," I said. "Eventually."

Marcus cleared his throat. "We would have two rooms for the night, if you please, good fellow."

Samuel nodded. "I have some left. I will show you up."

As Marcus prepared to follow Samuel up the stairs, I held up my hand. "Wait a moment," I said. "When last I was here, I asked you to sell Hestia for me. Did she find a new home?"

Samuel nodded. "Indeed she did. But she was too good for any other man, so I kept her for myself."

My heart leapt. "You kept her? Then she is here? In the stables?"

"Yes." He gave me a warm smile.

"Oh!" I could scarce believe that I would see my beloved mare again. "I must go to her!"

I ran out to the courtyard, which was lit by several braziers. Immediately, I saw a familiar face looking over one of the stable doors, and was there in an instant.

Unlike Samuel, Hestia seemed to recognise me immediately. She raised her head and whinnied in what I took to be a happy greeting. I put my hand up around her neck and rested my cheek on hers, and we stayed like that for a few blissful minutes. Not a horse and rider, but two old friends reunited.

Eventually I stroked her nose, and said, "I will see you again, old girl."

She snorted gently, nuzzled my neck, then nodded.

I went back into the tavern, to find Marcus and Samuel chatting quietly by the fire, each holding a tankard. A serving girl was filling these from a pewter jug. Samuel looked up. "Was Hestia pleased to see you, Mary Fox?" he asked.

The serving girl slopped some ale, missing his tankard and splashing the liquid onto his breeches. He frowned at her.

"Attention, Mabel!"

"Sorry Master,"

"Oh yes," I said. "Hestia was most pleased to see me. As much as I was to see her."

"Then you must have her back," he said, wiping at the spilled ale with his hand. "She has always been yours, not mine."

Once again, my heart leapt. "Are you sure?" I asked, my breath catching in my throat.

"Indeed so. You gave her for my safekeeping, and asked me to sell her. That I did not, so you are still her owner. I even have your saddle and bridle kept safe as well."

I ran to him and threw my arms about his neck. "Samuel, you are a prince among men!" I stood back and held his free hand in mine. "I cannot thank you enough!"

"Your delight is reward enough for me," he replied.

The serving girl gave a small curtsey. "Am I finished for the night, Master?" she asked.

Samuel nodded, "Yes, Mabel. And take more care in future."

"Yes, Master. Sorry, Master."

When she had gone, we settled by the fire. I explained to Samuel that Marcus and I had been returning to London from Ipswich, when were caught in the storm aboard *The Margarita*. I gave no more information about why we were in Ipswich, nor why we were returning to London. Samuel had known me long enough and supported me in a few of my escapades, so he knew not to ask too many questions. But our tale of the shipwreck was clearly upsetting to him, especially when I told him of Job Carver meeting such a dreadful end.

"I knew him," Samuel observed. "He would oft come here for a drink of an evening when he was home from a voyage. He has… he had… a young wife and babe, living on the hill above the Hey Bridge. His wife Miriam would occasionally join him here, and they once invited me to celebrate Candlemas with them in their little cottage. Charming, it was," he added, swilling the ale around in his tankard. "Painted in the brightest yellow. Sunny, just like Job and Miriam." He shook his head. "A sad, sad loss."

—0—

We broke fast the following morning, seated in the parlour of the Blue Boar. A few of Samuel's other residents were also breaking their fast around us.

Samuel himself was serving the plates of bread, cheese and gammon. When he came to our table, I observed that he must be the hardest-working landlord in all of Essex.

"It is that girl Mabel," he said with a rueful smile. "She has been with me but a few weeks. Not only is she clumsy, but now she is absent as well."

Something about his words caused a sudden sense of disquiet. The girl had spilled the ale, and now I thought more on it, she had done so immediately after Samuel had said my name.

Why had the girl reacted so, and why at that precise moment?

It was almost as if she was shocked to learn that I was Mary Fox.

But what would that be to her?

Unless…

A wave of cold fear almost stopped my breath.

Unless she was put there by my stepfather.

Unless she was part of a network of covert observers he had put in place a few weeks ago, after I had run away from him.

A network of observers who would report to him if ever I returned.

And no doubt she had reported back to him – and was now absent because she knew what was to happen.

I leapt up. "Marcus," I hissed, "we must go! Now!"

"Now?"

I grabbed his sleeve. "Come on! We have no time! I will explain later!"

Thankfully Marcus also knew me well enough not to ask any further questions. Together we ran out of the tavern and across the courtyard.

Hestia looked up enquiringly as we arrived in her stable. I grabbed the saddle and bridle that Samuel had thoughtfully left on a post. Quickly I saddled her. Marcus helped me onto her back, then clambered up behind me, his hands on my hips.

"Come Hestia!" I shouted. I squeezed her flanks, and we emerged from the stable like an arrow from a bow.

I crouched low over her neck as we made for the archway out on the far side of the courtyard.

Just as three men rode in, blocking our way.

The leader was an elderly, red-faced man in a well-cut doublet.

My stepfather!

I pulled Hestia up so violently that she reared onto her hind legs, as she and I both screamed.

I clung on to the reins, and Marcus to me, lest we would both fall onto the cobbles. As Hestia dropped down, I could see the evil smile on my stepfather's face. He had waited for this moment. He had planned for it. And now he had me.

His smile said it all.

I glanced quickly round. The courtyard wall to our left was high.

But not too high.

I knew my Hestia. Even with both me and Marcus on her back, she could clear it. I wheeled her round. "Come on!" I yelled, and gave her a small kick. She snorted and lifted her head, which I knew meant she was game for the challenge.

Then she dropped it again with purpose, and suddenly we were galloping towards the wall.

"What is beyond?" shouted Marcus in my ear, but I neither knew, nor cared.

Hestia put her ears back and stretched her neck.

We were coming to the wall almost too fast. Two strides away, I pulled back on the reins.

Hestia, my beautiful, courageous friend, rose into the air like a graceful bird, her forelegs tucked up beneath her, as we soared over the wall.

And landed, sure-footed, in some scrub-land beyond.

A few trees rushed up to meet us. Hestia picked her way round them without missing a step, and we emerged onto a lane between some houses.

"By Heavens!" Marcus yelled in my ear. "I would never have believed it!"

We galloped along the street, scattering cursing townsfolk like chaff in the wind.

I glanced behind, but the streets were too narrow to see if we were being followed. And I reckoned we had made a good head start by leaping over the wall.

More and more streets seemed to come upon us, with ever more screams and curses from townsfolk as we forced them from our path. As each street led to the next, I began to despair that we would ever get out of the town. But then I spotted a green hill on the horizon with a few houses dotted on its side. Our destination.

Finally the streets thinned out, and we started up the hill into the surrounding country. I glanced round again, dreading to see my stepfather and his men emerging from the town behind us, but still there was no sign.

"Come on Hestia," I urged, and she responded immediately with a burst of even greater speed. I had little doubt that our path would be easy for my stepfather to follow, he had only to find the streets strewn with the disgruntled men and women of Maldon, who would gladly point him in our direction.

Hestia made a small stumble, then bravely picked herself up again. She was not going to keep going forever, and this hill was becoming steeper. We would need to find somewhere to hide.

I reined her back to a fast trot.

"Who was that man?" yelled Marcus.

"My stepfather," I yelled back. "Sir Andrew Fox, of Marchington Manor."

"He meant you harm. I saw it in his eye."

"I know. He vows to kill me."

Marcus made no answer to this as we continued on. But I could guess his thoughts.

Just how many men are trying to kill you, Mary Fox?

Shortly after, we rounded a bend and I saw a small cottage standing alone on the edge of some woodland. It was painted in the brightest yellow.

"In here!" I yelled, and we trotted in amongst the trees, heading deep in until it was dark and still. I pulled Hestia up, and jumped down, then tied her to a small tree. Then we made our way back to the cottage and knocked on the door.

A small woman came out, carrying a mewling babe. Her eyes were red with weeping, and her hair hung like straw from her head.

"Miriam Carver?" I asked.

She gave a distracted-looking nod, as if the appearance of two wild-eyed strangers was nothing compared to her other news.

I guessed she had already been told of Job.

"Yes," she said, frowning as she clutched the babe to her breast. I saw a flash of the strong-will Job had spoken of. "Who is asking?"

"We have sailed with Job Carver," I said, then paused. "I am very sorry for your loss."

She did not reply, but looked down at the babe. I continued, "We spoke with Job, before the storm. We would tell you what he said of his plans and his love for his family."

"You spoke with him?" she asked, looking up. I nodded, with a small smile. "Then you had better come in and tell me all."

As we went inside, I thought I heard the thud of hoofbeats in the distance.

18

THE GOOD WIDOW

Miriam Carver settled the babe in his crib then sat at the table in her little parlour. The room was lit by a single tallow candle as the only source of light, as the two windows were covered with heavy sacking.

She motioned us to sit as well.

"So," she asked expectantly, "what did Job say to you?"

Marcus and I sat also. "Before I tell you, we have a small request," I replied.

She raised a curious eyebrow. "You have conditions, in order to tell me what my husband…" her voice cracked and she seemed to control a small sob, "…what my husband has said?"

"I know you are in distress," I said, "and we cannot begin to imagine your grief, but," I paused and held her eye, "but we are in mortal danger. Some noblemen are pursuing us, and wish us the gravest harm."

"Noblemen?" she asked with a frown, glancing at Marcus.

"Yes. They wish us harm."

"I see," she said, with just a ghost of a smile. "Then you wish for me to hide you?"

I nodded.

"But I know you not," she said, a hard expression clouding her face. "God knows noblemen are seldom righteous… but what if your pursuers are the ones in the right?”

To be fair, I had not thought that she might have such an objection. I had only thought that it was noblemen pursuing us and she hated such men. Also that our connection with her husband would make her take our part and help us hide.

I drew a couple of coins from my purse and held them up. “If we can help you now Job is gone…?” I suggested.

Just then the hoofbeats were clearly heard outside, together with the jingle of bridles.

“Please,” I said, taking out my purse and pushing the coins across the table. There must have been such a look of desperation in my eye, that I saw her expression soften. “Very well,” she said, scooping up the coins. “There is a cellar.”

Quickly we agreed what she would say, as she lifted a trapdoor in the corner of the room, and we scurried down into a cold, dark space. She closed the trap, and I heard her dragging the table across it.

I settled as best I could in the darkness.

Marcus was breathing hard beside me, so loudly that I feared it might be heard. I touched his arm. “Shh,” I cautioned. Although the hammering of my heart might have been just as easy to hear.

There was the tramp of boots coming in, then the loathsome sound of Sir Andrew Fox.

“You, woman, I seek two fugitives on a single horse.”

“Who are you, sir?” Miriam asked.

“That is none of your concern, woman.” I pictured my stepfather’s chin jutting with his customary belligerence. “Have they come here?” There was a silence, then he added, "Do not seek to dismiss me with a falsehood, woman, or I will see the consequences for you are dire."

There was another pause. Then Miriam said, "Some quarter hour past I did hear hoofbeats pass, but I did not see who it was."

"In which direction?"

"From Maldon, going towards Danbury, I would say."

"And this is God's truth?"

"On my oath," Miriam replied. "They are not long gone – you will soon catch them up."

"Hmm." There was another silence, broken only by a tapping sound. I thought this was most likely my stepfather's foot as he considered his actions. "Very well," he said, then there was again the tramping of boots out of the house.

A few minutes later, light flooded into the little space, as Miriam lifted the trap.

"They are gone," she said.

"Thank you Miriam," I said as we climbed out and she dropped the trapdoor down. "You are most kind. I am sure God will forgive your false oath."

"T'was not false," Miriam said. "I did hear you ride past, and saw you not. I simply did not mention how you then knocked on my door."

We sat again at the table and Miriam placed bowls before us.

"What will you do now?" she asked as she warmed a pot on the fire.

I settled in my chair, my heart resuming its normal beat now my stepfather was riding away, hopefully towards

Danbury. "If you are agreed, we will stay here no more than an hour, then we will leave you in peace."

"I am so agreed," she said. "Where will you go?"

"We were headed for London on the ship, so we will continue that way," I answered.

Miriam filled our bowls with broth. "So now please, tell me what Job said," she asked as we ate.

I told her how proud he had been of her and the babe, and how he planned to give up the sea and work the land, so he could be with them both.

"He will be with us always," she agreed. "But sadly, it must be in here," she tapped her chest. "Not in person." She paused, looking across us. "How did he die? The captain rode up yesterday, but only told me Job perished in a storm that nearly wrecked the ship and he was buried at sea."

I explained the storm, and how it had brought *The Margarita* almost to the verge of a capsize, then the lightning that had struck at the mast. "I fear Job was in the wrong place at the wrong time," I observed. "But it would have been quick, of that I am sure. He would not have known it was happening."

"I hope so," Miriam replied. "God must have decided to take him, but by His grace, the first Job would have known was when he was suddenly in the Lord's presence."

The conversation stopped on that thought. I am sure we were each considering how it must have been for Job, to be at one moment trying to stand on the deck, then next finding himself prostrate before the Lord Jesus.

After a while, Miriam glanced curiously at me. "You make all the conversation," she said. "Yet you are but a lad." She looked across at Marcus. "Do you not speak, sir?"

He gave me a sideways smile, "I find it serves little purpose when young… ah… Henry here, has such command of the situation."

I bit back a retort about him being more of a man, and smiled instead. "Master Kytson is most unassuming," I said. "I merely say what he is also thinking."

Miriam laughed. "You speak more as a girl than a lad," she observed.

Her words made realise how much I must concentrate on my male role. Suddenly I felt trapped in this little cottage, and needed air. Then an awful thought hit me. "I must go and check on Hestia, my horse," I said.

I stumbled out of the cottage and into the forest. It was dark amongst the trees, but there was just enough light for me to see Hestia standing quietly.

I gave a relieved sigh. "How are you, old girl?" I asked, putting my hand to her cheek.

I was so pleased to see her, that I did not hear the rustling of the undergrowth behind me.

Hestia looked over my shoulder and whinnied. It sounded as if she was warning me of danger.

But it was too late.

Before I could turn, my head seemed to burst open. A thousand sparks of light flashed before my eyes.

Then I slid down into total blackness.

—0—

I came awake with my head pounding as if a blacksmith was using it as an anvil.

I tried to move my hands, but they seemed stuck behind my back. My feet also seemed to be stuck together.

I was lying, bound hand and foot, in the dark on a solid floor – but I knew not where.

There was a vaguely familiar smell – of wood and sweat. I could not place it, but it made me feel very uneasy.

Then I gave a yelp as I was jolted back and my feet hit something solid. But the yelp never made a sound, as a rag was bound round my head and filled my mouth.

There was the sound of hooves, as I was thrown to the side.

Then another sound that I would never want to hear again.

Screech. Screech. Screech.

I tried to give a despairing scream.

I knew exactly where I was.

In the same squeaky-axle box cart that Sir Reginald de Courtney had used when he had tried to return me to my cursed life at Marchington Manor.

So now I was finally being taken back to that dreadful place.

To a life of servitude at the least.

Or worse, my stepfather was going to carry out his awful threat.

All breath left my body, just as if I had fallen into icy water.

I was being carried to my death.

19
WHAT TO DO WITH MARY?

After what seemed like a lifetime in the darkness, being thrown one way and another and collecting no end of bruises, the cart finally stopped.

There was a lurch and the sound of feet hitting the ground. Then footsteps on the gravel. The door opened and I blinked, closing my eyes against the sudden light. A man's head appeared, silhouetted in the doorway. "Come missy," he said, in a voice I did not recognise. "Home at last."

He grabbed my feet and pulled me roughly out, until I was sitting beside the cart. Then he scooped me up like a sack of coal and hefted me over his shoulder. As we walked along the gravel, all I could see was his lower back and rump. Then we came to a door, which he pulled open, and we were in the corridor which led to the kitchens. I tried to twist the right way up to see where we were going, but it was not possible, so I flopped back. Where were the feet of the cook or the kitchen servants; people who knew me and might come to my aid?

But the kitchens were strangely empty.

He took me up the stairs, along a corridor and through another door. I recognised the flagstones. We were in the Great Hall. There he slid me off his shoulder, so I dropped onto my side, curled up like a newborn babe.

"You have done well, Matthew," came my stepfather's voice. "You may go now. Leave her there."

A pair of dark leather boots appeared before me.

"I knew you were most likely still in that cottage," he said. "So I had Matthew wait until you came for your horse." He gave a mirthless chuckle. "Nice horsemanship, Mary, I will give you that. Jumping the courtyard wall with both you and the man on the beast's back; that was impressive."

Then one of his boots slid back.

I braced myself for the kick.

It caught me in the chest. I gave a grunt as the pain spread out over my whole body, but my cry was swallowed up by the gag.

"So, Mary, I finally have you back under my charge. Not running about the land masquerading as a boy!"

Another kick. This one lower, in my belly, making me curl up even more.

"Do you dare to defy me, you wicked girl? Weeks, I have been looking for you! Weeks, I have been interrogating all the men and women I put in place to report back if you were seen!"

A further kick, which caught my knee, so a little less pain.

"You make my name a mockery, you heartless little harridan!"

The knee, again.

"'There goes Andrew Fox,' they say, 'the man who cannot control his daughter. The man who tried to marry her to a good family, and who failed because she defied him. Because she acts most unnaturally. Because she's a disgrace to the memory of the fine woman who bore her; a woman who's shoes she is not worthy to touch, let alone fill."

The knee once more.

"That was for my friend Sir Reginald, who was nearly unmanned by your own knee, Mary, and who you left for dead in a lane."

Then the chest again.

"Well, do you know, my loving daughter, he recovered and returned to his home. But he says he will have nothing more to do with you."

Then back to the knee.

"He says he would not marry you now, if no other girl remained in all of Christendom."

The boots walked away and I uncurled slightly, trying to find a place in my head where there was no pain. For every part of the rest of my body was screaming, even if I could make no sound.

"So what am I to do with you?"

The boots stopped and turned back.

"I could make good on my oath that night by the gates of this very house, that I would end your useless and misguided life. And indeed, I am minded to do so."

One foot tapped on the floor.

"No other person knows I have you back, except my servant Matthew, and he will hold his tongue. Not even your brothers. So I could have your worthless throat slit and your unnatural carcass dropped in a ditch, or even the disused well that you so nearly perished in before, and no-one would be any the wiser. Except Satan, who I don't doubt is looking forward to receiving you in his pit of flame."

The boots came back by my head, then rocked forward as he crouched down. His red blotched face was thrust into mine. "I am that close, Mary." He held his thumb and forefinger in front of my eyes, pinched almost together. "That close – to carrying out my threat and being rid of you forever."

He stood up and moved back. "But I have decided not. At least not yet." The boots moved closer again. "Why? Because that would be too easy. No. I have decided that the only way to make you understand the pain of your unnatural behaviour, is to make you a prisoner. So you will be kept in confinement, here, in a sealed-off room on the east wing. For as long as I decide to keep you alive."

One of the boots moved back and I braced myself once more, but the kick did not come. Instead he used it to push my shoulder over, so I was lying on my back looking up at him.

"I might decide to release you one day, but not for many years. Not until you are a dried up, good for nothing old woman. Would you like that, Mary? Losing the best years of your life, as a result of defying me?"

It was hard to see his face as his belly obscured it, but there was no avoiding his words.

"Or belike I will die one day myself, and you will be forgotten. Left to wither away like a starved rat."

The pain in my body was nothing to the pain of his words. To be held captive without hope of release would be to lose my mind. Indeed, I could almost prefer the swift death to the life he was promising.

"So," he said, with a note of finality. "Let it begin." He walked away, and I heard him call out, "Matthew! You can take her upstairs, now."

—0—

The man Matthew dropped me on the floor of a plain wood-panelled room, then reached down and untied the bonds on my hands and feet. There was some relief as he also pulled off the gag.

I would have welcomed the chance to rain down upon him all the curses I knew, but my mouth was too dry.

Maybe some other time. Speech would come back eventually. Meanwhile, it was all I could do to gasp in air like a fish upon a slab.

Such was the pain of the kicks from my stepfather, on top of the bruising I had received from being thrown around inside the cart, that movement was also something I would also need to leave for the future.

For now all I could do was to keep still and hope the pain would subside. Eventually.

He went over to the door. "Fare thee well, missy," he chuckled. "I will bring food and firewood morning and evening, and change over your chamber pot for a clean one. You are to place it by the table where I can see it from the door, and step away to the other side of the room. If the pot is not placed by the table, or if I see you near when I open the door, I will close it again. So you will not be fed, nor have your pot changed that day, or until I choose. Understood?" I gave a small grunt of agreement. "Good." He paused. "Each week I will also bring a pitcher of water

197

and rag, so you may clean yourself. The same rule applies as with the chamber pot."

He went out and I heard a bolt being thrown on the other side of the door.

I know not how long I lay still on the floor, but after perhaps an hour, I gently tested movement in my legs. It was not easy, as my knees protested greatly from the attentions of my stepfather. After some very slow efforts, accompanied by gasps of pain, I finally managed to get them straight.

Encouraged by this small success, I tried my arms. They too required slow, careful moves, but eventually, I was able to bring them round to my front.

It took much more time and painful wincing, but I was then able to get up off the floor and walk slowly to sit on the pallet bed in the corner.

Time. That was a commodity I now had in abundance.

Time to look around the room that was to be my world; maybe for the rest of my life. It was a small chamber, possibly once used for one of the more senior servants. The wood-panelling was very basic, and above it were bare white plaster walls and ceiling. The walls were unadorned with any form of hanging or decoration. On the wall beside the door was a small table with a built-in bench seat – which I assumed was to avoid affording me a chair I could break up and use as any sort of weapon. The bed I sat on was a single pallet with no posts or curtains. There were no books, paper or writing implements to keep my mind occupied.

Truly my stepfather intended for this to be a punishment.

As I sat on the bed, I had nothing else to think on, except to reflect on how I had got into this dreadful situation; a lifetime prisoner of a vindictive and violent parent.

Was it poor judgement? Or poor fortune?

It had been misfortune that *The Margarita* had to put into Maldon after the storm.

Maybe it had been poor judgement to go to the Blue Boar. I could possibly have guessed that my stepfather would have spies in such places.

But it had good fortune to be reunited with Hestia. Not many mares could have cleared that wall with both Marcus and myself on their back.

Hestia! Poor fortune indeed that I had only had her back for a day. I hoped she had not been stolen by the man Matthew, and had remained in the care of Marcus after I had been beaten over the head and taken away in the cart.

If so, Marcus would use Hestia to make his journey back to London. I trusted that he would have good care of her – and that one day I might be with her again.

I groaned aloud. This small room, with but one window (barred, naturally) would most likely be my home for life. With little or no chance of release. All thoughts of seeing Hestia would have to be forgotten.

Unless Marcus would realise what had happened to me, and rescue me? I had done as much for him. I could hope for this, although in my heart I knew it would be better not to let my hopes be raised.

A spear of pain shot across my chest, making me cry out. My chest – repeatedly kicked by my stepfather. What damage had he done there? Was I to bleed to death?

I carefully unfastened my jerkin. The binding around my chest was revealed, and I strained to look down on it.

Thankfully there was no blood on the outside.

I took out the pins and gently unwound it, dreading to see red staining inside.

But by God's good grace, there was none.

Finally it was off, and I looked to see how badly there was bruising. There was tenderness, for sure, but only small bruising. Perhaps the binding itself had protected me from greater harm.

I pulled the jerkin back on to cover myself, then I realised there was no person to see my immodesty.

Until Matthew came with some food and to change the pot.

I looked balefully at the large earthenware bowl on the floor by the little fireplace.

At least there was a fire.

I would not freeze to death over the winter.

—0—

And indeed I did not.

The little fire kept me warm through the winter months, and as winter became spring then summer, it continued to give off enough heat to keep the chill away.

My bruises healed themselves in the first couple of weeks, and I was able to move freely without pain. Thankfully nothing seemed broken, nor permanently damaged.

Matthew continued to bring me food and firewood, and to take away what little I left in the chamber pot.

One time he brought me a simple servant's dress on the instruction of my stepfather, who had apparently decided I must dress as befits a woman. Matthew took away my jerkin and breeches, with the comment that they would soon be burned.

My hair grew long again, and he brought me a linen coif to keep it in place, but no pins.

Once it became sadly clear that my fears were correct, and Marcus was never going to come to my rescue, my thoughts then turned to escape. I concocted ever more desperate schemes to get away. These included hiding behind the door when Matthew came in, ready to throw the contents of the chamber pot in his face, then rush past as he was momentarily incapacitated. But on the day I tried this, he opened the door, and when he did not see the pot on the floor, he closed it again immediately.

I missed my dinner that day.

On another day, I left my pot in its place, but as soon as he opened the door, I ran at him, aiming to get past.

Sadly he was able to close it in plenty of time before I was near.

I missed both meals the following day.

And the one after.

I tested the bars on the window often, mindful of how I had managed to get such things away from Cruddon's house in Blackfriars. But these were well secured into the hard brickwork, and however hard I tried, they would not make even the slightest movement. It made me realise that my stepfather had prepared this room thoroughly, well in advance of my capture. He must have planned the whole thing on the basis that he would get me back eventually. It was consistent with the level of organisation he had put into establishing his network of spies.

The chimney seemed to be a possible exit route, so one day I let the fire go out, then clambered into the hearth to look upwards. A blackened and soot-covered grating been set into the brickwork at the start of the flue, but even if I had been able to get past it, the opening itself looked too small for my shoulders.

Truly, he had thought of all possible escape routes, and made sure they were inaccessible to me.

I took to gazing out of the window for hours at a time. It had a limited view across part of the roof of the main house, then to a small stretch of parkland and trees. At one time I thought I saw a rider crossing the park, and hammered my fists on the window – but I knew it was all in vain. The rider was too far away to hear me, and even if he did, how could he possibly identify where such a sound was coming from?

And it might have even been my stepfather himself.

—0—

One day he came up to see me.

It was as the trees in the park started turning golden for the autumn. I was lying on the bed with my hands behind my head, gazing up at the whitewashed ceiling, when there was the sound of the bolt being drawn back.

I sat up. Matthew was not expected for several hours.

The door opened, but it was not Matthew who walked in.

It was my stepfather holding a sword before him.

He closed the door and stood with his back to it, waving the sword in my direction.

I looked at the point, flickering in the orange light of the fire.

A sudden cold chill gripped me.

"Have you come to put me from my misery, father?" I asked, gesturing at the sword. "Have you decided to carry through on your original threat?"

He gave a slow, cold smile. "Nay, daughter. But that offer still stands, should I decide to act upon it." He lowered the blade. "I have done such a good job of hiding you away, that at times I have quite forgot you even existed. So I thought I would come and see you for myself."

"I am still here, I can assure you," I replied, unable to stop this sounding sarcastic.

"Indeed you are." He glanced down at the sword. "No, this is for my protection, for I am well aware of your capabilities. I have heard tell of your exploits, which put me in mind of some dreadful parody of a man. I understand you are well used to fighting with a sword or leaping through doors like a performing acrobat. So I thought it best to come prepared."

So, even though I was held a prisoner, he still feared me.

I supposed that was something.

"Like you prepared a network of spies to entrap me?" I asked. "Or set up this room as a secure prison in case I was ever taken?"

He raised an eyebrow. "I have never underestimated your quick wit, Mary. Had you been born a boy, it would have served you well. But in a woman – no. That is unnatural and ungodly. It cannot be allowed."

"Then what are you to do with me?" I got up from the bed. "You have held me here for what – nigh on ten months? Do you still propose to hold me for the rest of my life? Or is this not punishment enough?"

He shook his head. "No, Mary, it is not. I cannot conceive there is sufficient punishment that can be given you, in this world at least, to atone for your unnatural behaviour. I will leave you here under my justice." He opened the door to go out, then paused and turned back.

"Or until such time as Satan decides to take over."

20

MATTHEW

As the trees in the park turned golden once more, and the autumn rains became winter snows, it was a wonder I did not go mad, stuck alone in that little room.

Indeed I did find myself struggling to remember what life had been like before this prison became my whole existence. It all seemed to fade into some sort of half-remembered dream. Had I really lived as Prince Henry Fitzroy at Durham House, with Lady Kyme taking the part of my mother? Had I called her 'Lady Mother', and enjoyed the strange, and much missed, feeling of having her as a warm and supportive parent?

Had I been to Blackfriars and snatched Fitzroy himself from under the nose of Jacob Cruddon? And had I then been to Court and sat beside the King? Or gone to Ipswich and rescued Marcus, once again from the clutches of Jacob Cruddon? At times I struggled to remember the order of events. Was it before or after Court that I met Noah Robson in the Blackfriars house and stopped him from being consumed by rats?

Rats!

One thing only that pleased me in my prison chamber – and it was small comfort indeed – was the lack of any rats seeking to keep me company. But either this room was too high up in a far wing of the house for them to venture, or the cats kept by the housekeeper had managed to rid Marchington Manor of them all. So I was pleased not to be kept awake by the thought of being eaten in the night.

Which meant that the only company I had, apart the unpleasant visit by my stepfather, was from my gaoler, Matthew.

Outwardly he was an unremarkable fellow, of medium height and build, dark haired, and with no particularly distinguishing features. It seemed strange that he was content to visit my room twice a day, bringing me food and changing my chamber pot. It must have been a noisome task for him to empty each one I had filled, especially as every few weeks I added the bloody rags he gave me for my courses. What kind of man would be content with doing that?

I often wondered what he did each day, when he was not attending on his prisoner. Did he have other duties within my stepfather's household? I had not known him at Marchington Manor before I originally ran away, so he must have been brought in after I had gone. Maybe he had been recruited as one of the spies, then been taken into the house once the need for such subterfuge was over. Did he live in the servants' quarters, or did he have a cottage in a nearby village? Was there a wife, and if so, did she know what his tasks were?

I decided on one occasion that I would attempt to engage him in conversation. It was mainly to find answers to my questions, although I will admit it may have been more about simply having the chance to talk to someone other than myself.

"Tell me, Matthew," I tried one day, as I observed him from the far end of the room, "is my care your sole duty? Or do you do aught else between visits to my chamber?"

"Talk not, you little vixen," he growled, "or there will be no food for a day."

"Oh come now," I said with what I hoped was a winsome smile, "that is harsh when I seek only to make polite conversation."

"I am ordered not to let you converse, lest it leads to one of your cunning tricks to escape."

"Escape?" I exclaimed. "How does a mere discussion lead to that?"

"I know not, but I cannot take the chance."

"Then you have a high opinion of me, sir, that you think I may talk my way past you."

He frowned. "Your father keeps you here for that very reason."

I feigned surprise. "What, you mean that he does not wish me to talk?"

"You know well what I mean." He scratched his beard. "That you are not a natural woman, and use cunning and subterfuge to achieve your ends."

I spotted a flaw in his argument. "But you will agree that all women love to talk?"

He gave a deep sigh and a nod. "Aye, that they do."

He was married.

"Then if I merely wish to engage you in a conversation, does that not make me a natural woman?"

There was a silence, as again he scratched at his chin, then he said, "I know not what you mean by such arguments." He closed the door and threw the bolt across.

I was left wondering if I had made my life better or worse, and decided that even such a cursory conversation was better than none at all.

I tried again the next time he came, hoping to build on my earlier achievement.

"Good sir…" I began.

"Silence! I have said."

I ignored him. "You have a wife?"

He stared at me a moment, his mouth working. "That is none of your concern."

"She must be a fine woman."

"I said," he repeated, "that is not to concern you."

"Why not?" I asked, putting some sweet reasonableness into my voice. "I see you twice every day and no other. Why should I not take an interest in you?"

"I have said…" he tried once more, but I held up my hand.

"I know what you have said." I gave him a sideways smile. "But here is the heart of the matter. You know all about me. Why should I not know a little of you?"

"Because I have orders not to converse with you." He gave a small frown, as if he could not see why I found this so difficult. "And these I follow."

"Ahh. Orders. We must all take heed of these."

He made a hollow laugh. "From what I understand, missy, that is exactly what you do not do."

A small victory! I had got him to make a point of his own, rather than to respond just to mine. I chased this up quickly. "I follow only such orders as I agree with. Can you not do the same?"

"That is not what orders mean." He frowned again. "A man is not at liberty to pick and choose. He must follow them whatever."

"Most virtuous," I conceded, warming to my theme. "But what if…"

He shook his head. "Nay, 'tis enough." Then, as before, he was gone.

These two conversations seemed to have started to break the ice in our relationship.

In the months that followed, we engaged in longer and longer discussions. At first these would end abruptly, usually when I found some flaw in his argument and was just starting to press my advantage. But eventually, our discourse became wider and more animated, and we would spend much time on each. One time we even spoke across the whole day, so he must stop and fetch the evening tray. We became like old friends, as keen to debate each other as any pair seated in a tavern. I lived for his smiles and his approval, and positively revelled in the times when he decided to open a conversation himself.

I came to think I had some special connection with him – and not just because he was the only living soul I could communicate with. I would look forward greatly to his visits, waiting each morning and evening like some excited little girl, desperate to see him. And I believed he felt the same, as his mind became sharper; honed by my challenges and my refusal to accept ill-considered arguments.

It dawned on me that Matthew was not quite as plain-looking as I first thought. His dark hair fell in a pleasing way across his forehead, and his nose, which was maybe slightly larger than normal, had an interesting curve at the end. His eyes now impressed themselves on me; they were slightly greenish, yet with flecks of brown. His mouth turned up slightly at the corners, and he had a way of putting his tongue slightly out when considering his response to some point I had made.

How could I have ever thought him unremarkable?

Over time I also managed to learn more of his life outside his twice-daily visits to me. He did have a wife, and they lived in a cottage on the edge of Maldon. Sadly, God had not blessed them with children – something they both felt bitterly unfair. It had always been his dearest wish to raise a son; to teach him the ways of the world, and to take great joy in a boy's growth and strength. But he would have equally welcomed a daughter, watching her grow into a confident young woman.

Having such interaction with another did help keep me sound in my mind, for without it I feel sure I would have been left only with God to talk to. And more and more I had come to realise that conversing with someone in one's own head – even someone divine, yet who makes no discernible effort to respond – does little to preserve one's sanity.

But it was not only my mind I needed to keep sound, but my body also.

I ate very little – mainly because that was what I was given – but even so, I was concerned not to become portly like my stepfather through lack of movement. And should I ever be able to escape, then I would not wish to be recaptured through an inability to move quickly.

So sitting alone, I devised a series of activities to help keep me sound in body, as well as helping keep my mind occupied.

Each day I would rise with the sun, and each day I would lie down to sleep as the sun did the same. In between, I would conduct a series of runs and walks that made me physically tired. The walks consisted of striding a hundred times around the room without pause, then a break of maybe a quarter hour, then a hundred more the other way.

It took exactly thirty-six steps – no more and no less – to make one complete round of the room.

Once I had done my two walks in the morning, I would wait until the shadows started to lengthen, then do my running. This consisted of a quick dash from one side of the room to the other, a touch of the wall, then a dash back again.

Nine steps each way.

Of these, I would do a hundred pairs, then a rest as before, followed by a hundred more.

I started this exercise regimen soon after my stepfather's visit. After ten months of inactivity up to that point, I must have been in the poorest condition.

But by the time I greeted my third springtime, I fancied I had reached at least the strength and stamina I had enjoyed before being taken, and possibly even a little bit more.

Which was most opportune, because that was when I escaped.

21

CHANGING OF THE GUARD

It was one bright spring morning, some two and a half years after I had first been thrown into my little prison chamber.

There was the usual sound of the bolt being pulled back, so I put my pot down in its place and stood on the other side of the room, as I must do every day.

I found myself hopping from foot to foot with anticipation as I waited for Matthew to come in. I had thought of a new line of discussion; I wanted to ask him if he had heard any news of the Court, or if the Queen had been delivered of a son at all. It had been more than two and a half years since the birth of Queen Anne's daughter, so I thought it likely that she had given birth again. Maybe even twice. And if so, then surely Matthew would know of it. Such news is called out by every town crier, and even if he had not heard of it himself, then I felt sure his wife would have told him.

Matthew came in with his tray of food and drink. He put it down on the table, changed over the pot, then made to close the door without a word, or a look in my direction.

Then he seemed to hesitate; his hand on the door frame. He turned and looked at me.

Such was my excitement that I took this as my cue to ask my question.

I had scarce drawn breath, when I stopped. There was a deeply sad look on his face that suggested any topic of mine was not going to be appropriate.

I bit down my question, and waited for him to speak.

"I shall not be seeing you again," he said. "I will no longer be responsible for your care."

I gave a small gasp. Whatever I had thought he might say, it was not that.

"But…" I stammered. "That is not fair…"

"There it is. I am sorry, sweet Mary."

"But… but… why so?"

"I would not do this anymore."

Like a simple fool I repeated, "Why so?"

He looked down. "I have enlisted as a fighting man in the King's army. I shall be happy to follow my orders there, instead of those of your father here." He nodded, almost as if to reassure himself, and said, "You are not the harridan your father believes. You are a good woman." He shook his head. "So I cannot do this any longer." He moved back, pulling the door nearly to a close, then looked me directly in the eye. "May God go with you." He gave me the smallest of smiles, then said, "Fare thee well, Mary Fox. Fare thee well."

He closed the door, and there was the faint sound of the bolt being pushed slowly across.

I stood still for I know not how long, struggling to understand what he had said.

I had thought him my friend, but never forgot he was really my gaoler. Had I become too amiable with my conversations, that he had become confused himself? Had it made him lose sight of his true purpose?

I lay down on the bed and stared up at the ceiling.

In all the months since we had started talking, I had been able to bear my imprisonment, for he had given me both a purpose and something to look forward to each day. Now he was gone, what had I to keep myself going?

With a sigh I turned onto my side and curled up on the bed like a small child, even though the sun was still not high enough to say it was noon.

There I stayed, slipping in and out of a fitful sleep, until I heard footsteps coming up the stairs.

I sat up in alarm as the bolt was drawn back.

Quickly I put the pot in its place by the table and stood back by the far wall – such was my conditioning that I did this without any thought.

The door swung partly open; a slim hand holding the edge.

Then a woman's shoe appeared, followed after a moment by the hem of a serving girl's dress.

The door opened fully, and my hand flew to my mouth when I recognised who it was.

It was Miriam Carver.

—o—

Miriam closed the door and sat at the table.

"We thought you dead," she said. "Master Kytson and I." She observed me quietly a few moments.

I said nothing, for I was still too shocked to make anything more than the smallest mewling noise from the back of my throat. She continued. "All we knew was that you had told Master Kytson that your stepfather, Sir

Andrew Fox of Marchington Manor, had threatened to kill you. Naturally, we assumed when you disappeared, leaving your horse, that he had somehow succeeded. Especially after the man himself had forced his way into my house as I grieved for my Job, and brought with him such anger and spite." She rearranged her skirts. "So we thought where he might have disposed of your remains. We first went down to the Hythe Quay, and asked there if any man had fished out the body of a boy…" she smiled, "…for although Master Kytson told me of your true nature, we thought no person would think you a girl in those clothes and cut of hair." She paused. "And, of course, were you to be fished out and examined by the coroner, then it would be the finest news, heard by all."

I remained silent. The thought of my cold, dead body being undressed and its truth being exposed made me feel sick to my core.

"So then we rode up and down every ditch around Maldon, expecting to see your sorry carcass as food for the birds and the worms but, as you can understand, we found no trace of you."

And all the while the sorry carcass in question had been rotting in this very chamber. I managed a "Hmm?" and waved a hand at her to continue her tale.

"Eventually, we decided that maybe you had been taken here by your stepfather. I was all for having Master Kytson ride up and make enquiries, but he was less sure. He said if you were here, dead or alive, it would be most dangerous for him to come asking questions."

I could imagine Marcus being concerned, and now I thought it through, I could not fault him. Had my stepfather been confronted with a young man asking about me, then I would not give a fig for such a young man's chances of leaving again alive.

"I am sorry, but that was when we decided it was the end of the matter. That there was nothing more we could do for you. Master Kytson said he must reluctantly return to London, but impressed on me the need to contact him if there was any news of you. I started to make the best life I could as a widow and mother."

I managed to clear my throat and find my voice. "Then how are you here now, after more than two years?"

"Ahh, there is another tale." She gave me a satisfied smile. "I am friendly with Bridget Elias, who lives with her husband not far from my cottage. She has oft helped with the care of my little son Isaac, as she and her husband have not been blessed by God with any children of their own. She was telling me that her husband had decided to enlist in the army."

"Matthew… Elias?" I asked, starting to see how all of this might have occurred.

She nodded. "Aye. That is him."

I continued for her. "So Bridget Elias told you that the reason her Matthew was enlisting, was because he could no longer stomach working for my stepfather?" Again she nodded. "And Matthew had confided in Bridget the reason; that he was charged with being gaoler to a prisoner held in secret in the Manor?"

"Correct. And that this was not something he could continue to do."

"I see," I said. "So you came to the realisation that the secret prisoner must be me?"

"Yes, that was it," she said. "I went first into Maldon and found a rider travelling to London. I asked him to seek out Master Kytson, and tell him that the person we sought has been found, and that he must come quickly, and bring some men with him if possible. Then I came here, with a view to getting you away, as you had shown me great kindness and support after the death of my Job. Master Kytson had also told me of your bravery in rescuing him, as well as a young lad from kidnap. So I knew you were a good woman, and could not bear the thought of you being held prisoner – it seemed a most unchristian and greatly unfair. I resolved I would do something to help you. So I offered my service as a housemaid."

"And I am deeply grateful," I said with a warm smile, coming over and sitting beside her. I put my hand on hers. It was good to know there were such women as Miriam Carver in this world, who would act from kindness and compassion. Especially as she was a relative stranger.

This gave me a thought. Her being a stranger was indeed a piece of the greatest fortune.

"My stepfather must have seen an opportunity to have someone who was unknown to the other servants take up Matthew's secret duties," I observed. "It must have seemed a blessing from God when you presented yourself." I paused. "You did present yourself? You met him directly?"

"I did," she replied. "He explained to me that you were a young relative of most unsound mind, who was kept a secret lest his sons and the other servants were frighted by your ravings."

A disturbing thought occurred to me. I turned to her with a frown. "But you met him, when he came into your cottage. We heard from the cellar. Did he not recognise you?"

"Nay, noblemen like your stepfather pay no heed to common folk like me. I think it most unlikely he would recall a woman he met briefly over two years before in a dark cottage." She smiled. "And anyway, he made no such recognition when he assigned me my duties, and I used a different name to my own. To him I am Joan Porter."

"A sound idea," I said. "And he had no concern I might overpower you?" I looked her up and down. She had a particularly small frame, such that I felt something of a giant beside her, and I am not above average size myself. "You are half the size of Matthew Elias."

She shrugged. "He made no mention of any such concern."

I nodded. "Most likely he thinks my spirit is quite broken from being held for so long. He does not conceive I will try anything." I went over to the bed and sat. "So now you are here, Mistress Carver, shall we prove him wrong? Do you plan to help me get free?"

"Of course," she said. "But I have not yet decided exactly how this should happen." She was thoughtful a moment. "And I would want to wait on Master Kytson so we can get you away more easily."

I nodded as I thought this through. Now I had a gaoler who was not only on my side, but was also committed to my escape, such an enterprise must surely be possible to accomplish. And if Marcus was involved, together with some men, then we could factor this into the plans.

"I will also give it some thought," I suggested. "And we can discuss and agree on our plans over the next few days.

Hopefully that will be enough time for Master Kytson to get your message and gather some men." I sat back and leaned against the wall. "We must ensure that no harm comes to you or Master Kytson in this venture," I said. "So we must take our time and make our plans with care."

22

NEW HORIZONS

Over the next few days Miriam came morning and evening with the tray and change of pot, just as Matthew had done before her.

And just as with Matthew, we talked freely. But instead of the cut and thrust of challenging debate, my conversations with Miriam were focused on plans for escape.

Gradually these took shape – until finally, we were ready.

"It only takes Marcus Kytson to arrive and you to give him instruction," I said one evening, as Miriam laid out the new plate of food and cup of ale, then gathered the morning's empty ones onto her tray. "Then we can set the plan in motion."

"Yes," she agreed with a smile. "Then you will finally be free, Mary Fox."

Free? I looked around the little room, that had been my only home these past thirty months. As familiar to me as the backs of my own hands.

Thirty-six steps around.

Nine across.

Would I soon be able to say goodbye to it?

I dearly hoped so.

I felt a cold chill in my belly. Was I ready to make my way in the world outside once more?

I stood tall and raised my chin. I must push away such feelings. For sure it would be a challenge, but I must resolve to face up to situations I had not encountered in all this time. I must leave the relative safety afforded by these four walls and once again live a free life beyond.

I must hold on to the excitement, not the fear.

"That is my dearest wish, Miriam," I replied, with what I hoped was an easy smile of my own. "I have dreamed of freedom every day since I was first held here."

And indeed, I had done so – except that freedom was some distant, unattainable ideal, unlikely ever to happen. Now that it was here, really here, I needed to grasp it. I resolved to start thinking myself free in my head. To see not these four walls, but the open fields and paths that existed outside, so I might be more able to manage them if… no, when… they became a reality.

"You will let me know as soon as Marcus is here?" I asked.

"For sure." Miriam bustled out of the door. "The very moment."

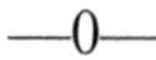

Two days later, Miriam told me that Marcus had arrived, and had brought with him two men. So we could set our plan in motion.

That night I lay awake on the bed, counting down the hours as best I could, feeling almost sick with anticipation.

Eventually I heard the softest footstep outside the room, and the almost imperceptible sound of the bolt being slowly pulled back.

Miriam crept in as quiet as a mouse, the bright flame of her candle flickering in the blackness. It gave her face a strange look; her eyes appearing only as pinpricks of light from under her hooded black robe.

She handed a similar garment to me and I slipped it on. Then I eased off my old hard-soled shoes and replaced them with the soft slippers she gave me.

She stood back, leaving the door open. I took a deep breath to steady myself.

I lifted my chin.

I walked out of my prison.

—0—

Beyond the room was a short passageway. Miriam closed and bolted the door, then held the candle beside me so I could see the steps at the end.

"Careful as you tread," she whispered in my ear. "I have laid blankets over the stairs for quietness, as we agreed."

I stepped down the stairs with great caution, lest the blanket slip away from under me and I fall with a great crash. Thankfully I was able to reach the bottom without a sound. Miriam gathered the blankets up behind me, then whispered, "This way."

We crept along a lengthy passage to the top of another set of stairs, which I thought were the ones leading down to the kitchens. Again we went down these with blankets to deaden the sound.

We came to the same passage that I had been carried through all those months before. I stopped a moment with my hand on the rough brick wall, again to steady my breath.

This led to the outside and freedom.

But first we must risk going through the kitchens, lit by the dull glow of the smouldering fire. Along one wall were the cots of the kitchen servants, who all slept in their place of work. We needed to reach the door at the far end. And this meant getting past all these cots without raising any of the occupants from their slumber.

Easy to say, but harder to achieve.

And necessary if we were to get safely out of the house.

I could just make out six beds in the light of our candle, each one with a darkly shadowed shape curled in sleep. The breathing sounds ranged from the lightest breath up to a full-throated snore.

Despite the noise, Miriam and I proceeded like the quietest of mice towards the door at the far end.

Then suddenly with a grunt, the snoring ceased. We stopped still, like two black-robed demons in the orange light. The snorer grunted again. Then he coughed. It was the cough made by one who is most definitely awake.

My blood froze as one of the figures rose up from its cot.

There was a gasp, sounding like one of surprise.

"By Heavens," growled a voice, "who goes there?" There was a slight pause. "Be human or from hell?"

"Run!" I hissed at Miriam.

Casting aside all thought of silence, we bolted towards the door.

There was a loud creak as the man clambered up from his cot. Heavy footsteps came after us, together with the shouts of "Intruders! Thieves! Stop them!"

We reached the door, and I wrenched the handle open, then pushed it wide. Together we ran across the gravel, not caring that we made the sound of a hundred soldiers on the march, and headed across the eerily blue moonlit lawns towards the gates.

It seemed as if they were receding as we ran, and in desperation I called out, "Come on!"

I could hear the man behind us. He was yelling and cursing as he pursued, calling for others to join him.

There were several more shouts from behind.

Was one my stepfather, alerted by the yelling?

Then thankfully we came up to the gates. There were two ropes hanging over the high wall just beside them. Miriam and I grabbed one each. Marcus's head appeared through the bars of the gate. "Hang on!" he called across, as we twisted the rope in our hands to get the best grip.

There was the sound of hooves on the other side of the wall and my rope jerked upwards. I swung my feet onto the wall and walked up as the rope pulled me to the top. Beside me I could see Miriam doing the same.

We reached the top and I grabbed the coping stone, letting go of the rope, then flipped round so I was facing back towards the house with my legs hanging down the far side of the wall.

A quick glance told me the man, a burly fellow in a dirty-looking nightshirt, was almost upon us.

Several more men were behind him, but I could not see their faces.

"Let go!" Marcus called. "I have you!"

With a small grin at the man, I pushed back and let myself drop.

For a moment I was falling freely, and feared I might land badly. Then strong arms grasped my waist as Marcus caught me and let me gently down. Another man had done the same for Miriam.

I slipped from Marcus's arms and ran over to the gate, peering through. The burly servant was running at the wall like a leaping toad, trying to get hold of the end of my rope. Marcus must have seen what was happening. He ran to the horse who had so thankfully pulled me up and tried to get the beast to move forward. This was a mistake, for he frightened the animal. It neighed and tried to bolt. The man must have caught the rope at that very moment. As the horse moved, the rope became taught and, with a sick grin of his own, the man was swiftly pulled up the wall.

I ran back to Marcus.

"You are pulling him up," I yelped.

Marcus stared at me with a white face in the moonlight. I grabbed at the bridle and tried to stop the horse. It raised its head but kept moving forward. So in desperation I pulled its head round. Reluctantly it turned, but it was not enough. The man's hands were now above the coping stone.

As his triumphant face appeared, I managed to get the horse further round, and pulled it quickly towards the wall. The rope went slack, and with a sudden expression of surprise and a shocked cry, the man disappeared.

There was a loud thump. I looked through the gate again. He was lying flat on his back. Several other men started to gather around his prostrate form.

"The second rope!" I called to Marcus.

Quickly he ran to the other horse. This time he took no chance. He pulled directly on the rope, so the end whipped over the wall before any man could take hold.

Marcus came back to me.

"Hello Mary," he said with a grin. "It has been a while." He enveloped me in a great hug, whispering, "I have missed you so, Mary," in my ear. Then he helped me onto the first horse. It was Hestia. She whinnied when she saw me, and I gave her a quick stroke on her neck.

As I settled in the saddle he helped Miriam up behind me. Her hands grasped me about my belly. "It worked," she said in my ear.

"Only just," I said over my shoulder.

"Come, Mary, and you Miriam," Marcus said, mounting his own horse, "we need to be away if we are to make our destination by first light."

23

THE THREAT TO THE PRINCE

The sun had barely crept over the horizon as we made our weary way into the town of Chelmsford, crossing the bridge over the river Can just as it opened.

Our party consisted of Marcus, myself, Miriam, and the two men Marcus had brought with him from London, Ed Benson and Hal Dugdale.

We had hardly spoken on the journey, such had been our exhaustion after the escape, and we had barely stopped in case my stepfather was following us. I had no doubt he would have been awakened by the noise, and there was every chance he had opened the gates and ridden out as soon as he was able. I could only hope he had no clear indication as to which way we had gone. Especially as we had first headed south as if we might be making for the docks at Tilbury, making sure to leave many hoofprints and breaking off branches to create a trail. But after a few miles we had doubled back and headed north-west through the forest towards Chelmsford.

Even then, our destination was not within the bustling town itself. It was a place called Writtle, a few miles beyond, where Miriam's brother and his wife were tenant farmers on a smallholding.

The plan was for Miriam to stay there a while with her little son Isaac, in case my stepfather managed to identify who 'Joan Porter' really was. To that end, Miriam's brother had fetched Isaac a few days earlier, so she need not leave him alone while effecting my rescue, nor have him with us on such a wearying journey.

We arrived in Chelmsford after around two hours' ride.

The town was a hive of activity, even this early. People thronged the wide central thoroughfare, forcing us to ride closely together lest the flow of the crowd might separate us.

"This is good," Marcus observed as we picked our way round what seemed to be an abandoned cart. "We are so surrounded that it will be hard to follow us, let alone pick up our real trail."

I had a passing thought that he seemed to have learned something from his earlier failure as a pursuer through Greenwich, but in truth, I was more distracted by all the people crowding around me.

"What ails, Mary?" he asked. "You stare about you with the look of a frightened deer."

"I am not used to this many folk," I whispered, unable to find much voice.

"Mistress Fox has had little other than her own company these two years and a half," said Miriam from behind me. "How would you fare if you went from that to…" she waved a hand at the sea of people around us, "…to all this?"

Marcus glanced at me with concern on his face. "Indeed, I see what you mean." He gave me a smile. "Hold firm, Mary. We will soon be through and out into the country beyond."

I nodded silently, and tried to force myself to look only at my horse's ears and pretend that I was not within such a crowd. I succeeded for a few minutes, until a man jostled hard against my leg. My loud and urgent scream brought a swift rebuke from the man, and Marcus back to my side.

"I will ride beside you," he said, and waved at Hal to take up a position on my other side. Ed then rode in front, so I need only look at his horse's hindquarters.

"Thank you," I whispered to Marcus. "I will soon be in much better spirits, I assure you."

"I know you will, Mary," he replied, and we rode this way without further incident.

The crowds thinned out as we came to the narrower streets on the far side of the main thoroughfare, and I began to feel a little more comfortable. I allowed myself a brief look across at Marcus, and it was the first time I had seen him properly in the daylight.

He seemed older than I remembered, as if he had aged more than the actual time that had passed. His face seemed harder, and his brow more pronounced, and I fancied that the hair that flowed out from under his cap was maybe a little thinner than before.

"You must tell me what has been happening these past months, Marcus," I said, as we rode into a narrow, and thankfully, fairly empty street. "Has the Queen been delivered of any further babes? And how is the Prince? Fully recovered from his ordeal at the hand of Jacob Cruddon, I trust?"

He looked over at me with a face of sorrow. "Indeed 'no' to both of those," he replied. "The Queen has had no more issue – at least none other than two miscarried and stillborn sons. Regarding the Prince there is both good news and bad." He gave a small nod of his head. "The good news is that when I returned to London, I found that he was greatly recovered, as Lady Kyme had hoped and prayed. He has since been undertaking many duties on behalf of his father the King. He is even married."

"To the girl he was betrothed to before I was taken?" I asked. "Mary Howard?"

"That is the one, yes, although they have never lived together, as the King thinks they are too young."

I felt a chill of fear as I asked the next, most obvious question. "And the bad news?"

"In the last few weeks he has relapsed again into the same malaise he originally contracted when held by Cruddon. It seems he was able to show recovery for some time, but then perhaps the disease has never really left him. Now it has returned, and he has once again taken to his bed."

"In Heaven's name!" I cried, almost pulling up Hestia. "Is he dying?"

Marcus shook his head. "We hope not. He has recovered once, and we are most hopeful he will do so again. He is young and strong, and much like his father at the same age. So there is every hope this illness will finally leave him for all time."

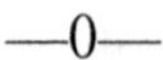

There was silence again as we rode out of Chelmsford and set out on the path to the farm at Writtle. This time the lack of conversation was based on my discomfort at the news that Marcus had shared.

Had my efforts to rescue the Prince all been in vain?

For if this was a continuation of his earlier malaise, brought on by Cruddon's appalling treatment of him, then it was no different than if Cruddon had tried to put him to death with a sword. Which was what the one-eyed villain would have done on Queen Anne's orders, had I not snatched the boy from under his nose.

The Queen! She must still wish the Prince harm, for she had not been delivered of a male heir – at least, none that were alive. So he was still a Catholic threat to her Protestant daughter.

Yet Marcus said the Prince had been seen in public many times, which would have given the Queen plenty of chances to have Cruddon take him again.

I asked this of Marcus when we were finally arrived at Miriam's brother's farm and had stepped out of the little cottage together.

"To understand this, there are some things you would need to know," he told me. "There was an Act of Succession last year, which recognised the Queen's child Elizabeth as the legitimate heir, and the Princess Mary, daughter of Queen Katherine, as illegitimate and therefore unable to succeed."

"But then the Queen has no cause to wish the Prince any harm," I said. "If her daughter is the only legitimate heir."

"Sadly not." He shook his head. "In truth, nothing changes. Now there is a Protestant heir – Elizabeth – and two illegitimate Catholics; Mary and possibly the Prince. Were anything to happen to the King, the Catholics would naturally favour the male over the female claimant. So it still benefits the Queen to remove the rival claim."

"I understand," I said, nodding. "The Queen is still a threat to the Prince."

"Exactly," he replied. "Lady Kyme has conferred on me the duty to guard her son at all hours. Hal and Ed here, plus two others, have been assigned to assist me in this task. We have been on our duty whenever he has been at official functions, and even while he sleeps. The other two men are with him now. I warrant our presence has been enough to deter Master Cruddon, and I would even warrant the man has now realised he cannot get close to the Prince." He seemed to look past me, as if he was seeing Cruddon before him, and he put a hand to the hilt of his sword. "Although if I ever meet that rogue again, I would be pleased to put my blade through his cold heart." Then he looked back at me and his face cleared. "So no, the Prince is extremely well guarded."

I was curious. "And all this has been without the King's knowledge?"

"Aye." He touched his hilt again. "We keep close to the Prince in public, except when he is in the royal presence, as Cruddon would not get close in such a situation." He was silent a moment, then he said, "The King knows not that he was originally taken, nor that it was on the Queen's orders." He gave a short laugh. "Although I fear she will not have such influence for much longer. It is said that the King is less enamoured of her, especially as she has now miscarried twice. It is well understood that his eye has settled on one of her ladies, Jane Seymour."

"Then this Queen will be cast aside?" I asked.

"Most likely. It is assumed she will be divorced and banished from Court, like Queen Katherine before her." He paced away, then turned back, a look of concern on his face. "But you, Mary? You have had some hard times. Tell me all."

I let out a slow breath. "There is little to tell, Marcus. Two and a half years passes uneventfully when one is in the same room, and with only a gaoler for occasional company."

"But there is a top and tale to this story?" he asked. "When you were first taken, and when you finally escaped?"

I saw no reason to keep the truth from him, so I said, "I was brought to Marchington Manor in bonds and subjected to my stepfather's anger, before being taken up to my prison chamber."

"Anger?" He raised an enquiring eyebrow.

I shrugged. "He felt I had dishonoured him and the family name. A daughter who refused to do as she was told. To marry the man he had chosen. So when he finally had me helpless before him, he vented his frustrations on me." I paused. The memory of all those kicks was one I tried to keep out of my head. "By means of his boots," I added, rubbing at the knee that still occasionally ached on cold days.

"By Heavens, Mary!" Marcus looked shocked. "I would run him through in a heartbeat if I had him at my mercy."

"Well, you do not, and the further away we are from him, the better," I said.

"Agreed." He nodded slowly. "And indeed, we must be away soon, Mary," he said. "For we have little time."

"Time for what?" I asked.

He put his hand on my shoulder. "Little time before the Prince has his next duty to perform, which he cannot do from his sickbed; the Garter Ceremony."

I must admit I did not see immediately where this was going. My imprisonment must have softened my wits.

"Then that is simply not going to happen," I said. "If he cannot rise from his bed."

"Indeed not," Marcus replied. Then he added softly, almost as if the thought had just occurred, "unless someone were to stand in for him." Then he gave me what I could only describe as a 'significant look'.

I gasped in shock, and somewhat in anger. Was this why Marcus had been so ready to come to my rescue? He and Lady Kyme wanted my services as her son again?

"Well, that will not happen either," I snapped. "He was a boy of fourteen when I stood in for him before. Now he is nigh-on seventeen and I warrant, a man. How can I possibly hope to convince any person, let alone his father, that I am he?"

"You are older too, Mary. You are twenty years yourself."

"Yes, but as you can see, I am a woman of twenty." As if to confirm this, his eyes dropped to my chest. I dare say it was heaving in my anger. "This is utter madness!" I snapped.

"It is only for a short time, until the Prince is again recovered, as we are certain he will be. The Prince is small of stature, Mary, so you are still a match for him in body." He searched my eyes, as if willing me to accept. "Please Mary. Lady Kyme and I are convinced it is the only way.

We, and the Prince himself, are begging you to do this for him."

"Begging?" I asked "Lady Kyme?"

"Yes, you must know she loves you as a mother; something she has oft said to me. And as a mother, she looks to her daughter for help." He nodded. "She was distraught when we thought you dead, and talked of you often afterwards. When we had news you were alive, she near fainted in relief."

"She loves me as a mother?" For a moment I could hardly take in such words. I was a beloved daughter? Suddenly I could not wait to see her again, and to throw myself in her arms. If I did become the Prince again, it would only be for her sake, for all the thought once again filled me with the dread of being exposed as an imposter.

But something Marcus had said did not make sense.

"But what did you mean by 'it is the only way?'" I asked.

"The King is so close to reversing his earlier decision and making the Prince the heir," he explained, "that if he is not seen at these events; not seen to support the King, then there is every chance it will not happen."

He put his hand on my arm. "Did you know, His Majesty had a jousting accident recently and almost died? What if he had? Should we have England at war with itself again during two-year-old Queen Elizabeth's minority?" He frowned. "The Prince is a good man, and an able one. He would hold the realm together. Can you imagine if he is denied his birthright when he again recovers? Can you live with yourself if England goes to war because you would not help? That unpopular Boleyn woman would naturally try to claim the protectorate, and there are many factions at

Court who would not accept this." He shook his head. "The Mary Fox I once knew; she would not countenance such a thing. Not for one second."

He gazed at me with an expectant look.

"And not to forget, the offer of a hundred sovereigns still stands…"

I took a deep breath. "Very well. I will do it."

What else could I say?

24

LADY MOTHER

We travelled to London the following day, having said our farewells and given our heartfelt thanks to Miriam and her family for all they had done, as well as a suitable number of coins to compensate them for all their troubles.

The money had come from my purse, which Marcus returned to me with a smile.

"When you gave some coins to Miriam the day you were taken, you left this on the table. By God's good grace your father did not see it in the dim light. I have guarded it well ever since, lest you were ever found."

I took it with a grateful smile. "I thank you, Marcus." I checked inside. The paper I had found in Blackfriars was still there.

It had been a sad parting from Miriam, for I had grown quite fond of her and wished her the very best in life. She seemed sorrowful too and gave me an embrace, whispering in my ear, "You are a good woman, Mary Fox, and we have been through much together. I wish you the greatest good fortune, and hope you find yourself an equally fine man to share your life." She glanced across to where Marcus was mounting his horse. "And you may not have to look too far," she added with a conspiratorial smile.

"I rather think not," I said. "But thank you for the suggestion."

"Do not dismiss him too readily," she whispered. "I saw how he threw his arms about you as soon as you came over the wall. He has a place in his heart for you, Mary Fox."

"He thought me dead," I observed.

"Yet told me he could not countenance another woman since. I warrant he would marry you, if you would have him. I know it."

"As may be," I replied, "but my mind is quite fixed."

She inclined her head to one side. "You are a woman," she said softly. "Minds can change."

I pondered her words as we rode back to the city.

Marcus Kytson had a place in his heart for me?

I looked over at him, sitting tall in the saddle. He must have sensed my gaze, for he turned and gave me a broad smile.

I looked quickly away, unsure of what to say.

Did he think to take me to wife?

What of the vow I made to myself? The one to stay apart from any man? To use the promised hundred sovereigns to make my own way in the world? To be my own mistress, and never servant to any master? Why should I be beholden to a man just because he had feelings for me? Was that reason enough to lose my independence? It was the reason I had refused a previous proposal from a young man called Robert Fitzwilliam.

Marriage may offer a woman security, but at what cost? She becomes her husband's property. Even her money becomes his.

And she becomes the mother to his children – that is, if she survives giving birth. Childbed fever had taken my own mother. How could I take the risk that it would not do the same to me?

I glanced again at Marcus. There was no denying he was tall, handsome and possessed of a quick wit. If I should marry, then I could do a lot worse than Master Marcus Kytson, youngest son of Sir Robert Kytson of Huntingdon, in the Diocese of Ely.

But could I trade my independence for the security of marriage?

There was a strong reason to say 'yes'. I had just escaped from my cruel stepfather – who would no doubt be livid with rage. Were I to be re-taken, I could imagine his vengeful response. He would not imprison me again, but cut straight to his promise of permanent disposal. To be a married woman would afford me a husband's protection.

So there it was. Independence and freedom, or the security of marriage?

Which to choose?

Hestia seemed to sense my confusion. She snorted and nodded her head a few times.

"What must I do, old girl?" I muttered under my breath. "Should I open my heart to Marcus, or keep my freedom with the money I am promised?

She turned her head and gave me a hard stare from her clear brown eye.

I knew her well enough. This was her way of telling me that now was not the time to decide.

"Very well, old girl," I muttered. "First I will help Lady Kyme – the nearest person to a mother I have ever had, by standing in once more as her son. I will help the Prince secure his future, once he is again recovered. Then will be the time to decide – to ride away with the money I had been offered, or to make a life with Marcus."

She nodded a few times and snorted her agreement.

—0—

We trotted into the courtyard of Durham House and grooms ran out to take our horses to their stables.

Lady Kyme met us in the Great Hall.

"Mary! Oh my Mary!" she exclaimed, pulling me into a warm embrace, "I have missed you so much! We thought you dead!"

"Still alive, Lady Mother," I replied with a smile.

"Oh!" she put her hand to her mouth. "You call me that again! It warms my heart more than I can say!"

"Mine too," I replied. "You have been as a mother to me, when I have none of my own."

She let me go and stood back. She had aged in the time since I last saw her; lines had crept around her eyes and across her brow, and there was a slight pallor to her skin that could not be concealed by rouge. "I have heard that the young Prince is poorly again," I said. "I was sorry to hear this."

"Yes," she said, with an expression of deep worry. "He was doing so well in the time since you last saw him. Then a week ago, he started coughing and took to his bed. By good fortune there has not been any need for him to appear in public during this time, and we have a few days before the Garter Ceremony." She looked up. "He must be recognised as the true heir, and for that he must be seen, hale and hearty, in public. And for that…" Her face cleared

242

and she seemed to manage a small smile. "For that we need you, my dear Mary, so that you can take his place while he stays abed." She put her hand on my arm. "Then all will be well. He can resume his public duties as soon as he recovers, and you can be away to wherever you wish to go, a hundred sovereigns better off."

"But he is a man now…" I wanted her to acknowledge the key problem, if not my deepest fears of being exposed. In fact, the little confidence I had felt as the Prince before my captivity had evaporated like a morning mist. Now it turned my belly to ice just thinking about the danger I would be in.

"I know, Mary, I know." She let go my arm and walked over to the table, returning with a goblet of wine for me. "But we must be clever with our artifice. We must make best advantage of what we have."

I raised an eyebrow. "Which is?"

"My Henry is not yet seventeen. He is slight, as you are. And yes, his face has grown more a man, while yours is naturally more a woman, but with your hair cut again and with your cap pulled low, you are still such a strong likeness. Indeed, it is almost uncanny." She came up to me and studied my face closely from left and right, which I found a little uncomfortable.

She nodded, as if to confirm to herself something she had suspected. "I say you have become more a woman, Mary, and it is true. But have we been fooled by the length of your hair and the fact you wear a servant's dress? Your face is thin. Marcus tells me you have been held a prisoner these two years or more, and no doubt fed very little?" I nodded. "Indeed," she continued. "It shows. Your cheeks are somewhat hollow, and your eyes sit deeper under your brow." She stood back, her hands on her hips. "This plays to our advantage; very much so. It makes your face more masculine, and…" she narrowed her eyes. "And, dare I say it, more a match for my Henry."

She gestured at Marcus to come over.

"Does not the thinness of her face give her more a manly air?"

Marcus came up beside her. "I do believe it does, my lady," he observed, studying me carefully, making me feel as if I was a butterfly pinned to a board for their inspection. "And I see your point. The thinness caused by Mary's imprisonment does give her more the appearance of a boy. With her naturally identical look to the Prince, I am confident she can once again play the role."

"And her voice," added Lady Kyme. "I note she has a more husky tone since she has been held. I warrant it is a combination of poor nutrition and her increased age."

I wanted to shout that I was present, and could hear them perfectly well. But I held my peace, and even managed a small smile.

I know when I am beaten.

"Then we had best begin, had we not?" I said, keeping my voice low, and as she had noted, more manly.

Lady Kyme gave me a warm smile, which seemed to remove much of the worry from her face. "I agree. There is no time to lose if we are to get you ready for the Garter Ceremony. Come, let us bathe and dress you, and have your hair cut once again."

I followed them up to start the process of change.

25

WINDSOR CASTLE

The twenty third day of April is St. George's Day; traditionally set aside for the meeting of the Chapter of the Order of the Garter. A vote can be taken from the existing members so that new Knights can be appointed. As a leading Knight, the Prince was expected to be present and cast his vote.

So I must be there in his place.

The meeting was to take place at St. George's Chapel at Windsor Castle. The Prince had briefed me the day before on the castle and its various buildings, as he had resided there for a time.

"I know the place well," he said slowly, in between coughs from his sickbed. "I have rooms in the castle." He gave me a short set of directions for finding them, which I must confess, I found a little hard to follow. Then he told me of the Garter Ceremony, and my voting requirements.

"You must cast your vote for Viscount Rochford and Sir Nicholas Carew," he told me. "Rochford is the Queen's brother George Boleyn."

"Why would you vote for him, after all his sister has done against you?" I wondered.

"It is a matter of political expediency," he replied. "He has been on the ascendancy for some time, as have all the

Boleyns, raised by the Queen's favour. If she does finally bear a son, then she will be untouchable, and so will he."

"But if she falls?" I asked, recalling what Marcus had told me.

"Then you… I… also vote for Carew, who opposes the Boleyns and supports the woman who has now caught the King's eye, Jane Seymour. Plus," he added, "there is the look of the thing. Rochford has power and influence right now. It is hardly surprising to vote for him, even if he does fall sometime in the future."

"But your preference would be Carew?" I asked.

He nodded. "It would be. In the end the vote is but advisory. The final decision rests with the King. If he chooses Rochford then there is clear support for the Queen." He broke off for a fit of coughing. "But if he chooses Carew," he continued, once he had regained his breath, "then it will be clear to all that the Queen and her family will fall soon."

I rode to the castle the day before the meeting, along with Marcus, Ed and Hal. They were all splendidly bedecked in the Duke of Richmond's livery, so we must have made an impressive sight as we wound our way through the villages and towns to the west of the city of London. Eventually we came through the Henry VIII Gate into the Lower Ward and rode into the stables. As we came out on foot, I scarcely had time to take in the magnificent Round Tower and the chapel of Saint George, before a well-dressed courtier strolled out from under a covered gallery and came over in our direction.

"Richard Long," Marcus whispered in my ear. "Gentleman Usher."

The man came closer. Without taking my eyes off him, I hissed at Marcus out of the corner of my mouth, "Does he know the Prince well?"

"Yes. But he has no reason to doubt you. It has been more than a year since you last met."

I cannot say I was reassured. Now I was here at Windsor, it hit me just how much danger I was in once again. If this man exposed me as an imposter, all would be lost. And this was just the start. Every further interaction was going to place me in even greater peril.

Long came up to us and bowed. "Your Grace," he said, "welcome back to Windsor."

"Master Long," I said as he straightened. He was tall in stature, with a prominent nose and such heavy brows that his eyes were all but lost beneath. "I am pleased to be here once again."

"As we are to have you back, Your Grace," he replied with an easy smile. "Your usual rooms were not available, so different ones have been prepared."

"Thank you," I replied. At least I would not have to remember the Prince's directions.

Marcus stepped forward. "Well met, Master Long," he said, sweeping off his cap with a small bow of his own.

"Master Kytson."

The formalities over, Richard Long led us across the Long Gallery, then through a further maze of passages and doorways until we were shown into a set of chambers. There was a single bedchamber for me, with a separate room for Marcus, Hal and Ed through a door set into the wood panelling. A bright fire crackled cheerfully in the grate.

"I thank you, Master Long," I said. "Tell me, is my father the King in residence?"

"He is indeed, Your Grace," he replied. "And the Queen also."

Long bowed and went out, while Ed and Hal withdrew into the second chamber, leaving me and Marcus alone.

"There," he said, with a broad smile, as he thumped a fist into his palm. "Long had no idea you are not the real Prince. You have his look and have near mastered his voice. You passed the first test with style."

I was not so well assured. "If Long has not seen the Prince in more than a year, I warrant he would have expected a boy to have grown and changed. But what of the King? What of all the others who have been in the Prince's company more recently?"

"You will carry it off, I am certain," he said. "I have every confidence you will."

"'Tis well you have such certainty," I replied. "I wish I shared it."

He put his hands on my shoulders. "Come now, Your Grace. Let us not have doubts. I know the Prince as well as any man, and I say you are still as like as two twins. Put you both together in the same clothes and even I would struggle to tell you apart."

"What if the King suspects? He knows of doubles, for he has one himself; a fellow by the name of Nathan Rose, if I recall correctly. And last time at Whitehall, it was at his request that I stood in for the Prince. But then he said I should not stand in again. He knows not that we seek to deceive him now." I bit my lip as I looked into his eyes.

"He would not even send me to the Tower if he found out;
I would go straight to a noose at Tyburn."

—0—

We processed into the formal meal that evening in St.
George's Hall.

Once we were all in place we stood as the King entered
with the Queen. He was as tall and as broad-shouldered as
I recalled from over two years before, drawing the gaze of
every man and woman in the room as if he was the brightest
sunflower, alone in a field full of weeds. His long doublet
was in the purest white and edged with gold, while the most
enormous cod-piece protruded from beneath. It was
coloured in gold-trimmed purple with stripes of white, and
demanded as much attention as did its owner. It made me
feel almost sorry for the man, that he felt such a need to
make a public display of his virility – almost as if he was
trying to compensate for his lack of legitimate sons.

Beside him was the Queen, and this was the first time I
had ever seen her.

She was small by comparison to her husband, but I
warrant she would have stood taller than me if we were side
by side. Her dark hair was severely drawn back under a
black hood edged with pearls, and her eyes, which had a
stern, cold air, were constantly flicking around the room. It
was as if she were looking for something or someone.

Then her eyes stopped on me, and it seemed as if she had
found what she was seeking. Her expression hardened into
one of anger. It felt like a pail of cold water had been

thrown over me, as this woman stared at me with ill-concealed dislike.

I knew she hated the Prince enough to send Cruddon to take him prisoner. So it must have galled her greatly to see the young man she would have disposed of, recovered and in seeming good health.

I returned her gaze with as much confidence as I could muster.

But did she know that it was me she was staring at, not the real Prince? Noah Robson, or even Cruddon himself – would have told her that there was a double; a girl called Mary Fox, and that this Mary Fox had stood in for the Prince at Whitehall. But did she know that the person she was staring at with such venom this day was not in truth the recovered Prince, but actually his double, Mary Fox?

Then her eyes narrowed, and she frowned. My breath caught in my throat.

She knew!

Or at the very least, she suspected.

What should I do? Make a run for it? With the number of guards around, I would not get very far. I checked the main doors. It was covered by two fearsome fellows in silver breastplates and kettle helmets, carrying large halberds; the blades and points gleaming in the candlelight. There had been several others in the passageway earlier. I could imagine they would have little care for my welfare if the Queen pointed at me, and demanded I was stopped. And they would be none too gentle when they took me to a dungeon somewhere in the castle, so I could be held pending my punishment.

I rubbed my throat. There was little doubt as to what that might be.

But thankfully, she kept silent. She and the King reached their seats. Grace was said, and we all sat.

Servants started running out with the food and wine, but I do not recall eating or drinking, such was my concern over the Queen.

She knew; I was certain.

I tried my utmost to keep calm. I forced myself to smile and make polite small talk with the men on either side, whose names I never learned, or soon forgot.

Then things became even worse.

Marcus, who had been placed elsewhere on a side table, came up to me. He put a hand on my shoulder and whispered in my ear.

"Do not look immediately, but Henry Howard, Earl of Surrey, is seated on the far table to the left, third from the end."

"Henry Howard?" I whispered back.

"The Prince's brother-in-law. They virtually grew up together. I told you of him, and some of the escapades they had."

I recalled stories of drinking and carousing in the town of Windsor, and the writing of love sonnets to various young ladies. Apparently Howard was something of a poet.

I glanced up at him. "Why is he here?"

"To be fair, we did not expect it. He is not particularly in favour, and is not a Garter Knight." He patted my shoulder, then added, "But there it is, Your Grace. He is here indeed."

"And will expose me for certain," I hissed, now seeing danger coming from two sides.

"By what reason?" Marcus replied. "He has not seen the Prince in a few months. Courage, Your Grace. You can do this."

As Marcus walked back to his seat, I stole a quick glance at this Earl of Surrey. He was a youngish fellow, with the long nose of his father and, to my eye, a weak-looking chin covered in a thin beard. As I glanced at him, he caught my eye and smiled, then gave a small bow of his head in greeting.

How would the Prince respond to such a close friend?

There would be some banter between them. So I raised an eyebrow and smiled back, then bowed my own head, as if mimicking him.

His smile turned into a broad grin, then he cocked his head to one side, as if to acknowledge my bow.

I breathed a sigh of relief, and turned as the man beside me made some innocuous remark, that demanded an equally innocuous response.

As soon as the meal ended the King stood, then took the Queen's hand. As they processed from the hall, he nodded and smiled at the company.

Like everyone I bowed my head as he walked away, but he turned and caught my eye as I stood straight again. For the briefest moment he frowned, and my heart stopped as I expected him to roar in rage and point at me – but this did not happen. Instead his face cleared as if he had just recognised me, then he smiled a somewhat vacant smile, and continued on.

Nobody moved until the King and Queen had passed the guards, then a few stood, and started to make their own way out.

Once my heart had resumed its normal rhythm, I took this as my cue to leave. I stood and bowed to the men on either side, saying something to each about being tired after the day's journey and wishing to retire early.

I nodded to Marcus, and he fell in beside me as I headed for my chambers. We walked silently through the Long Gallery, then the maze of brazier-lit passageways beyond. I closed the door and dropped the latch once in my chambers, then fell backwards onto the bed fully clothed, my breath coming out like steam from a boiling kettle.

Marcus sat down beside me.

"You see?" he said, smiling down. "I told you it was no problem. The Earl gave no indication that he suspected anything. And the King – he seemed positively delighted to recognise you. Well done, Mary."

"It is not the Earl, or even the King that concerns me, as much as the Queen," I muttered, staring up at the curtain hangings.

"What of her?"

"She knows of me." I reminded him about Robson and Cruddon, and what they would have told her. "It led me to you in Ipswich, but it also told me that she knows the Prince has a double. She even knows the name Mary Fox," I added.

"I see."

"But, there is something I hold," I said, as I sat up and pulled open my purse. I took out the folded paper, with the incriminating legend for the Queen. I handed it to Marcus. He studied the image on the front.

"Is this Durham House?" he asked.

I nodded. "This paper was placed to convince me to seek you in Ipswich. Which was a trap, but I managed to avoid being taken by Cruddon."

Although not ultimately by my stepfather.

"If all discovered, hie back to Ipswich forthwith," he read. Then he looked hard at me. "So why did you keep this?"

"Look at the reverse,"

He turned it over and studied it as carefully as he had the other side. He looked up at me with a frown. "I see nothing," he said.

I pointed at the tops of the letters along the tear. "What do those words say?"

"Hmm." He let out a series of short breaths as he squinted at the letters. "The Queen has ordered it, but will deny," he said slowly, picking over each word. "I assume that is Queen Anne?"

I nodded. "I believe it is. So here is something I could use if it is needed."

"Let us hope it is not," he replied.

"That is the ideal," I agreed. "But I have it, in case." He gave me back the paper and I put it in my purse. "Yes. So tomorrow I must proceed with the other Knights to St. George's Chapel," I said. "I will take part in the vote, but I must do so without making close contact with the Earl of Surrey. And I should avoid the Queen at all costs."

26

THE GARTER CEREMONY

I fear I lay awake for every minute of the night.

The perils of my situation kept spinning round and round in my head like unwelcome flies around an old pie. In every imagined scenario I was exposed as an imposter by different people, from the Gentleman Usher Richard Long to Henry Howard; from the Queen to the King himself. And in every scenario, I ended up being flung into some foul dungeon; there to remain only as long as necessary to arrange my transport to Tyburn and the hangman's noose.

As dawn broke, I hoped my fears would subside, but they remained in full force.

Marcus came in as I was breaking fast.

"I trust you slept well, Your Grace?" he enquired.

"Not at all," I said quietly in my normal female voice. "I would we ride out immediately and forget all this play-acting."

"For sure we must not," he replied. "Have you forgot that we stand on the brink of another civil war if the King dies without naming the Prince his heir? You must be seen as the Prince, and on each occasion like this, until such times as he has regained his health, or the King will be less likely to name him."

"But it scares me, Marcus," I whispered. "What if Henry Howard exposes me? Or the Queen?"

He stared hard at me a moment, then shook his head. "No. No, I can scarcely credit this. Where is the Mary Fox I met some two or more years ago? The Mary Fox who fought several men in a tavern, besting each with her sword? The Mary Fox who found the strength to pull me from a fire? The Mary Fox who then rescued both me and the Prince from our respective captivities? Or even the Mary Fox who leapt her horse over a high wall to escape her father?" He paused while I said nothing. "Where is that Mary Fox, with her strength, her courage and her keen wit?"

"I fear she was lost in the prison chamber at Marchington Manor," I replied. "She was crushed in captivity."

"Then we must find her again," he said decisively. "Come Your Grace, let us get you ready for the Garter Ceremony. You will feel better when the mirror shows that you are the Prince himself."

I was not sure, but I let him assist me to dress in the Garter robes and insignia. I made little move to help as he put the white silken hose and chemise onto me, then a soft, embroidered doublet over which he attached my ceremonial sword belt. This was followed by a heavy blue overgown trimmed with ermine that featured the red cross of Saint George on one shoulder. A black cap with the insignia of the Prince's dukedoms of Richmond and Somerset was placed on my head. Finally, Marcus hung the chain across my chest, before kneeling and securing the blue and gold garter upon my left calf. Both the chain and garter showed the legend of the Order, *Honi Soit Qui Mal Y Pense*.

As I stepped into a pair of black leather shoes, he stood back, looking me up and down. Then he took out a polished metal mirror and nodded in apparent satisfaction.

"Shame upon him who thinks evil upon it," I observed as I studied my image in the mirror. While it was clearly of the Prince, I could only imagine how I might give myself away with an unfortunate word, phrase, or action.

"Eh?"

"I fear the translation of the Garter legend is far from apt this day," I explained, gesturing at the regalia I now wore. "I am still concerned by this. Most concerned. I am about to take the place of one of the foremost knights of the Most Noble Order. Me, Mary Fox of Marchington Manor, who has never been elevated to any honour, not even in the eyes of her own family. Any man who thinks evil of such a deception should feel no shame; only anger."

"Come now, Mary," he said, "you are so like the Prince, that no one will question you." He came closer. "Not Henry Howard, and certainly not the Queen."

"Why not? I am convinced she has her suspicions."

"Because she has more to lose than you. What if you were to reveal she was behind the plot to kidnap and kill the Prince? What if you were to share that paper you showed me last eve? That would be greatly against her interests."

I felt my eyes narrow as I stared at him. He was right, of course. I must not forget I held a critical piece of evidence against Queen Anne. In my fear over my own situation this morning, it had slipped my mind that she was also concealing secrets herself.

I nodded slowly. "You make a good point, Marcus. Forgive me for doubting you."

"There," he announced with a smile. "There she is. I caught a brief glimpse of the real Mary Fox."

I took a breath. In the deeper voice of Prince Henry Fitzroy, Duke of Richmond and Somerset, I said, "Then come, Master Kytson. I have a ceremony to attend."

27

QUEEN ANNE BOLEYN

I do not recall a great deal of the Garter Ceremony, other than being marshalled by some heralds in quartered tunics into a line, before being marched with the other knights through the upper, middle and lower wards of the castle to St George's Chapel, with its long, narrow quire and the banners of each knight hanging in rows above. There I found my seat, as designated by the Prince's insignia on a plaque.

There were interminable speeches and prayers, during which my main concern was to remain awake after my sleepless night. Eventually we were called to vote, and I duly raised my hand when the names of Viscount Rochford and Sir Nicholas Carew were called out.

As I voted, the King looked directly at me. Again, he gave me a vague smile, then his attention drifted to the next man, as if his thoughts were very much elsewhere.

For a moment I thought this most odd. Then my attention alighted on Queen Anne Boleyn, seated on a finely-carved throne beside her husband. It was not far from where I sat.

The Queen continually looked at me, which I found unnerving. I became quite practiced at maintaining a stony, noncommittal expression every time her gaze slid in my direction.

There is no finer way to make a person feel guilty, than by making frequent suspicious looks at them.

Especially when that person really *is* guilty.

When the ceremony finally ended, we were formed again into a line, and processed back the way we had come, until we were all seated once more in St. George's Hall for supper.

By good fortune – and, of course, my elevation to a higher rank of nobility – I was seated some way from Henry Howard. So I only needed to make occasional grins in his direction, and all propriety was maintained.

Throughout the meal I was starting to gain in confidence, thinking myself into the role – and the mind – of the Prince. I had made it through the ceremony, which was itself an achievement. Now all that remained was to finish this supper, and as soon as the King had risen, get to the safety of my chamber. I could then celebrate that I had done all I could for the Prince, his mother and Marcus, in their quest to ensure he was made heir, and be away to London at dawn.

As I supped on a piece of venison and drank some claret; probably more than I should, I felt myself starting to relax. My role was nearly finished, and I could decide what would be the next move in my life.

It was with this lightness of mind that I walked down the Long Gallery after the meal was ended, looking forward to reaching my chamber and getting a good night's sleep. Marcus had stayed back to talk to someone, and such was my weariness, I had left him and gone on alone.

There were a number of recesses on each side as I made my way down the gallery, and in my wine and tiredness-induced state, I did not pay heed to any of these. Instead my gaze was fixed on the door at the far end, and my chamber a few passageways beyond. So I had almost walked past one of these recesses, before I took notice of a sharp, repeated greeting.

"Your Grace? Your Grace?"

Once this had finally seeped into my mind, I stopped and looked back. There was a woman in the darkness but I could not see who it was. So, with curiosity piqued, I made my way in, and confronted her.

She moved forward, so the light from the main gallery lit half her face. It gave her the look of an evil sprite.

The Queen.

For a moment I was frozen to the spot, then I made the slightest move, as if I was about to walk back into the gallery. She shot out a hand and clutched at my sleeve.

"You stay here, Your Grace," she snarled, "for I would talk with you."

"Your Majesty," I conceded with a small bow, deciding to play the respectful prince. "What is your pleasure?" I shook my arm to dislodge her grip.

"My pleasure?" she asked. "My pleasure is to talk."

"Then please do, but I would ask Your Majesty to keep it brief, for I would go quickly to my chamber. I am greatly tired by the ceremony today."

"Ah, yes. The ceremony. I observed you well. You voted for my brother. He is not a supporter of yours, nor you of him. Why did you vote that way?"

I recalled the Prince's words when I had asked the same question. "Your brother has power and influence, Your

Majesty," I replied. "I felt he would make an excellent member of the Order."

"Better than Carew?" she snapped, her eye glittering in the light of the candles behind me.

"He also has merit, and possesses a sound mind. I would equally value him as a member."

"I see." She was silent a moment. I wanted to know where she was going with this. Did she indeed suspect me, as I had believed? Or was she not sure, and wanted a conversation to make her mind up? Or perhaps this was exactly what it seemed on the surface; the Queen simply conversing with her husband's son?

The least likely option.

"Tell me," she said. "I have forgotten something. Something only you can help me with."

Suddenly I was on my guard. She was going to ask me a question that none but the real Prince could answer.

So she knew – or thought she did.

"Tell me, Your Grace," she began, with a false-sounding pleasantness to her voice. "When my daughter Elizabeth was but two months of age, you visited her nursery, and you made a jest as you looked at her. You called her by a particular name." Her face hardened, and her look was tinged with triumph. "I would remember; what was that name again?"

I took a deep breath, and tried the only tactic I could think of, based on what I knew of the Prince.

"You are mistaken, Your Majesty," I replied with care. "For I do not believe I ever looked on your babe at that age."

Her face soured, and I concluded I had hit on the correct answer. My guess had been based on the fact that the Prince was, to the best of my understanding, still in his sickbed at that time.

She tried again. "Forgive me, Your Grace, as you say, I must have been mistaken. Perhaps you could tell me instead…" she paused, and I could see she was considering her possibilities. She must have decided to push harder on her suspicions. "…How it was that my good servant Noah Robson came to have a badly broken leg?"

I gave a small smile. "I am sorry, Your Majesty, but there you have me at a disadvantage. I am not acquainted with your serving staff, so I have no knowledge of this man, Noah…" I paused, as if trying to recall the name. "…Robson, was it?"

"So you deny you had anything to do with it?" There was now a sneering tone to her voice.

"Of course. What on earth has your serving man, or indeed his leg, got to do with me?"

Could I continue to bluster my way through this?

The sneer now progressed to her face and it was clear she had no more patience. "Oh come now, you little piece of shit," she snapped, "admit it. You are no more the Duke of Richmond than I am. You are not even a man. You are a wastrel girl called Mary Fox, acting as a double for the Prince! I shall advise the King and have you arrested!"

I decided she gave me no other choice than to fight fire with fire.

"How dare you accuse me of such a thing, madam?" I growled. "I am Prince Henry Fitzroy, son of the King, Duke of Richmond and Somerset, Knight of the Most

Noble Order of the Garter. And as I am sure you are aware, the motto of the Order translates as 'Shame upon him who thinks evil upon it'. You would do well to remember that, madam."

But something she had said was starting to bother me, like a worm eating into my head.

'A double!' Was that what she had said?

I had a sudden image of the King at the previous night's supper, and at the ceremony, giving me a vague smile. It was not as if he had doubted me, but rather he was pleased to have recalled who I was.

That was it!

A double!

Then perhaps her threat to have the King arrest me was a hollow one.

"Tell me," I said to the Queen. "Where is His Majesty the King this night?"

Her eyes widened. "He is abed upstairs," she whispered. "Like you, he was tired by the ceremony."

"Nay," I said. "Where is he really? Hampton Court? Whitehall? Is he sick? For the man we saw at the ceremony and in St. George's Hall this night, that was Nathan Rose, was it not?"

"How do you know…?" she began, but did not continue.

"So perhaps your threats against me are empty," I cut in. "For if you persist in this stupid nonsense about me being a woman or somesuch, I will start asking questions about who exactly is masquerading as the King." I decided to play my full hand. "And I might also start enquiries as to who was behind the plot to have me kidnapped nigh-on three years ago, and held in Blackfriars." I took the paper from my purse and unfolded it carefully before her eyes. Then I read from the torn reverse. *"The Queen has ordered it, but will deny.* Does that mean anything to you, madam?"

She did not reply, but her mouth opened and closed like a fish.

I refolded the paper and put it in my purse. "So I suggest you forget this nonsense, or else I will let the King, your husband, see this paper. And by that," I added, "I mean Henry Tudor, eighth king of that name, not Master Nathan Rose."

Again she said nothing.

"Goodnight," I said. "I trust we shall not meet again any time soon."

Then I stepped out of the recess, and started to walk again along the gallery.

I heard the rustle of skirts behind me and her foot on the floorboards.

"Your Grace," she hissed. I came to a stop and looked over my shoulder. She had her hands on her hips. "Your Grace," she repeated, "I only have one thing to say to you." I raised an enquiring eyebrow. "If you truly are the Prince, then it will concern you, for sure. But if you are indeed this girl, Mary Fox, it will strike fear into your heart. And so it should, for it is no idle threat, but a promise."

"And that is?" I asked.

"To have Jacob Cruddon come for you once again," she whispered. "But this time he will come with enough force to achieve my original aims."

28

A TRAP FOR A ROGUE

I could not get away from that castle fast enough, with the threats of Queen Anne ringing in my ears and the chance that at any moment someone – such as the Prince's childhood friend, the Earl of Surrey – would also expose me.

Marcus, Ed, Hal and I set out as the spring dawn had just started to paint the sky red over Windsor. We galloped through the lanes and many villages towards the rising sun as if the devil himself was on our tail.

Arriving tired and dusty at Durham House with our horses breathing hard, we jumped down and let the grooms lead them to the stables with steam rising from their flanks.

I threw a blanket across Hestia's back and asked her groom to make sure she had plenty of water and mash, then I patted her neck.

"Many thanks, old girl," I whispered, "I know it was a hard ride, but necessary." She flicked her ears at me, which I took as a sign that she did not mind overmuch.

I came into the Great Hall just behind the others. Lady Kyme was breaking fast alone, a tankard half-way to her lips.

"Master Kytson, Master Dugdale and Master Benson!" she exclaimed, jumping up from her seat so swiftly that some ale slopped onto the table. The others swept off their caps and bowed.

I stepped out from behind them and her eyes widened. "Henry!" she cried. She frowned as she replaced her tankard and shook its contents off her hand. "But you are not my Henry, are you? He is lying abed upstairs." She came over and looked on me with troubled eyes. "Forgive my mistake, Mary Fox," she murmured, "I have been praying so hard to the good Lord to save my Henry from this dreadful illness, that when you came in, as alike him as if twins born…" She hesitated a moment, then concluded, "…I almost forgot the truth of the situation."

"I do understand, Lady Mother," I replied, matching her slight smile with one of my own. "It must be hard for you."

She gestured us to sit with her and to help ourselves to the poached eggs, meat, bread, cheese and ale that was laid out.

"How was the Garter Ceremony?" she asked once we had sat.

"It went… well," I replied, pouring myself some ale.

She noted my hesitation. "But?"

"But – I met with Queen Anne."

"Who suspected that the Prince was not in truth, the Prince," Marcus observed. "The Queen has said she will send her man Cruddon with enough men to try and to take him again," he paused, "or Mary here, of course."

Lady Kyme's eyes widened and she put her hand to her mouth. "What are we to do?" she whispered.

"I assume the Prince cannot be moved?" I asked.

Lady Kyme shook her head. "I would not counsel it," she said. "He is not yet strong enough."

"I thought as much," I said. "So we must keep him here so he can get the rest he needs."

"But how do we make him safe?"

I had been giving this some thought to this as we rode back from Windsor, and I believed I had a possible plan. "We do some more play-acting, Lady Mother," I said. "We make Cruddon and his men believe that neither the Prince nor I remain in this house."

"Why you as well?"

"He knows of me," I explained. "So when the Queen tells him of her suspicions concerning the young man at Windsor, Cruddon will be sure to believe it is me not the real Duke. He will be looking to take us both."

"And he means you harm?"

I thought back to our last encounter, when Cruddon had taken such pleasure in trying to shoot me with his crossbow. "He means to kill me," I said simply.

Lady Kyme looked distressed as she put her hand over mine. "I am so sorry, Mary, that we have put you in such danger."

"Nay," I replied. "In truth, he has wanted to kill me since before I first met Master Kytson."

"Such a dreadful man," she said. "I recall you told us before how he blames you for the death of his son." She squeezed my hand. "Which you said was but an accident."

"It was," I agreed. "So he remains a threat to both the Prince and to me."

"Which is why we need to make him think neither Mary nor the real Prince are here," Marcus said.

I then talked them all through the plan I had devised. When I was finished, Lady Kyme nodded slowly. "It makes sense," she said. "And you think it will work?"

"I believe it will," I replied. "With luck it will stop his evil plans for good."

—0—

It took four days of preparations, but eventually the Prince's full household was packed and ready to make the move from London to another of his houses; this one at Tonge in Kent.

On the morning of the fifth day, a fleet of carriages were lined up outside Durham House. Each was being loaded with wooden chests of household possessions and clothes, under the watchful eye of Christopher the steward. As the horses snorted, stamped and shook their heads in their traces, manservants scurried in and out of the house with the final pieces of luggage.

I was dressed as the Prince, sitting on Hestia accompanied by Marcus, Hal and Ed. As we waited for the final part of our show to take place, I glanced across to the gates and the trees beyond. Two men were standing in the shadows on the far side, just as they, or their fellows, had been doing day and night since our return. I smiled to myself. It was a vital part of our plan that Cruddon's men – and it had to be his men – were keeping watch on the house. I wanted them to be under no illusion that the Prince and his entire entourage were heading out of London.

I turned my head as some shouts came from the house. Two well-built coachmen appeared, carrying a fine-looking chest. As I watched, one of them stumbled slightly and appeared about to drop it.

"I said, take care!" barked Christopher, as the coachman recovered and the chest was taken to one of the carriages. The back door opened and the distinctive figure of Lady Kyme in her travelling cloak stepped out. She then supervised the loading of the chest inside, giving her instructions in a loud, imperious voice. The two coachmen then climbed onto the carriage seat and settled themselves with the reins. Similar drivers did the same on all the other coaches.

Eventually everything was ready, and the gates were opened. All the coachmen touched the horses' rumps with their whips, shook their reins, and slowly the carriages rolled down the path, through the gates and onto the street.

Marcus and I then fell in at the rear of the procession, following the final carriage through the gates. As we passed through I took the greatest care not to stare at the watching men, lest they realise we knew of their presence, and had put on much of this show purely for their benefit.

Once we had reached the end of the street and turned east, I leaned across to Marcus. "Let us hope the message soon reaches Cruddon; that the Prince and his entire household are heading to Kent."

"While the real Prince remains in Durham House in the care of his mother and doctor," he agreed.

I settled in the saddle. "Let us hope Cruddon now falls into the trap we are setting for him."

29

CALL ME MISTRESS

The sun was setting in the west as our carriages finally rolled up to the Prince's house in Tonge, Kent.

I climbed stiffly down from Hestia's back and glanced quickly round. The house was small by royal standards, a two-story brick building with a few twisted chimneys, at the end of a lane that led from the centre of the town.

"Do you see anything?" Marcus asked as he also dismounted.

I made another sweeping glance round, and caught sight of some dark shapes beside a tree.

"Aye," I muttered. "I think I see them. They are observing us even now."

"We must give them what they expect," he replied, with his customary grin. "Let us show them the noble young Duke who has arrived at his Kent dwelling leading his household inside." He stood aside as our horses were taken by a groom. "Lead on, Your Grace."

I put my shoulders back and raised my chin. Then I swept past Marcus and on up to the house.

Ed Benson and Hal Dugdale, still dressed as a coachmen, were waiting for us at the top of the steps.

"Your Grace," Ed said, as they both took off their caps and bowed to me.

"Master Benson. Master Dugdale." I acknowledged them with a small grin at their play-acting. "You are ready for the next part of the plan?"

He nodded. "Myself and Hal will marshal all the fighting men we brought here disguised as coachmen and servants. I will assign them all to their positions, and give them weapons, so that if – or when – this man Cruddon attacks, we will be ready for him."

"That is so," Marcus confirmed.

"And it is you he wants to take, or to kill?" asked Benson, his grey eyes on mine.

"It is," I replied. "Both as myself, Mary Fox, and as the Prince."

"Then it is good fortune – nay, good planning – that the real Prince has remained in London, with some of my fellows looking to his safety." He paused. "So you must act on the next part of the plan, and spirit yourself back to London, so you cannot be taken."

"I will," I said. "This very night." I took his hand. "I am indeed grateful for your service. You are an honourable man."

"And one who relishes a good fight," he replied, putting his hand to the hilt of his sword. "I greatly look forward to putting an end to this rogue Cruddon's scheming."

Leaving them in the hall, I made my way up the stairs to put my own element of the plan into action.

I found Hannah, the ladies' maid who had seen to my bath when I had first come to Durham House all those years before, in one of the chambers. She was standing at the end of the bed talking to the steward Christopher. She was still dressed in the fine gown and hood she had worn in her role as Lady Kyme for the journey east.

She gave me a small curtsey as I came in, no doubt out of habit – which I found reassuring that even those who saw the Prince every day treated me as if I were really him.

But we had much to do, and no time for such reflections. "Are you ready, Hannah?" I asked.

"We are, Your Gra… Mistress Fox," she replied, standing away from the bed to reveal a kirtle, a gown, a pair of women's stockings, a French hood and a pair of shoes spread out.

"Good," I said. "Then let us get on with it."

First I stripped down to my chemise, handing the garments to Christopher as I removed them. He folded each one and placed them in a small travelling chest. Then he bowed, lifted the chest with a grunt and left the room.

I was alone with Hannah.

"Now then, Mistress Fox," she said, "let us make you once again a young person of beauty – a fitting lady-in-waiting for my mistress."

An hour or so later, I was once again bound up and trussed like a goose for the roast, wearing the constricting women's clothing I disliked so much. Hannah seemed oblivious to my discomfort, pulling on the ties at my back until I could scarcely breathe. My breasts, so used to being bound tight to my chest, had enjoyed only the briefest moment of freedom before being equally constricted into the tight bodice of the gown.

Once I was dressed, she took out some pots of rouge and kohl, and set to work on my face. It took some minutes before she appeared satisfied with her work. Then she took out an ivory comb, parted my hair in the middle, secured it under a dark coif, then added the hood.

"You have little hair for a girl," she observed as she adjusted the headpiece and stood back to see the effect. "But under this hood, it is well hidden."

She held up a mirror, and I must admit I gave a small gasp as I stared at my reflection.

Gone was the Duke of Richmond, a boy of nearly seventeen years.

In his place was an elegant lady of twenty, her face glowing with colour and her slim waist proclaiming her every inch a woman.

"By the Holy Cross, Hannah," I breathed, "I do not even recognise myself."

"I have only revealed your natural beauty, mistress."

I gave her a conspiratorial grin. "Well, let us hope it fools the men on watch; those who mean me and the Prince harm. Let us hope that they make no connection between Lady Kyme, her lady in waiting and her steward who leave by carriage, and the young nobleman who arrived so publicly this evening."

"Indeed, I do hope so, mistress."

I suppressed a small chuckle. To have a woman dressed as a lady calling me 'mistress' seemed quite wrong. I said nothing as she helped me into a fine travelling cloak.

Hannah put on her own cloak and said, "I believe Master Christopher will have made the carriage ready by now." She seemed to have regained her composure, which reassured me. I needed her to be as confident in her role as she had been when ordering Hal and Ed as coachmen back in London.

"Come then," I said, as I swept from the room.

The carriage was waiting outside the front entrance. Two horses were standing in the traces and the driver sat on top with his cap pulled low. Two large flaming braziers either side of the door gave everything a flickering orange glow. I walked round to the far side – I hoped in full view of Cruddon's watching men. I permitted myself a small smile; I had made sure I was silhouetted against the flames, so they could not see my face too clearly. I stood aside as Christopher helped Hannah up, then allowed him to help me also. He climbed on board himself, settled opposite Hannah and me, then rapped on the partition.

"Drive on," he called out.

"Very good sir," came a voice from outside. There was a jolt, then the carriage moved forward, and we were on our way.

"Keep from staring out of the window as we turn onto the street," I instructed. "The watchers will be suspicious if they spot us looking for them." Hannah and Christopher nodded, their faces orange in the glow of the braziers. Then we passed into the bright moonlight, making their faces change to a ghostly blue.

We rattled across the cobbled streets of Tonge; first past a few fine houses, then those that were crowded together and rickety looking, until we came to the edge of the town and the houses ceased altogether.

I leaned out of the window and looked up. The coachman was a black shape just visible against the dark of the night sky. "Did you see the watchers?" I called up.

"Yes," he replied. "Still trying to hide in that alley, but I saw them more clearly from up here."

"How many?"

"Five, maybe six." He paused. "And horses behind them."

"I assume they will be joined by more. And most likely Cruddon himself."

"Most likely."

I sat back inside. Christopher leaned across. "How many men in total are defending the house?"

"Master Benson and Master Dugdale are the two that have command. All the servants are really fighting men drafted in for the purpose, and they number a further six."

He nodded. "Let us hope the numbers remain in our favour. The watchers would have seen naught but serving men, when in truth it was a defensive force that should be able to repel even the most determined attackers."

"There were serving maids as well," I pointed out. "Three of them. Although they were also swordsmen in disguise." I turned to Hannah. "You made a fine Lady Kyme, too."

"It has been fun," she agreed. "Although I had not realised how heavy are the gowns that she wears."

Nor how constricting, I thought.

"I look forward to getting to Durham House, and I can be myself again," she said. She paused a moment, and her face fell. "I do worry so."

"For what?" I asked.

"That I will be punished for my presumption."

"You were asked to do this by Lady Kyme herself," I pointed out.

"Yes, but I am afeared all the same."

"It will be fine," I said. I bit my lip as the carriage rattled along the road heading west towards the city. In truth I was reassuring myself as much as her.

The next half hour was spent in idle chat, which eventually petered out as the fatigue of the day overtook us. Christopher's eyes drifted shut, and Hannah's head made its way onto the window post. I too felt tiredness creeping upon me, and decided not to fight it, but to welcome some sleep before we came to London. I settled back in my seat and allowed my eyes to close.

Once we were back in Durham House, we would be safe…

The Prince would recover and resume his own life…

Then I could soon cast off the disguise, and decide where to go next…

A neigh from one of the horses.

A sudden jolt.

The carriage speeding up.

I was awake in an instant, every sense sharpened to danger. I leaned out. "What is it?"

"Two horses behind," the driver replied. "Gaining fast."

"What can we do?"

"Keep going," he snapped. "Or we can stop and fight."

"Keep going for now."

"Cannot out-run them."

I turned and looked back. There were two dark shapes behind. Even as I looked they became larger, and could clearly be seen as two riders, crouched over the necks of their horses, the sound of their hooves beating through the ground.

I dropped back into the carriage. Hannah and Christopher were both wide awake, staring at me.

"What is it?" he asked.

"Two horsemen," I replied, my voice strained.

"Do they mean us harm?" Hannah whimpered, looking white in the moonlight.

"I warrant," I said. "I doubt they ride after us for any other reason."

"What must we do?"

"We sit up straight," I said. "You must play the part of Lady Kyme once more, and play it to the full. Can you do that?" She nodded wide-eyed, but I was pleased that she did sit a little straighter.

I made a small curse under my breath, that I had thought to keep Hannah as Lady Kyme, when I could have swapped roles and played her myself.

Ahh well, 'twas done now, and we must make the best of it.

"Chin up," I said. "You are a noblewoman, widow of a baron and mother to a prince. You have been the King's mistress. Ruffians on the road must respect your position. Take no nonsense from them."

Christopher leaned across and patted her knee. "Come, Han… My Lady. Be strong."

As he sat back, I caught his eye, and gave him a small nod of reassurance.

I felt below the seat for the knife I had secured there earlier.

The sound of hooves grew louder.

30
THE WOMAN WE SEEK

One of the horsemen rode past the carriage; making a dark, thundering shape in the night that momentarily blocked out the moonlight. Then I heard a neigh as he must have stopped in our way. We were jolted as our driver pulled his two horses up.

I glanced out of the window. The man had his horse across the path, and was dismounting. I looked behind and was briefly able to see his companion, before the moon went behind a cloud and all became dark. Now the man was only a stark silhouette against the night sky.

"What is the meaning of this?" barked our driver. "Do you mean to rob us? That is a capital offence, and I'll see you hang for it."

I admired his bravado. They say it is better to attack than defend.

"We were curious," replied the man in the rough voice of a common soldier, "what you were doing stealing away in the night."

"By the Heavens sirrah, how is that any of your concern?" snapped the driver. "We have naught to hide. Be out of our way, knave, and let us be about our business."

"If you have naught to hide, why do you leave under cover of darkness?"

"We can leave whenever the fancy takes us. We have no need to answer to you."

The man seemed to ignore this. "I would see who you have in there."

"No you will not!" The carriage rocked as the driver jumped down, and there was the sound of a steel blade being pulled from a scabbard. "Or it will be the last thing you do."

"Do you threaten me?" There was the sound of another blade being drawn.

"By all the saints, yes, I do."

I waited with my heart in my mouth for the sound of blades clashing, but it did not come. Instead there was the thudding of hooves coming from behind, then a horse being pulled up and a man dismounting. Footsteps crunched towards us. I had no time to say anything to Hannah and Christopher, before a swarthy bearded face appeared at the window. The door was pulled open.

"Get out," the man barked, and there was the dull glint of a sword. "All of you." For a moment we hesitated. The moon came out from behind a cloud again, illuminating the whole scene in a blue glow. "I said out!" the man repeated.

"You make a grave mistake," said Christopher, waving a hand towards Hannah. "Do you know who this is?"

"I do not give a monkey's cuss," the man replied. "Get down from this carriage, or I will drive you out on the point of my blade."

Hannah and Christopher got out, and I followed, my knife concealed up my sleeve.

I will give Hannah her due; she made a strong effort to be a stern Lady Kyme, but her nerves and her inexperience showed clear. "I am Lady Kyme," she quavered, "travelling to London with my lady in waiting and my steward. I will know the reason for this impertinence."

There was a silence as the second man stared at her, and everyone was still. Then he looked me up and down, before turning his attention to Christopher.

He gave an evil-sounding chuckle. "Lady Kyme, my arse!"

He studied me again with a sneer twisting his coarse features, "And who are you? The Queen of England?"

Suddenly his eyes narrowed, and it was as if a cold wave of fear engulfed me.

I saw the exact moment when he recognised who I really was.

"By the Lord, I warrant you are the woman we seek! The one we are charged to kill! You are Mary Fox!"

I shifted the grip on my dagger and pulled it from my sleeve. It must have glinted in the moonlight, for the man looked down, then yelled, "She has a knife!"

He pulled his arm back, then swept his sword at me.

I tried to step away as the blade swung in, but was encumbered by my heavy skirts. I screamed as my foot caught and I fell to the ground, just as the point flashed past my face.

I landed on my back with a jolt that knocked the breath from my body, and tried to raise my knife, as if some sort of protection.

But the man stepped forward and put his boot onto my wrist.

The pain of his weight was excruciating, but I could make no movement while he had me pinned to the ground.

He stood over me, both hands on his sword hilt and the blade poised to drive into my chest. His eyes glittered in the moonlight as he gave a triumphant smile.

"I will be well rewarded for this, Mary Fox!" he crowed.

"In hell, perhaps," said a voice from behind him, and suddenly the man seemed to grow a new sword; one with a reddened point that emerged from directly from between his ribs.

He looked down, his eyes wide with surprise at the length of steel that had spit him like a roasting boar. Then the blade disappeared as our driver pulled it out from behind with a ghastly sucking sound. I nearly spewed in disgust as the man's blood rushed out and landed on my chest and on the path.

The man staggered and raised his sword again, but this time there was nothing in his eyes; neither murder, nor even a soul. For a moment I feared his death would be mine as well, for he looked as if he would now fall onto me with his sword. With a cry I tried to wriggle clear.

A hand grasped the man's shoulder and pulled him backwards, away from me.

He spun round, and this was enough to make him overbalance, releasing my wrist. He swayed a moment, then dropped to his knees beside me.

He remained there a moment as if in prayer. Then he slowly fell forward onto my skirts, and was still.

Desperately I tugged at the trapped fabric, but the man's weight was too great. "Get him off me! Get me free!" I cried, my chest feeling as if it would burst. "In Heaven's name!"

A dark shape leaned over the body and pulled it off me.

"There," came the voice of the driver. "No need to panic, Mary."

I lay back, unable to move or speak.

"And in case you were wondering, I dealt with the other fellow first. He should not have run forward when you produced your knife. He forgot I was there a moment." He gave a small a grin. "A bad mistake indeed."

I looked up at the driver, who had taken off his cap and was shaking out his blonde hair.

"But I will say, that was fun," he observed.

I managed to find my voice. "Nice swordsmanship. Thank you, Marcus."

—0—

Marcus dragged the bodies as deep as he could into the undergrowth, judging by how long he was gone with each one. I used the time to massage my wrist, and it seemed that, thankfully, it was only bruised, not broken.

When Marcus returned, we unhooked our own two horses from the carriage traces and changed them for Cruddon's men's beasts. "Your Hestia is not a carthorse, and neither is mine," Marcus observed. "We will let them run alongside on a short rein."

"I would not have left her in Tonge," I said. "So it was necessary to use her to pull the carriage." I patted her neck and got a most disapproving stare in return. "Oh," I muttered. "Sorry, old girl."

I got back into the carriage. Christopher and Hannah were looking white-faced, and Hannah seemed unable to take her eyes off the splashes of blood remaining on my chest, even after I had tried to wipe them away with a kerchief.

"That man was about to kill you, Mary," she whispered. "Then Master Kytson pushed his blade into… into …" Even in the moonlight I could see that she was more green than white. Perhaps close to vomiting.

"He did what had to be done, Hannah," I replied.

"He was dead in seconds," Christopher said. "He would have known little before finding himself facing eternal judgement."

Hannah swallowed hard. "Would Lord Jesus have welcomed him?" she wondered.

"He worked for Cruddon," I observed. "So I fancy his journey would be downward to meet Satan, along with his companion."

"Oh!" Hannah gasped, and swallowed again. "Master Kytson dispatched him as well."

Marcus's face appeared at the window.

"I have tethered our horses, and we are ready to go," he said.

I looked at Hannah, who was, if anything, even greener, and swallowing continuously. "Wait a moment, Marcus," I said. "I think Hannah might need to step outside first." She nodded. I got down and helped her out, then led her to the side of the lane and held her by the waist while she vomited copiously. "There," I said, once there seemed to be no more to come. "Better?"

She gave me a wide-eyed nod, so I helped her back inside, calling up to Marcus, "Let us be away!"

As the carriage started forward, she whispered, "If I had held my silence – if I had not been so hesitant as Lady Kyme, would those men still be alive?"

"I doubt it," I replied. "They were already suspicious, else why would they have stopped us? And anyway," I added, "who can say what would have happened otherwise? No doubt they would have dispatched us all."

"Oh!" She put her hand to her mouth as if she realised the truth of this. "Then it was good thing that they did not believe me?"

I smiled. "What is done is done. The outcome was good for us. That is all."

She was silent again, as we rattled through the night towards London.

—0—

Dawn was spreading its red glow as we turned into the gates of Durham House. I searched across the nearby trees and hedges as we turned in, and saw no sign of watchers. As I hoped, Cruddon must have called them all to Kent, in preparation for the attack we were expecting. Perhaps even the two men Marcus had dispatched in the night had previously been the watchers here.

Lady Kyme met us in the Great Hall.

Hannah, who was still white-faced, quickly excused herself with a perfunctory curtsey, saying she must resume her normal attire. She lifted her skirts and ran out. Her steps could be heard pattering towards the back stairs.

After she had gone, Lady Kyme asked, "How went the plan?"

"Up until a few hours past, it went exactly as we hoped," I replied. She raised an enquiring eyebrow, so I told her of our encounter with Cruddon's men. She was suitably shocked as I related the tale of their deaths, but was most matter-of-fact about it.

"What have you done with the bodies?"

"There was an overgrown ditch a fair way off the path," said Marcus. "I threw them in there."

She nodded. "And all your men are in place, should this fellow Cruddon attack?"

"Aye," Marcus replied. "There are eleven men in all, but I must join them." He turned to me. "Now I know you are safely returned, Mary, I plan to ride back this day." He touched the hilt of his sword. "The ruffian took me, burned my flesh and kept me a prisoner. I want to be the one who puts a blade through his cold heart."

—0—

Marcus left a few hours later, once he had eaten well and his horse had had time to recover its strength. We took our leave of each other at the stables.

"I will return once we have dealt with the ruffian Cruddon." He looked down at me once he had mounted. "I only hope I do not arrive back in Kent to find him already dead," he added with a small chuckle.

"Take care," I muttered. "Do not forget that he is dangerous, as are his men."

"Thankfully we still have the element of surprise," he replied. "Which we would not have done if those two in the night had been able to warn him of our plan." He hesitated a moment. "You take care also, Mary. You do not know if some watchers may return."

I smiled. "I will keep away from windows, and stay in my female clothing, in case I am seen."

"Belike you can now find it in your heart to accept such attire?" he asked. "Even if only on occasions?" There was a slight look of hope on his face.

"It is not my pleasure, that is for certain." I shook my head with a small smile. "It is not what is in my heart."

He hesitated a moment. Then his face cleared and he resumed his customary irreverent grin. "Your heart has always been a challenge to me, Mary," he said. "I wonder how any man can find a way into it. So I have an offer for you."

I waited to hear what this might be.

"Mary Fox," he began, then stopped to swallow hard. "I would you do me the honour of becoming my wife."

I stared at him, speechless.

"But," he added quickly, "I know you are not as other girls," he said. "And that you desire to spend much of your time scheming and fighting like a man. So I do understand that a conventional marriage would be to imprison your heart, just as your stepfather imprisoned your body for all those years."

I nodded. It appeared he did understand me well.

"Thus, I would not be a controlling husband, but we will have a partnership of equals. One where we work together to right wrongs; where we go forth as a pair, taking on those who would do evil and undertaking whatever is necessary to conquer them. I am offering you the only marriage that

I believe you will accept, Mary." He gave me a look of hope.

"I… I know not Marcus…" I stuttered. "I must give it thought. I cannot answer you now."

He nodded, as if this was what he expected. "Then I will look forward to your answer when I return. But please, I pray you think on it most carefully."

"I will." I replied. "Think on it, I mean."

He laughed. "Please do. Farewell, dear Mary, and I will return soon, with, I trust, news of Cruddon's timely end."

With that he kicked his horse and cantered out of the gate, leaving me standing like a statue, trying to comprehend what he had just said.

A marriage where the woman was an equal partner? Where both husband and wife would go out into the world together to conquer evil?

Marcus was indeed correct about one thing; it was the only kind of marriage I could possibly accept. With this on my mind, I walked slowly back into the house.

Lady Kyme was in the Great Hall.

"Is all well, Mary, my dear?" she asked.

I took a long breath. "Marcus Kytson has just asked for my hand in marriage, Lady Mother," I said slowly.

She was all smiles, and enveloped me in a warm embrace. "Oh, Mary! I am so pleased! I have known for some time how he feels for you, and have oft told him to find the courage to ask. And now he has heeded my advice."

"He sought your approval first?" I asked.

"Of course! I have known him since a mischievous boy. He has always relied on my council."

"And you gave your blessing?" I asked. "Even though he recognised I am not as other girls?"

"I did, for nothing would give me more pleasure than to see you two happy together." Then she frowned. "You said 'yes', of course?"

"I said I needed to think, and would reply on his return."

She gave a small gasp. "But you will accept?"

"I do not… do not know. Maybe."

"But you must! He is a good man" She paused a moment, her eyes on mine. "Did he ever tell why I took him into my household?"

I shook my head. "Not really. Something about pranking you that he was an Austrian prince."

"Nay, it was a while after that. I had not long since given birth to Henry, and was granted a grace and favour apartment at Court. One day, Sir Robert Kytson came to Court with Marcus, and he asked to see me. It had been some time since we had last met, so I was pleased to see him again."

"Had he grown?"

She nodded. "He was much more a man. We talked over old times, then he asked to see my Henry. I said he could, so long as he did not wake the babe."

I pictured Marcus as a young man, scarce more than a boy, and smiled. It was an amusing image.

"We walked in. The wet nurse was asleep in her chair, and a fire was burning in the grate…"

Lady Kyme paused, and I could see there was a memory troubling her deeply. "But then I saw there was a piece of burning log that had been spat from the fire. It was smouldering in the rushes. As we watched, it sprang to flame. Before we had time to react, it had taken hold of a clump of rushes, and was moving quickly towards the babe in his crib.”

“Oh no!” I gasped. “What happened?”

“Marcus moved fast, and started stamping on the flames. But they had taken too strong a hold, and remained alight.” She swallowed hard. “So he fell on them, and rolled side to side, putting them out with his own clothing and body.”

“So he quenched them all?” I asked. “And no harm came to the babe?”

She nodded again. “Aye. He suffered some burning himself, which I treated with lard and soothing oils, but at least the fire was stopped.”

I was silent a moment.

Marcus had taken burns for the Prince, just as he had taken burns for me.

---0---

The next few days passed with little incident; Lady Kyme and I spent much time in idle conversation, almost as if we feared to discuss what was in truth uppermost in our minds; the possible battle taking place in Kent. I occasionally looked in on the Prince, who was still coughing and unable to rise from his bed, but who was not, in my opinion, or his doctor’s, getting any worse.

Lady Kyme and I were sitting by the fire in the parlour one evening in a casual discussion, when there was a knock at the door, and Christopher came in. He stood, twisting both hands, as if to stop them from waving around.

“What is it?” Lady Kyme asked.

"It is Master Kytson, my lady. He has returned."

"Oh that is excellent," Lady Kyme stood up. "Has he good news for us? Are all the men returned?"

"I fear not, my lady," said Christopher, looking as if he might burst into tears. "He is alone. And he is wounded."

31
PREPARING FOR CRUDDON

Marcus staggered past Christopher and dropped into a chair like a felled tree. There was a strip of linen bound around his upper thigh, with a deep scarlet stain filling one side.

"We were routed," he whispered, staring into the fire. "Completely routed."

"Marcus? What happened?" I asked. His whole downcast demeanour, his wound, his words; these all sent my heart out to him. Was the thought of nearly losing him opening that very heart, in a way I had never expected?

"We should have had more men," he muttered. "We were but twelve in all, and 'twas not enough. They had at least twice our number, even without those two lying in a ditch. They attacked us in the middle of the night." He frowned, "Nay, it was the darkest hour of the morning just before dawn. We were slow; having not thought they were coming that night. We were off our guard." He looked us each in turn, his eyes betraying his weariness. "We fought bravely," he continued, "and sent a few of them into Satan's arms, but it was not possible to have a sword in every direction at once. It ended with me, Hal and Ed fighting back-to-back against Cruddon and six... no," he shook his head, "...maybe eight of his men."

I felt the blood drain from my face as I stared at him. "I should have been there," I whispered. "I should not have run like a base coward. I should have been there, fighting by your side."

He looked up, his eyes wide in his dirty face. "Nay, Mary, it was the best thing for you not to be there. Cruddon attacked us with the express aim of seeking your death. He kept shouting for you to come out, for all I told him you were not there."

I shook my head, scarcely able to breathe as the full impact of this hit me hard. "But good men died in my cause," I said. "I should have seen this might happen. I should have been there."

"Not just your cause, Mary. The Prince's as well." He drew a deep breath. "Cruddon also called for the Prince. I warrant the rogue is still under the orders of the Queen to take him."

Lady Kyme paled. "We must redouble our guard on Henry," she whispered. "He remains in danger."

Marcus transferred his gaze to her. "That he does, my lady. Cruddon will no doubt regroup, and I assume he will make his attack on us here in a few days."

"But how did you get away?" I asked.

"When Ed and Hal went down…" he began, then stopped and took a deep breath. "…When they went down, I knew one person must get away to warn you. So I fought on with one eye on the door, and when I saw a chance, I made good my escape. I ran to the stables like I was Achilles himself, mounted and was away before they even had a chance to follow."

"And your leg?" I pointed at the bloodied bandage."

"Oh that." He shrugged. "I must have taken a cut without noticing in the fighting. So once I had ridden clear, I stopped and tore a strip off my chemise to bind it." He glanced at it. "I fancy 'tis much worse than it seems."

"I will take care of it," I said softly, and from the corner of my eye I saw that Lady Kyme's head had snapped round to look at me. "But first you must bathe and change your clothing."

—0—

The wound was indeed quite superficial. I knelt beside Marcus, making sure it was clean, before applying a fresh bandage. Then I tied it tight to keep the edges of the wound together.

"You will have a fine scar there," I said, once I had finished. "But it will soon fade, I warrant."

I did not mention the other scar, a puckered burn mark further down his thigh, and nor did he.

"Thank you, Mary," he said, and for the first time he seemed to manage a weary smile. "You make a fine nurse."

"Better than a swordsman, I fancy," I replied. "One who should, in truth, have been there fighting by your side."

He leaned forward and put his hands on my shoulders. "Nay, sweet Mary, for then you would have been slain along with us all, or taken prisoner by that knave." He hesitated a moment, as if this pained him greatly. "Anyhow, he will doubtless try and attack here as well, so you will have ample opportunity to fight him in the coming days, I warrant."

"I welcome it," I said.

He moved his hands up to my cheeks. "And the offer I made before leaving for Kent. Do you welcome that also?" He gave me a nervous-looking smile.

"I am sorry, Marcus, but…"

"You refuse me?"

"Nay," I shook my head. "I just need more time. I have not yet decided."

"More time? How long?" he asked softly.

"I do not know." I stroked his hand. "But be assured I will tell you, one way or the other."

"You promise?"

"Of course. The very moment I have come to a decision."

"Please do," he said.

"I will," I said. "But first we must prepare for Cruddon."

The thought of Cruddon making an attack on Durham House caused me the gravest concern. It was one thing to have him attack the house in Tonge, where every man in the place was a dedicated swordsman, but quite another for him to attack this London house, with Lady Kyme, the Prince and the servants here. Especially as his previous attack had resulted in the loss of so many of our own men. What chance would we have unless we could secure reinforcements – and quickly?

"We need to outwit him," I said slowly. "We need to find a way to prevent him from making an attack in the first place, so Lady Kyme and the Prince are not put in any danger."

"Well, you are the one who devises schemes, are you not, Mary?" He looked into my eyes with an almost hopeful expression. "I am sure you can come up with a plan."

"Perhaps," I replied. "But it needs to be soon, as we do not know when Cruddon's attack may come."

—0—

If I was hard pressed to come up with a scheme quickly, the following afternoon this seemed to pale by comparison to the news we heard.

Lady Kyme, Marcus and I were having a quiet conversation over our meal. We had been suggesting many and various plans to deal with Cruddon, and I was pleased that an idea of mine had been discussed and enlarged into something resembling a possible course of action.

Suddenly Christopher rushed in. His eyes were wide and his hair, which he usually kept neat, was most tousled, as if he had been running his hands through it. He burst through the door without a knock or his customary bow and marched straight up to the table.

"What is it, Christopher?" asked Lady Kyme.

"It is the Queen, my lady," he said. "She has been arrested and taken to the Tower."

"Arrested?" Lady Kyme gasped. "By what cause?"

"She has been accused of adultery and treason," the steward whispered. "Along with Sir Henry Norris, Sir Francis Weston and Sir William Brereton. And even a musician by the name of Mark Smeaton."

There was a long silence while we each digested this information.

"She will need to be brought to trial," observed Marcus. "She will have a chance to clear her name."

"I warrant the King wants rid of her," Lady Kyme replied. "Master Cromwell will ensure she is found guilty."

"What then?" Marcus asked. "A nunnery?"

Lady Kyme shook her head slowly. "I suspect not. She is accused of treason. The only punishment for such a crime is death."

There was another silence as we all considered this further. Lady Kyme was looking almost puzzled, as if she was unsure whether she should be pleased to see one who would harm her son in such danger, or upset that a fellow partner of the King was likely to be executed. Marcus had his customary half-smile, as if he found it all amusing when the mighty were made to fall.

"What say you, Mary?" he asked.

"I have no love for the Queen," I said, "and nor should any of us, after what she has put us through, and how she has caused men to die because of her." Marcus's smile disappeared and he nodded in agreement. "But my concern is that now she has set him off, Cruddon is propelled by his own desire for revenge. I fear this changes nothing." I shook my head. "Cruddon will still come. It is not a matter of 'if', only of 'when'."

32

THE QUEEN'S EXECUTION

I was partly right about Cruddon – he did make his move, but it was not for another fortnight.

Meanwhile, we followed the unfolding events as the Queen's life progressed inexorably towards its violent end. We heard of her trial, which as Lady Kyme had said, was naught but a sham; her own father and her uncle Norfolk making sure she was found guilty. We discussed in hushed tones the news that the Queen's own brother George Boleyn had been accused of an incestuous and treasonous bedding. And we were shocked when we heard that the marriage had been annulled, disinheriting the Princess Elizabeth.

"My Henry is sure to be elevated to the succession now," Lady Kyme said, when we talked over this topic later. "If only his health were to take a turn for the better."

The doctor had visited the previous day, and had told us that there was neither improvement nor any worsening. "He still coughs greatly," the little bald man said, "but there is no blood in the phlegm."

Lady Kyme bit her lip at this. "As a mother I find it hard when we cannot see improvement."

"But he gets no worse," the doctor added, as he replaced his cap, bowed and prepared to leave us. "Hold on to that thought."

"The man does little to help," muttered Lady Kyme after the doctor had gone. "Belike I will find another."

"I agree," I said. "The Prince needs to recover soon, so he can take his rightful place at his father's side." I paused. "I understand the Queen… or Mistress Boleyn, as we should now call her, is due for execution on the morrow, and the Prince has been instructed to attend?"

Lady Kyme nodded. "That is so." She paused, considering me with her head to one side. "But given the state of his health, it is not possible for him to go."

I knew what was to come next. It was a clear as night follows day.

"So, my dear Mary, you must attend in his stead."

"Very well," I replied. "For all I would rather not see her meeting her death, I have no love for the woman. If I must see it, I will."

"Do not forget you are there as the Prince, not yourself," she said. "Your feelings are not the ones that govern this situation."

"After all she has done, I warrant the Prince will be just as pleased as I will to see her dispatched," I muttered.

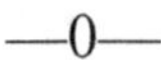

The following morning I made my way across the city to the Tower, accompanied by Marcus and Christopher in the Prince's livery. The fortress loomed large above us as we rode into a stable block alongside the edge of the moat. An old ostler came out, bowing, and asked if we were here for the execution of the Queen. He made it sound like something as ordinary as a May fayre, as if such a momentous event were all in a day's work for him. I supposed after the number of high-born nobles who had been dispatched within these grim walls, even the death of a queen must have been nothing special.

I made sure Hestia was securely stabled with some food, then joined Marcus and Christopher to continue our journey on foot.

We walked under the Middle Tower, over the moat bridge and through the Byward Tower entrance. It felt as though we were coming into the belly of a fearsome stone beast as we walked along the inner wall until we came to the Wakefield Tower and made our way onto the bright open Inner Green. As we turned left, Marcus touched my elbow, then pointed over to our right.

"St. Thomas's Tower," he murmured. "Beyond is the Traitor's Gate."

I gave an involuntary shiver. Just the word 'traitor' left me feeling weak and cold – for once again I was masquerading as the Prince without the knowledge or permission of his father. What if I was exposed here, just as I had feared I would be at Windsor? No need for the Traitor's Gate – I could be marched straight to the darkened Tower dungeons, there to await my fate.

"Chin up, Your Grace," Marcus said. "Less of the look of a nervous foal and more an expression of triumph. You are one of the land's foremost nobles, about to witness the execution of his bitterest enemy."

"True," I replied, lifting my head and assuming the stern expression demanded by the occasion, tinged with a little of the pleasure of seeing an enemy vanquished. This was not just my emotion – it was that of the Prince himself. I knew this from looking in on the boy the previous eve. I had wanted to tell him that I was to attend in his place, but he had further ideas for discussion.

He had seemed worse than I remembered; hollow-eyed, grey-skinned and unable to breathe without the sound of coal being poured from a scuttle. "I am grateful, dear Mary," he whispered. "It is good that I am seen in public, hale and hearty, rather than news of my illness is known by all."

"Indeed, Your Grace," I said. "Once you are fully recovered, no-one will be any the wiser."

He gave me a thin smile. "If I do recover."

"Of course you will," I protested. "You are young and strong."

"Yet I have been in and out of this sickbed ever since that man Cruddon held me in his damp, rat-infested cellar."

"But you have been better for long periods," I said. "So can be again."

He coughed deeply for a while; the phlegm rattling in his chest. "I do hope so, Mary," he whispered once he had his breath back. "But I fear God has other plans for me."

He was a boy of near seventeen, but with the face of a dying man in his later years. At that moment I could see that maybe the Lord did plan to take him very soon. But I wanted to keep his spirits up. "I am sure God plans great things for you, Your Grace, with a long and fruitful life."

He gave a small shrug, as if to say that what the Lord willed, he would accept. Then he made a ghostly smile. "Whatsoever happens to me, at least that woman dies on the morrow." His smile broadened. "Now there, God has planned correctly." He seemed about to say something more, but was interrupted by another severe bout of coughing. I waited until he was again the master of his breath, then he said, "I know it is not a Christian thought, Mary, but I am pleased at the news of her end. She meant me harm, and it was her actions that first put me in this sickbed. So I want you to do something for me."

"Of course, Your Grace," I answered, wondering what he might want.

"As the woman's head is parted from her body, I would have you smile. Openly and clearly. I want the world to know that the Duke of Richmond welcomed her execution." He looked up at me, and I could see there were tears at the corner of his eyes. "Will you show what I think of her?"

I hesitated a moment, but I could see he was sincere in this wish. "Yes, Your Grace," I said. "If that is what you desire."

So now Marcus, Christopher and I were joining the crowd of nobles and warders who were thronging across the green to where a wooden dais had been erected. I glanced back at the White Tower. It was a giant presence, standing four-square in the middle of the space, with tall spires at each corner and many arched windows. These gazed at us like eyes, and I fancy they were judging the enormity of the occasion about to happen; the execution of a queen. Had the Tower ever seen the like before? Most likely not – and perhaps never would again.

An elderly gentleman wearing a fine red and gold doublet, embroidered with the Tudor rose and the King's monogram, suddenly appeared, blocking my way. Two warders stood behind him, their gleaming halberds crossed.

"Your Grace," he said. "I am Sir William Kingston, Constable of the Tower."

I nodded weakly, finding my knees were shaking. Was this to be the moment of my arrest?

Then I saw there was a grim smile on his fleshy features.

"I assume you would like a good view of the… ahh… proceedings, Your Grace. A space has been held for you close to the dais. Please follow my warders, who will escort you there."

The warders shouldered their halberds and started walking through the crowd. I hurried after them, with Marcus and Christopher following close behind. When we arrived at the front, the warders indicated our space, then took up guard positions nearby.

I could now see the dais clearly. It was a raised platform standing on wooden legs with a banister rail and crossed supports running all around, apart from the steps to one side. Fresh-looking straw had been laid across it.

"To sop up the blood," Marcus whispered.

"I thank you, Master Kytson," I replied, unable to keep the sarcasm from my voice.

"See the muscled fellow with the sword?" he asked. I nodded. "He is from France. I am told the King decided that instead of suffering the pain of being burned for treason, the woman would be beheaded."

"Not by an axeman with her head on a block?" I asked.

"Nay. The King was concerned that an axeman might take several blows. He wanted this to be quick and clean."

"How thoughtful of him."

"Apparently this fellow is much practiced with a sword."

The man in question was standing to one side, with his hands on the hilt of a large broadsword that had its point resting between his feet.

There was a small flurry of activity behind me, and a man in clerical dress walked out, followed by Sir William Kingston. They climbed the steps and talked quietly for a while.

A few minutes later, a guard arrived, followed by three women dressed in black, all looking very solemn and perhaps even close to tears. These were followed by two more guards, with a tall woman walking between them, wearing a plain cloak and a simple white coif.

Anne Boleyn.

She looked neither to her left or right as she walked up the steps, but had her head held high, almost as if she was feigning confidence to hide her fear. For all I disliked what she had done to me and the Prince, I could not help but respect her at that moment.

She reached the top and spoke quietly to the constable a moment, then he beckoned the swordsman over. She spoke to him also, then handed him a coin.

"Payment for a swift execution," muttered Marcus.

The cleric stepped forward, and she bowed her head to him. He spoke softly a while, before making the sign of the cross over her.

Anne Boleyn then asked something of the constable. He nodded, and she stepped to the edge of the dais, and looked outwards. The crowd, who had been muttering amongst themselves, fell silent.

"Good Christian people," she began, her voice clear on the still morning air. "I am come hither to die, for according to the law, and by the law I am judged to die, and therefore I will speak nothing against it. I am come hither to accuse no man, nor to speak anything of that, whereof I am accused and condemned to die, but I pray God save the King and send him long to reign over you, for a gentler nor a more merciful prince was there never: and to me he was ever a good, a gentle and sovereign lord." As she said this, she looked down, and briefly she caught my eye.

The corner of her mouth twitched, and she appeared to forget what she was about to say. She gave me a look of such hate that I swear that if she were truly the servant of the devil, as many had said, then she was cursing me for all eternity. Thankfully the moment passed as swiftly as it had come, and I doubt if any man, save perhaps Marcus, had even been aware of it.

She raised her head and continued. "And if any person will meddle of my cause," she glanced briefly at me again. "I require them to judge the best. And thus I take my leave of the world and of you all, and I heartily desire you all to pray for me. O Lord have mercy on me, to God I commend my soul.'

They say that the curse of a witch condemned to die is a powerful spell, and for a moment, I felt my hands shake and my knees tremble. With an effort I stopped myself.

What nonsense, Mary Fox! Do not be frighted by such foolish thoughts!

Her women stepped forward, helping Anne Boleyn out of her cloak, to reveal a plain grey gown. They then tied a blindfold about her face and one of them held her hand to support her as she knelt.

"To Jesus Christ I commend my soul; Lord Jesus receive my soul," were her last words aloud.

The executioner then kicked off his shoes and stepped silently up behind her, while she continued to mouth her prayer.

I reached for Marcus's hand and whispered, "I cannot watch."

"Watch," he hissed back. "Your Grace."

I forced myself to take in the scene, almost as if I was seeing a performance by some mummers – nothing but make-believe – so that when one of them died a gruesome death, he would pick himself up at the end to take the applause.

But that was not going to happen to Anne Boleyn.

The executioner leaned round to her left, and said something sharp. She immediately turned her head to that side; her mouth still moving silently. As she did so, he stepped to her right, then swung the blade back.

He brought it round in a slicing sweep so fast, that I could scarcely follow it.

It passed through Anne Boleyn's neck with the heavy sound of a falling branch, and there was the immediate metallic smell of hot blood.

Her head fell away to the side, her mouth still moving even as it flew through the air. A red fountain sprayed out behind, and a bright stream flew high from the neck.

There was a thump as the head hit the dais, a scream from one of the ladies and a collective gasp from the throng.

The headless body stayed in a kneeling position for a few moments, as the blood flow slowed to a steady pour, like wine from a pitcher. Then the body moved slightly, as if a hand were pushing it gently from behind. Over a few agonisingly slow seconds it gained pace and fell faster and faster forward. It landed with the neck close to the side of the dais.

A bright stream of blood suddenly appeared, and flowed down over the edge and onto the grass below.

I smiled.

—0—

After a few minutes some servants came up to the dais carrying a wooden chest, that looked to me as if it was more used to holding arrows or suchlike. The women lifted the body and carried it over, and proceeded, along with many small cries and gasps, to force it inside. The chest certainly appeared too small, even for a headless corpse, but eventually they managed to pack it in. Two of them and the servants then carried it off the platform, while the third woman carefully picked up the head and placed it in the cloak, then bundled it up and hurried off after them. I saw them making for the Chapel of St Peter ad Vincula, to one side of the green.

"The show is over," Marcus observed. "We had better get back to Durham House."

"I feel sick," I muttered.

"Some wine will settle your stomach," he said.

Red wine pouring from a flagon. Red blood cascading off the dais.

"Maybe some ale."

We made our way through the departing crowds towards the Byward Tower. As we walked, I heard snatches of the conversations around me.

"She died well."

"Nay. Good riddance, I say. Naught but a meddler."

Or, "It was a fine speech."

"She had no right to speak any of it. She was godless. We have lost the true faith because of her."

I glanced at Marcus as the crowd thinned out so we could speak without being overheard. He said, "She saw you. It stopped her for a moment."

"Aye. I thought you noticed that."

"Anyway, she can no longer trouble us." As he strode on, I looked round for Christopher. He had not been as able as myself and Marcus to push through the crowd, and had fallen some way behind. No doubt he would soon catch us up.

He was still not with us as we passed through the gate, and onto the bridge across the moat.

At the far end I noticed there were some men standing in our path. They were facing towards the Tower, as if they were waiting for someone.

"Those men will need to stand aside," I observed casually, "or we will not be able to pass."

"Your Grace!" Marcus called. "Stop!"

The urgency in his voice halted me immediately. I glanced back. Marcus was still, staring white-faced at the men blocking our way.

Behind Marcus three more men stepped onto the bridge at the Tower end. These had their hands on the hilts of their swords. They stood shoulder to shoulder, blocking our retreat.

We were surrounded.

Marcus must have seen the horror on my face, and he also looked behind.

The men at the front started to walk forward. Now I could see they were led by one in the middle who seemed familiar; his cap at a low angle and one hand on his sword hilt.

He swept off his cap, so I could see him clearly.

He had one eye dissected by a scar down his face.

Now I felt I really was about to be sick.

"Hello, Your Grace," Cruddon said with a small bow. "Or should I say, Mary Fox?

"You are mistaken, knave," Marcus spat. "I know not why you think such a strange thing. This is his grace Prince Henry, Duke of Richmond, as you can see by the livery I wear. Certainly not a woman. You are making the gravest of errors."

Cruddon gave a lopsided smile. Half his face did not move, so it seemed more a sneer. "You are well met, Master Kytson. How is the arm? Healing nicely, I trust?"

"You will pay for that, Cruddon."

"Tsk tsk," Cruddon shook his head as if in sorrow. "Faithful to the last, Kytson, if misguided." He drew his sword, then settled his stance, resting the point between his feet. It was so much like the executioner who had so recently taken off Anne Boleyn's head, that I shivered and took a step back. Immediately I felt a hand on my shoulder, and glanced round. It was one of the men from the other end of the bridge, pushing me towards his master.

"Unhand me, sirrah," I snapped in my best Duke of Richmond growl. "You dare not touch the person of a prince."

"Oh, but he may touch the person of Mary Fox, a known killer and evader of justice," Cruddon said. "For that is who you are in truth. The Mary Fox who killed my son in Essex. The Mary Fox who snatched the real Prince from my cellar in Blackfriars. The Mary Fox who reported a fire in my Ipswich home, as a ruse to spring this self-same Master Kytson from my keeping. The Mary Fox who left Tonge under cover of darkness pursued by two of my men, and the Mary Fox who no doubt can tell me why there are traces of dried blood and vomit on the path, and why my men have never been seen since." He paused. "That Mary Fox."

"I know not…" I began, but he flicked his sword point up to my throat. "Silence, woman! I know that you masquerade as the Prince while he lies in his sickbed, for I accosted the little doctor who left the house in London, and he told me all."

I dared not think how Cruddon had forced the information out of the man, and did not want to ask. Some things are better left unknown.

"So you will come with me, Mary Fox and Marcus Kytson. We can settle our scores for once and for all."

33
NOW TO END THIS

Cruddon and his men surrounded us, then forced us to march off the bridge. We had little choice; both Marcus and I were being pushed forward by concealed knives pricking at our sides.

There was no possible way we could escape. We were too closely surrounded by their sickening foul-smelling bodies to get away.

Unless I could attract people to come to our aid.

Several passers-by crossed our path – almost close enough to touch. All it would take would be a shout that that we were being kidnapped.

That the Duke of Richmond was being kidnapped.

Again.

One man's eye caught mine; a tall fellow who looked as if he would be good in a fight. Here was the opportunity. I drew breath to shout for help. But the cry died in my throat. A sharp pain from the blade nicking into my side told me my guard was well aware of what I planned.

I managed to catch Marcus's eye, and he gave me a look which clearly said we should bide our time.

Reluctantly I nodded.

On that thought I walked on.

—0—

There was no sign of the ostler as we arrived at the stables. I glanced across to where Hestia was waiting, nodding her head and whinnying. I deliberately looked away, lest Cruddon realise she was mine, and decide to do her harm as well.

We were marched up to an old carriage that was standing to one side of the yard with two horses skittering in the traces.

"Where do you take us?" I asked Cruddon, trying to stop my voice from shaking.

"You will see," he snapped. "Now get in."

Marcus and I climbed up; each with our own guard keeping his knife in our sides. We were directed to sit together on the rear seat. There were leather loops above each side of the carriage; put there for passengers to hold onto as it went around corners. These ones had a length of thin rope added. The guards had us lean across and put both wrists through, then they each used the rope to secure us. When they seemed sure we were unable to get away, they sat back on the other seat and observed us through lowered brows.

We were jolted as the carriage started forward, then it bounced across the cobbles.

I tried the guards, to see if they might be more forthcoming than Cruddon. "Where do we go?" I asked. "Blackfriars?"

Neither responded. Instead they continued to stare at us, with faces that suggested they thought us vermin.

Marcus gave a small chuckle. "It seems Master Cruddon has recruited deaf mute knaves to his cause," he observed.

"Silence, sirrah!" hissed one of the men, holding his knife up. "Lest I cut out your tongue."

"So maybe not deaf mutes." Marcus muttered. "But still knaves withal."

"I said silence!"

Marcus shrugged, but held his peace.

A heavy silence descended as the carriage rolled on.

—0—

After perhaps a half hour, I was aching with the strain of having my arms raised and tied to the strap. I was also aware of a dull pain in my side; presumably where the knife had nicked my skin. So I was relieved when we slowed and turned into a pair of gates, then rolled up a short driveway to the main entrance of a fine building.

"Durham House," I breathed to Marcus.

He nodded with a worried frown.

What was Cruddon planning? And did it involve bringing harm to Lady Kyme and the Prince? After all we had done by drawing Cruddon away to Kent, was he now about to do as we feared; bring the fight to Durham House?

He was.

The carriage came to a halt outside the front entrance. The guards untied us, and pushed us out with their blades. As we staggered down onto the gravel, nursing our sore wrists, Cruddon dismounted and came over.

"So now we know where you have taken us," I said, "What do you mean to do here?"

"You will see," he replied. "Inside."

The two ever-present guards each took hold of an arm and pulled them up behind our backs. As I gasped with pain, there was a hiss in my ear, "Silence girl, or I will skewer you like the rat you are." I choked back my intended curse, and staggered forward into the house.

Lady Kyme came to meet us, paling visibly as she saw how Marcus and I were being held.

"What is the meaning of this outrage?" she demanded, with only the smallest break in her voice.

Cruddon stepped forward and stood in front of me.

"Lady Kyme? Allow me to introduce myself." He swept off his cap and bowed. "Jacob Cruddon, at your service, my lady."

"Well, Master Cruddon, if you would truly be at my service, I suggest you take your person and your men off this property." She took a step forward with her hands on her hips and I silently commended her bravery. "And I also suggest you release Master Kytson and my son, the Duke of Richmond."

Cruddon turned and I caught sight of the side of his face that showed his emotion. It was feigning surprise. "Your son, my lady?" He turned back. "Nay, this is one Mary Fox, a known murderer and unnatural adventuress, who is merely masquerading as the Duke. I understand your true son is abed upstairs with a severe coughing sickness."

"How do you know…?" Lady Kyme began, but Cruddon cut her off with a raised hand. "Silence!" he snapped. "Enough of the pleasantries! We must be down to business." He indicated that two more of his men should come forward. They took hold of Lady Kyme's arms and spun her round.

"Unhand me, you dogs!" she snapped, but the men ignored her.

Cruddon marched past and said, "To the great hall." He led the way, seeming to know the layout of the house well; no doubt having familiarised himself with it when he first took the Prince all those years ago. As we arrived in the hall, Cruddon directed us to the chairs at the high table and had us sit.

There were several pitchers of ale and wine on the table, making me realise just how thirsty I was. I reached for one of them and a goblet, and was about to pour for myself, Lady Kyme and Marcus, when I felt my arms being pulled behind the chair, and my wrists once again being tied. A quick glance either side showed the others were being similarly served.

Lady Kyme caught my eye. *Christopher*? she mouthed. I gave her a quick shake of my head, and mouthed back, *Not taken*. She nodded, with a small look of relief, and we both faced forward again.

Fortunately this exchange seemed to have gone unnoticed by our captors.

Just then Hannah ran in, taking in the scene with a small shriek. Cruddon immediately went to her in a few strides and took an arm. He dragged her, still shrieking, to an empty seat and thrust her onto it. "Hold your peace, woman," he growled, "or I will silence you with a gag." She whimpered to a stop and was quiet, apart from an occasional small choked-down sob.

Cruddon barked an order at two of his men. "Search the house. Find me every other living soul within and bring them here."

"Even the sick boy?" asked one of the men.

"Leave him. His death approaches anyway."

Lady Kyme gave a small cry. "Nay, he recovers!"

"If you say," Cruddon waved his hand as if he were swatting away a fly. "Believe what you will. It will not change the outcome."

"By Heavens, Cruddon," Lady Kyme snapped. "You are the very spawn of Satan!"

He rounded on her. "Am I?" he snarled, and I swear even the immobile half of his face went red as his voice rose to a shout. "I am a father who has lost a son, taken from me by the evil woman who pretends to be your sick child!" He pointed at me, for all his eye was fixed on Lady Kyme. "The same woman who left me for dead in a forest. The same woman who ripped out part of my house in Blackfriars…"

"So she could rescue my son, kidnapped by you."

Cruddon did not seem to have heard her. Instead he moved his hand to indicate the fire beyond me, dancing merrily in the grate as if none of this was truly happening. "…And who falsely reported a fire at my home."

"So she could rescue me from your captivity, sirrah," Marcus cut in.

Cruddon turned on him. "Because you were trying to follow the Queen's man through Greenwich! A low, dirty spy! It was the least you deserved."

Before Marcus could respond, the door opened and a precession of twelve servants were forced into the room by Cruddon's two men. I recognised a couple of maids, some house servants, a stable boy, a gardener and two ladies who were in waiting to Lady Kyme. The others appeared to be from the kitchens, as they were preceded by the cook. All looked confused, frightened and, in some cases, angry. One of the maids even had a red weal across her face, which she kept touching gingerly. Her appearance drew a fresh cry from Hannah.

Cruddon broke off to supervise all the new arrivals having their hands tied, before being lined up along one wall. One of his men then passed a rope behind them all, and tied each end to heavy furniture, so they were secured in their place.

As he returned to us, I said, as loudly and as firmly as I could, "Your true quarrel is with me, Cruddon, and me alone. Take me and let these others go free."

This seemed to anger Cruddon again. He came up to the table and leaned his fists on it, his face so close to mine that I could feel the heat of it. His scar seemed to burn redder than the rest of his face, and his milky white eye seemed so at odds with the fire in his other.

"But they are all complicit, Mary Fox," he snarled. "Your deception of the King at the Garter Ceremony – oh yes, I know of that, for my mistress the Queen said as much, God rest her soul – such planned actions would have involved the whole household from Lady Kyme downwards. So it is the whole household that will be held to account."

I could no longer contain my own anger at this. "That is nonsense and you know it!" I yelled, causing him to move his face away from mine. "These good people have had nothing to do with any of our plans! Let them go."

"What, and have them tell what has happened here?" Cruddon sneered. "I think not."

"Have you no Christian mercy?" I shouted.

"Christian mercy? Do you, a proven murderer, an unnatural woman, accuse me of this?" He raised his hand and I braced for the blow. But no amount of bracing could have prepared me enough. I thought he had broken my neck with the force of it. Flashes of light exploded all around me, as if fireworks were being set off, and it felt as if a live flame had been set against my jaw. It was all I could do to avoid crying out. Marcus and Lady Kyme both pulled at their bonds, as if they would break free to avenge my pain, but how could they do so when we were held captive by this madman?

"Christian mercy?" Cruddon repeated. "I thank you not to use your shrill voice on matters you do not understand!"

He stepped away from the table.

"Now to end this!"

He marched over to the fire, and selected a kindling stick from the scuttle. As we watched in horror, he held it to the fire until it was blazing, then he raised it up to the edge of one of the wall hangings.

It was a linen-based tapestry with images of a hunt, no doubt as dry as an old bone.

"You once called the watch to my house in Ipswich with a tale of fire," he said, his voice now chillingly calm. "It was a false tale then, but now it will become truth." He held the stick closer to the tapestry, clearly delighting in the looks of disbelief and fear he was provoking in every member of the household as the flame crackled and sparked so close to the material.

I felt Marcus shudder and draw a sharp breath beside me.

"I am sure the watch will be called when Durham House is ablaze for real," Cruddon continued. "but I cannot imagine they will get here in time to save any of you, or the boy upstairs, from being burned alive."

At this Lady Kyme gave a cry. "Let me go to him!" When Cruddon shook his head, she broke into sobs. "You will have your reward in hell for this day's work!"

"Nay, lady, for mine is righteous vengeance." He studied the flame in his hand, and the hanging above. He held it closer, but not yet touching.

"I bid you all farewell."

The door burst open.

"Stop that!"

It was Christopher.

He ran to the table and grabbed a pitcher, then in one smooth movement, swept it towards Cruddon's stick. The ale flew out and immediately doused the flame with a hiss and a puff of smoke. Much of it also soaked Cruddon, too.

Before Cruddon could respond, six guardsmen in brightly burnished breastplates and kettle helmets marched in, their halberds raised.

"What in heaven's name is the meaning of this?" barked a loud voice.

It was one that had the authority to command absolute attention.

As the guardsmen stood back, a tall, broad, imposing figure walked in, dressed in white and gold.

I bowed my head. "Your Majesty," I said. "Not a moment too soon."

34

THE NIGHTMARE MADE REAL

The King strode to the centre of the room and gazed about him with his hands on his hips; his feet splayed outward. His presence was so large, so commanding, that it was as if the sun itself had fallen from the sky and landed in our midst.

But His Majesty was not prepared to shine on us like the sun. Instead he burned with anger.

"You, Richmond," he barked at me. "Tell me what is going on here."

Here was my chance. I took a careful breath to steady myself, then said as calmly as I could, "This man is an agent of the late Queen, Father." I looked pointedly at Cruddon. "He was acting under her orders when he took me, my Lady Mother and Master Kytson by force. He has bound us securely, along with the rest of the household, and was about to set the house on fire. We would all have been killed."

"By Heavens!" the King thundered. "You! One-eyed man. Is this true?"

Cruddon swept off his cap and bowed. "Jacob Cruddon, gentleman of Ipswich, at your service, sire."

"I did not ask your name, knave! I care not what you are called or where you are from!" The King glared at him. "Is what my son said true?"

Cruddon gave a lop-sided smile. "What this person has said has some little truth, sire. But this person is not your son. In fact it is not even a boy. She," and he put great emphasis on this word, "is called Mary Fox. She has been masquerading as your son for some time, while the boy himself lies dying upstairs. Upon discovering this, I have held all concerned so I can determine the full truth of it, before bringing the same to your attention, sire."

The King stared wordlessly at Cruddon. Then he frowned. "What of the burning stick?" He waved a hand at Christopher. "Had this fellow not doused you in ale, you were about to set the place on fire."

"An idle threat, sire, 'tis all. Designed to get the Fox woman to admit the truth. I would never have carried it through."

Again the King was silent. I glanced around. Marcus had a grim smile, as if amused at Cruddon's bare-faced lie. Christopher seemed shocked; no doubt at how close we had come to being burned. Lady Kyme was looking aghast, and I felt sure she was unable to think of anything other than what she had been so casually told; that the Prince was dying. I wished I could reassure her, but in truth, the last time I had seen the boy, I had thought much the same. Cruddon's men appeared uneasy; one or two were giving quick looks at the guardsmen, as if sizing up their chances of making a swift exit. The servants were all pale-faced, almost visibly shaking from the narrowness of their escape. Either that or it was from being in the presence of the King.

The King gave Cruddon a suspicious sideways look, then approached the table, his attention now fully on me. "Stand up, boy," he said.

"I would, Father, but I am tied down."

"Hmmm. You, Crudface. Untie him."

"Her, sire."

The King's face reddened. "Do you correct your Sovereign Lord, man?" he snapped.

Cruddon said nothing, but scurried round behind me, and I felt him fumbling with the knots.

Once I was free, I stood, and faced the King with my steadiest expression. He came closer, studying me, his small eyes searching across mine, as if he wanted to lay my deepest secrets bare. I held my breath.

How long had I feared being exposed to the King? How much had I played over and over in my mind the scene where I was denounced, then hauled off to a dungeon by guardsmen with halberds, there to await my fate?

And now here I was, living that very nightmare.

I had seen a woman executed before my eyes. It was a real fate, that could so easily happen to me in the next few hours. Depending on what this great man before me decided.

The King's eyes narrowed.

"This man says you are a woman, not my son at all," he growled. "Is that so?"

I found my throat had closed up, too dry for speech.

I shook my head.

"Speak up, boy."

"Nay, Father," I managed to whisper. "You know me well."

"Hmm."

There was another long silence.

His eyes bored into mine.

Then something changed in them.

In that moment, I knew.

I knew that I had won.

That my nightmare was at an end.

"Indeed so." He turned to the room, and to Cruddon who had come round the table after untying me. "This is our son, and we recognise him well."

"But sire," Cruddon began, "may I ask you to reconsider?"

"No, you may not." The King gestured to a couple of his guardsmen. "You. Arrest this man and take him to Tyburn. He is a traitor to his King and to our only son. There he must be hung, drawn and quartered, and his head placed on London Bridge for all to see. Then all shall know of his treachery, and be warned not to do likewise."

Cruddon seemed stunned into silence. Two of the guardsmen took him by the arms and started to march him out.

As he went, he managed to turn briefly, and his one eye caught mine.

'You win, Mary Fox,' it seemed to say. 'Finally, you win.'

—0—

Once the King and his guardsmen had gone and all the servants had been released and given leave to have restorative drinks in the kitchens, Marcus and I stayed in the Great Hall with Christopher and Hannah.

Lady Kyme had already run upstairs to be at her son's side.

The fire was burning as merrily as before, and but for a splash of ale staining the base of the hanging nearby, there was no sign of the near-death struggle we had just experienced.

"The King was magnificent," Hannah breathed, as she sipped at some wine. "How fortunate you were able to get to him, and to persuade him to come here, Christopher." She gave him a coy look over the rim of her cup. "What on earth did you say?"

"Oh, naught but the truth of the matter," Christopher replied, with what seemed a little too much nonchalance. "That I saw the Prince and Master Kytson being taken, and followed them back to this house. There I observed Cruddon having them bound and led in. I knew he would be up to no good, so I only had to make it clear that the Prince was in danger. The King was most keen to stop any such mischief."

"That was so clever of you," Hannah sighed. "We owe you our lives."

"Yes," I agreed. "Not only by securing our royal visitor, but also by throwing that ale to douse the flame. That was good thinking."

Marcus looked at my cup and picked up a pitcher. "Some more wine, Your Grace?" he enquired. On my nod he poured some, while giving me a conspiratorial wink.

A wink.

That was what the King had done earlier, as he studied my face so attentively.

A wink.

The one little thing that told me that all was going to be well.

Because the man in front of me was not, in truth, Henry Tudor, King of England, eighth monarch of that name.

No, he was actually one Nathan Rose, the King's royal double.

I had been concerned that somehow, as unlikely as it might seem, Christopher might have actually found the true King, and somehow persuaded him to come to Durham House. Our plan had always been for Nathan Rose to come if needed, as he could be briefed in advance to play the part as necessary. That was why Marcus, Christopher and I had sought him out a few days before, and met him in a local tavern.

Out of his kingly garb, he was just a tall, heavy-set man in a long jerkin and breeches, with a leather cap to hide the redness of his hair. Marcus and Christopher were in plain doublets and I was in a serving girl's dress and coif. I doubt if the four of us raised any suspicion as we conversed quietly in a corner.

"It is a full-time task, being the King's stand-in," Nathan observed. "I must be ready to be dressed at a moment's notice, lest the King suddenly decides he does not feel like appearing. Sometimes he has a headache, or is tired, or more recently has wanted to stay abed with his new love, Jane Seymour." He shrugged slightly. "Of course for you, it has been full time since the Duke of Richmond has been so unwell." He considered me a moment. "You play him excellently. When I saw you in Windsor, no man could have told you two apart. I suppose if God wills you to have another's face, then he means for you to use it for good purpose."

"Indeed so," said Marcus, "which is why we need your help."

We then explained our concern that Cruddon might attack us in Durham House at any time, and how we would need some means of stopping him. Thankfully, Nathan agreed readily.

"Anything to help a fellow stand-in," he said. "Just get word to me however you can, and I will come."

"Will you be able to bring some guardsmen?" I asked. "Cruddon will have men of his own."

"For sure. The King cannot travel without a guard; if I am playing his part, they come as a matter of course."

"And you will be at Whitehall?"

"Indeed so. I stay close to the King." He gave instructions as to how he could be contacted, which thankfully Christopher noted well.

And Nathan had truly been magnificent, as Hannah had observed.

I sat back and took a sip of the wine Marcus had just poured. There had been none of the hesitancy and vagueness I had observed from Nathan Rose before in Windsor. This had been Henry VIII in a state of full kingly anger, raging against a villain who promised death and destruction.

At least that was now to be Cruddon's fate, not ours.

But then I had a sudden moment of unease. A worrying thought occurred.

"Nathan had no royal authority to order Cruddon's execution," I whispered to Marcus. "What if the King discovers what is ordered in his name?"

Marcus shrugged. "I very much doubt he will find out, less care. He has just had one wife disposed of, and will no doubt be marrying another soon. He has much greater things to occupy himself than the execution of an insignificant traitor."

I nodded. This made sense.

Just then Lady Kyme came in, with tearful streaks down her face. She hurried round the table to my side and threw her arms about me. "Oh Mary," she sobbed, "he worsens so much. He makes no indication he knows I am there, and his breath rattles most awfully in his throat. It is such a painful sound. I fear what that dreadful man said is true; my Henry has very little time left." She pulled back and I could see the anguish in her eyes. "We must call his father to his bedside before it is too late."

35
ONE LAST THING

The following day the King came to Durham House to see his son.

The real King.

Lady Kyme met him at the door and led him to the Great Hall, together with a priest and four of his guardsmen. I studied them carefully, but thankfully, none seemed to be the same ones as had accompanied Nathan Rose the day before.

Marcus and I were there, but stayed in the background as if part of the household, not wishing to intrude on the distress of the Prince's parents. I was dressed once again in my women's finery. The last thing I wanted was to parade in front of the King as if I was his dying son. So I had used as much rouge and kohl as I could, and stood with my hands clasped and my head down, lest he catch sight of me and think me somehow familiar.

They stood apart and spoke quietly for some time; she giving small sobs as she talked, while he held her hand and patted it affectionately. But there was no doubting his concern; he was bowed over her like a much older man, with none of his usual kingly confidence and assured swagger. It was almost as if he needed Nathan Rose to play the King, so he could get on with the more human thing of being a man; and particularly a father desperately concerned for his only son.

Eventually they went upstairs, accompanied by the priest, while we waited below. I felt the whole house shake with the weight of the King's heavy tread upon the stair, then there was quiet for many long minutes, as I imagined the King kneeling at his son's bedside.

I was just about to say something to Marcus – I forget what, as it was but a trivial comment – when I was silenced by a sudden loud noise from upstairs.

It was a howl.

It was like the echoing bellow of a wounded bear, and it pierced the air as if no other sound could possibly exist before or after it. I felt my blood turn to ice and took Marcus's hand, clinging on to him for support, lest I collapse to the ground.

For there was only one reason why the King would make such a cry.

The pain in Marcus's eyes showed that he thought the same.

The King had just lost his only son.

My heart felt heavy in my chest. After all our hopes for his recovery, God had decided to take the Prince now. To deny him a long and fruitful life.

There was nothing more to be said. We sat in silence for what seemed like hours, until eventually there was a heavy tread on the stair, and the King came back in with Lady Kyme and the priest.

One look at Lady Kyme's tears showed she would need help in the days to come. So I knew I must stay with her to offer her my love and support.

"Our son Prince Henry, Duke of Richmond, has been taken into Lord Jesus's arms," she said, her voice trembling. The King was silent, his mouth working as he seemed to be trying to hold back his tears.

We all made the sign of the cross and bowed our heads.

—0—

A few hours later, the King took his leave. He had spent a long time walking in the gardens alone with Lady Kyme, before making his way down to his barge.

An uneasy pall hung over the house after he had gone. Marcus, Christopher and I sat in the Great Hall, all lost in our own thoughts. Lady Kyme came back in and sat with us, looking like an empty seashell whose insides have been scraped away.

"Arrangements must be made," I observed, trying to bring her back with some practicalities. "A funeral and burial." I paused, as she made no indication she had even heard. "I am happy to take on the management of this, Lady Kyme."

Eventually, she looked up with watery eyes and sniffed loudly. "That may need to wait a while," she muttered.

Marcus frowned. "Why so?"

"The King has said it is politically inconvenient for the Prince to be declared dead," she said in a flat monotone. "And to have a funeral at this moment,"

"What?" I exclaimed. "He would leave his own son unburied? Why, in Heaven's name?"

"Because he has a new Act of Succession," she said, in the same tone. "It was intended to finally legitimise the

Prince. If it was known that my Henry is dead, then the act might not pass."

"Why is that a problem?" I asked. "The Prince is never going to succeed now."

"He did explain, but I am not sure I was really understanding his words." She paused. "Sufficient to say it was something to do with removing both Princess Mary and Princess Elizabeth from the succession, and giving the King the power to name a male successor of his choice, should the new Queen Jane fail to give him a son. My Henry would be the obvious choice, so if it is known he is gone," she sniffed again, "then the bill may not pass." She shook her head, as if she was not sure she had remembered correctly. "Or somesuch."

"But he must realise he cannot conceal the death forever," I said.

Or I might end up having to play the Prince for life…

"Nay," she said. "It is only until the opening of the new Parliament next week, and the time it takes for the passage of the bill. Then, once the Act becomes law, he will announce the death and conduct the funeral." She stared at me with a blank expression, as if she was quite empty of all emotion. "You must play the Prince one last time, Mary. He asked for it. He wants you to do it."

"What?" I squeaked. "He knows it was me?"

"Not by name, no," she replied. "He knows only of the 'young lad' who played the Prince a few years ago. While he said at the time he never wanted the Prince to be substituted ever again, now, of course, things have changed. He asked me to find this lad once more, and press him into the part." She raised her eyes to mine. "Will you

do this one last thing for me, Mary? Will you play the
Prince once more, for the opening of Parliament?"

36

GO WITH GOD, MARY FOX

The 8th day of June 1536 is recorded as the last time the Prince was seen in public, hale and hearty, before his death was finally announced on the 23rd of July.

Many men saw me there, leading the King in the procession and carrying his 'cap of maintenance', as we processed from York Place to the Palace of Westminster. Then there were interminable speeches and discussions. These I found hard to follow in detail, as my mind kept wandering towards the thoughts as to what I should do once I was free to go, with a hundred sovereigns weighing in my purse.

I was still leaning towards cutting my ties with Lady Kyme and Marcus, and heading out alone to see where my fortune took me. But I did keep returning to Marcus's offer; that we would be more a partnership and less a conventional marriage. The best of both worlds – to have adventures alongside Marcus, yet to be offered the stability and 'respectability' of being a wife.

If I truly believed he would keep his word, it was tempting…

Yet, how likely would it be for him to change his nature? How soon would he decide that what he really wanted was a docile little wife and mother to his children? Would I then be entrapped, unable to escape a lifetime of servitude? Would I too die in childbirth, as my own mother had done?

Once the speeches finally drifted to a halt, we filed out of the hall, and processed back to York House for a mass and a banquet. I know I circulated and spoke to many of the nobles there, discussing such subjects as I had been briefed on by Marcus. I know I was expressing concern that one of my servants, Giles Forster, should be given the stewardship of Banbury, a post left vacant by the execution of Anne Boleyn's co-conspirator, Henry Norris. I used this as a primary talking point, and it seemed to cover much of my needs as I moved about.

At one point I found myself talking with a small, thin, elderly Savoyard, who Marcus had pointed out as being Eustace Chapuys, the ambassador to the Holy Roman Emperor. I was aware this was a man who reported on all the events of the Court to his master, and who therefore knew everything about everyone.

"Your Grace," he said, bowing low. "How do you fare this day?"

"I fare very well, Master Chapuys," I replied, slightly guarded. This man had quite a reputation for drawing his own conclusions, even if they were not born out by the facts.

"This Act of Succession, it favours you greatly, does it not?" He gave a thin smile. "The King your father is free to name you as his heir, should he so wish."

This was a loaded question, for talk of succession in open company could easily be misinterpreted as the treason of 'imagining the death of the King'. I was not sure if he was genuinely interested or just trying to stir trouble.

"That is a matter for His Majesty and not for me to speculate upon," I said. Then I thought to counter with an attack of my own. "I should have thought better of you, Master Chapuys, than to suppose I had any motive in this, other than a deep love for my father and a willingness to do whatever is his wish."

At this he gave me a sneering smile, then slid away to talk with some other man who had caught his attention.

The King came up to me, and I bowed low myself.

"Henry, my boy," he boomed. He gave a small frown, then said quietly. "I saw you talking to the Ambassador. Is all well?"

"Indeed, Your Grace," I replied, aware that he was really asking if I had managed to fool Chapuys that I was the real prince. "The Ambassador was asking only for my thoughts on the Act of Succession. I told him that was a matter for you, not for me."

"A good answer," he agreed. "A good one indeed." He clapped me across the shoulder and gave me a conspiratorial smile. "You are doing well, young man. Very well." Then he whispered in my ear, "I would to God that you did not need to be here, but I am pleased that you are. Thank you."

—0—

I stayed with Lady Kyme until the death was announced. It seemed churlish to leave her while she grieved, so I remained. She had instructed that the Prince's remains be taken to St. James's Palace, as she could not bear to have them near her. It was then agreed that the announcement would be made that the Prince had died there.

I wanted her to see me as her loving daughter, not remind her of the Prince while his body was lying cold in a casket, so I dressed as a girl at all times. It was difficult for me to spend weeks dressed and behaving as a true woman, but I did so for Lady Kyme. I even allowed myself to join her in womanly pursuits, such as sewing and embroidery. Many an evening was spent before the fire, with me squinting at the stitches I was supposed to be threading on my sampler, which looked lumpy and rough compared to her neat work.

"You will have to try harder, Mary, my dear," she observed one evening, looking over at my poor handiwork. "One day you will run a house of your own. You will need to keep yourself well occupied. Were you never taught needlework skills?"

"My mother died of childbed fever when I was born," I said.

"Ah yes," she said. "Apologies, I had forgot you had told me." She gave me a concerned look. "Childbed fever is such a dreadful cruelty from the Lord. Why does he take a good woman, so soon after she has been blessed with a child?"

"We cannot know," I agreed.

We continued sewing for a while, while the fire crackled merrily beside us.

"I lost my cousin Eleanor to childbed fever," she observed in a conversational tone. "It must have been around twenty years ago."

I looked up in surprise. "My mother was also called Eleanor," I said.

"What a coincidence." Then suddenly her mouth opened and her eyes widened. "Where did you grow up, Mary?" she breathed.

"In Essex," I replied. "A place called Marchington Manor."

"No!" Her eyes seemed to get even wider. "My cousin Eleanor lived at a Marchington Manor. I forgot that she had married a man called…"

"…Richard Fox," I finished for her. "My true father…"

We stared at each other for some moments, both seemingly unable to comprehend the enormity of this revelation. Then she said, "My cousin Eleanor died giving birth to a baby girl, a few months after she had lost her husband Richard in a hunting accident."

"And married his cousin Andrew Fox," I said. "My stepfather."

"Who we always suspected of causing the accident."

Now it was my turn to stare wordlessly. "My stepfather killed my father?" I gasped eventually. "In truth?"

"Oh, my poor Mary!" she wailed softly. "I am so sorry. We had no proof, but always suspected Andrew. He was also in the hunting party when Richard was hit by a stray arrow. It could have been fired by any of maybe half a dozen men, but Andrew was there. It could have been him."

"Then it was," I asserted. "He always hated my father for marrying the woman he thought he loved. He married her within weeks of my father's death, even though she was already with child."

She put down her embroidery and came over to me.

I stood and we took eachother in our arms.

"My poor Mary," she said, stroking my back, "My poor, poor Mary. I am so sorry."

"Lady Mother."

Then a thought occurred to me. I let her go and stood back. "The Prince was my close relative," I said. "That is why we looked so alike. We were second cousins."

—0—

Once the death was announced, it was the Prince's father-in-law, the Duke of Norfolk, who was entrusted with the funeral arrangements. He decided to make it a low-key affair as the body was now in a very poor state of preservation. He therefore ordered it be transferred to a lead-lined casket, lest it become clear from the odours that death had actually occurred many weeks earlier. He then asked for the coffin to be placed in a sealed cart – as he was heard to mutter that it would be a further guard against any man 'sniffing out' the truth. However, such a cart was not available, so a straw-filled alternative was procured.

Marcus and I were asked to attend at St. James's Palace as Lady Kyme's representatives, although instructed to keep in the background and not engage with Norfolk unless absolutely necessary.

The Duke was the same long-nosed curmudgeon as all those years ago. I had thought him like an undertaker then – and now here he was, making all the arrangements for the internment. This provided me with some amusement, and I made the mistake of mentioning this to Marcus. Thereafter it was all we could do to stop ourselves from laughing every time the man barked an order or saw to a detail.

We managed to keep away from being addressed by Norfolk directly until the morning that the cortège was due to set off. We were talking together in the hallway of St. James's Palace as the Duke marched past.

"You there," he snapped at Marcus. "You are here on behalf of the mother?"

Marcus swept off his cap and bowed. "Indeed we are, Your Grace. Marcus Kytson, gentleman, at your service."

His gaze raked across to me. "And your companion here?" he asked.

I curtseyed. "Mary Fox, spinster. I am also charged to represent my Lady Kyme, the grieving mother, Your Grace."

"I see," he replied. He drummed his fingers on his staff as if considering options, then he said, "I need two attendants to accompany the cortège. You will perform this service for me." It was a statement, not a request. "You will ride behind. Do not get too close. When we reach Thetford Priory, where my family are entombed and the boy is to join them, you will act as the mourners."

Which is how Marcus and I were the only two riding behind the cart on our way to Thetford. I had long since retrieved Hestia from the Tower stables, and I had two hundred sovereigns in my saddlebag, courtesy of Lady Kyme.

"A hundred was promised to you as a fee for standing in for my son," she had said, as she hefted the heavy bag of coins and handed them over. "So here it is. Plus a further hundred, because you did much, much more."

"No, I cannot accept," I began, but she cupped my cheeks in her hands and looked deeply into my eyes. "I will not accept refusal, Mary." I could see a tear spilling onto her cheek. "After all you have done for me and for my Henry, it is the very least I can do." I must have frowned, for then she added with great perception, "Think not that it is such a base thing as payment for services, Mary, but that it is a gift from me. From your cousin, and one who would be as your mother. The mother you never had."

Another tear joined the first. "I have loved you as a daughter, and nothing would give me more happiness than to have you always by my side. But I know that is not what you want, and you are most likely not to return. So go with God, Mary Fox, and remember you will always be in my thoughts and prayers."

I had told none of this to Marcus, and as we rode through the east of the city, he said, "Do you accept my offer? I would have an answer Mary."

"Soon Marcus, soon," I replied. "When I have finally decided."

The cortège passed out of the city and into Essex. Once again, I felt the familiar tinge of fear that we were in the same county as my stepfather. So I kept my head down and my hand close to the knife strapped to my thigh throughout our time in the county. I only allowed myself to relax a little once we were safely into Suffolk, and then on into Norfolk.

The Priory of Our Lady of Thetford was a magnificent monastery, and the Benedictine monks were ready to begin the funeral service almost immediately after we arrived that evening.

Marcus and I had little to do as the coffin was carried into the Priory Church by at least ten of the strongest-looking monks.

The service was short and perfunctory. Prayers and blessings were said, before the coffin was carried away to the Howard Mausoleum. Norfolk himself appeared to be in unseemly haste to depart, and as soon as the service was over, he briskly thanked the monks, showing very little sincerity. Then he mounted his horse, gathered the men who had ridden with him, and was quickly gone.

One of the monks watched him ride away. Then with a small sigh, he turned to us both and said, "You will stay, I take it, at least for one night?" But before we could answer, he frowned at us, as if something was troubling him. "By the Lord's Mercy," he exclaimed, "the two travellers who were caught in the fire!"

Now I could see he was familiar, if a little older, thinner and greyer. And still with broken yellow toenails poking out of his sandals.

"Brother Ignatius!" I said. "Is it you? What are you doing here?"

"Yes, it is I," he replied. "Our monastery was indeed dissolved after the fire, as I thought it would be. So a number of us came here, to continue God's work." He studied us with a quizzical frown. "Three years ago, you said you were on a clandestine mission. I trust you were well guided by the Lord and achieved all you desired?"

I glanced at Marcus and we shared a brief moment of understanding. How many times had we faced failure, or even death, in our quest to support the Prince? We had both been held captive but escaped; we had both been near drowned at sea; we had fought and he had killed men on the road in the night, and I had accidentally caused the death of one in Blackfriars. And we had been within seconds of being burned alive in Durham House.

Individually, we had also faced jeopardy. I had died a thousand deaths from fear of capture every time I donned the garb of the Prince; while Marcus had fought against superior odds in Kent and only just managed to get away. How to tell all of this to Brother Ignatius?

"There were many obstacles to overcome," I murmured. "And the end of our tale was not the one we envisaged at the start. But for all that, we did have some successes."

"That is good," Brother Ignatius beamed. "And you are still together. That is wonderful! Am I to take it you are now joined in holy matrimony? Together in the eyes of God?"

"Not yet, Brother," said Marcus. Then he turned to me with a soft smile. "But that is my dearest wish."

"Ahh, indeed." Ignatius gestured to the church behind us. "You are in the right place. I am sure we can arrange a ceremony most immediately." He gave a conspiratorial smile. "We can even dispense with the banns in such exceptional circumstances."

I felt Marcus's hand seeking mine.

It was warm, strong and reassuring, as if when we held ourselves together, nothing could tear us apart.

As if we could accomplish anything, just by being joined.

But was that sufficient? I looked into his eyes. "Tell me, Marcus," I said softly. "Why is it you wish to marry me? Really?"

His smile faltered a moment, almost as if he had not considered an answer. "Because, Mary, because I think we are cut from the same cloth, you and me. We are birds of a feather."

"And that is enough for you?"

He nodded. "Of course, Mary. I have ne'er before felt so close to a girl."

"Close?"

"Aye, indeed. You must feel it as well? You do, I am certain." He squeezed my hand. "Will you have me?"

So there it was. All I had to do was to say 'yes' and Brother Ignatius would take us inside the church and marry us.

I would then be Mistress Mary Kytson, wife to an honourable – if somewhat sardonic – man.

A man who thought it was enough that we were 'birds of a feather'.

Could I compromise my own needs, to be always under my husband's protection? To be safe for ever from my evil stepfather? To be with a person who might, one day, just possibly, say he actually *loved* me?

Or…

My attention was caught by the sun setting beyond the Priory.

It was a golden glow. One that suggested the alternative… *freedom*.

The freedom to be myself rather than Marcus's wife, always at risk of him demanding more of me than I could willingly give.

The freedom to go where and when I wished.

To be beholden to no man, by virtue of my own wit and my skill with a sword.

And of course, my two hundred sovereigns.

Freedom.

I pulled my hand away from Marcus's and shook my head. "No," I said firmly. "I am sorry, Marcus, but I cannot do this. You are a good man, and I agree we are similar, but your needs for the marriage do not meet with mine." I smiled in sorrow. "The answer is 'no'."

He looked at me with an expression that I took to be sadness, although maybe tinged with understanding. Of expectation, even.

"You are sure, Mary?"

I gave an emphatic nod. "Yes, I am. As sure as I have ever been. I will always remember you fondly, Marcus Kytson, but I am not ready to settle down as your wife. I am sorry, but that is my decision."

"Maybe in the morning you will see things differently?" he tried.

The morning?

"No, Marcus," I said. "I have made my decision. I must go now."

He said no more, as I walked to the stables and mounted up on Hestia, checking that I had my saddlebag with the money. He stood aside as Hestia skittered round to face the gate.

"Farewell, Marcus," I said.

He gave me a last smile. "Farewell, Your Grace."

With that I squeezed Hestia's flanks and we left the Priory at a canter.

THE END

Mary will return soon in her new adventure:

THE RIVER OF FIRE

Sign up for Jonathan's newsletter to be the first to know about Mary's new adventure – and other news, at:
jonathanposnerauthor.com

When I first sat down to write this book, there were two key events in the life of Henry Fitzroy that intrigued me. The first was the fact that the Prince was seen in good health at the Opening of Parliament in June 1536, yet died of consumption only six weeks later. The second was that his funeral was a small private ceremony at Thetford Priory with only two mourners, and he was interred in a lead-lined coffin at his father-in-law Norfolk's insistence.

Why so? It seemed amazing to me that the King's only son, one of the foremost nobles in the land, was disposed of in such a peremptory fashion. And that a progressive disease like consumption (tuberculosis) could have carried off a strong young man so quickly.

Maybe there was some subterfuge going on behind the scenes? Maybe the Prince had someone doubling for him?

I thought back to other stories of royal substitution, such as *The Prince and the Pauper* by Mark Twain and *The Prisoner of Zenda* by Anthony Hope (brilliantly parodied by George Macdonald Fraser in *Royal Flash*). In those stories, a double was used to stand in for a royal – and all of a sudden, I had my story! Why not have my heroine Mary Fox stand in for the Prince? This would explain the progression of his fatal condition while she presents him as hale and hearty to the outside world.

But what about the low-key funeral and lead-lined casket? I decided to make it that the Prince had actually died several weeks before the death was actually announced. Then the body would have been in such a poor state of preservation, that such a drastic measure would have made sense.

Armed with these two key plot points, I then set about building the full story. But the more I researched the Prince, the more I found there were so many people around him that substituting Mary would have been difficult to keep a secret. So I decided to simplify his household down to Lady Kyme and the fictional Marcus, Christopher and Hannah.

Lady Kyme has also been largely fictionalised. In truth, she would have been absent from the Prince's life at the time of the story, as she was up in Lincolnshire looking after her three children by Baron Kyme, and marrying a man called Edward Clinton. But I had Mary Fox's key motivation to consider – her deep need for a mother figure in place of the one she never knew. So I brought Lady Kyme in to fulfil that role.

It is known that there was no love lost between the Prince and Anne Boleyn. The reasoning for this that I present – that he was a potential Catholic claimant to the throne – is perfectly plausible. And it is documented that the Prince was present at her execution – and was seen to smile as she died.

So yes, I hold my hand up and freely admit I have played fast and loose with much of the actual history surrounding the Prince in the three years up to his death. But I have interwoven as many real events as possible, and tried to make the Tudor setting feel authentic.

I hope that works for you, and you can accept my changes to history in the service of the story.

If you have any comments or questions, please contact me through my website.

jonathanposnerauthor.com.

Please also leave a review on Amazon, Goodreads or BookBub.

As an author it is always good to get feedback, good or bad.

Thank you in advance!

ABOUT THE AUTHOR

Before becoming a full-time author in 2021, Jonathan worked for many years as a marketing and advertising executive. He now lives in the South West UK, and when he is not writing, he enjoys walking, theatre and presenting regular shows on a local community radio station.

He is fascinated by Tudor history, and has written a series of novels that address the question 'what might happen if you time-travelled back to the 1560s?' He has also written three full-length musicals, a one-act play and two books of short stories.

For more information, visit his author website at
jonathanposnerauthor.com.

**Winter & Drew Publishing Ltd is a publisher of historical
action and adventure – with a difference.**

**Winter & Drew Publishing specialises in helping
independent historical fiction authors self-publish their
books under the Winter & Drew imprint.**

Do you have a historical action adventure novel of your
own – and are looking for options to have it published?

Visit the website to find out more.

winteranddrew.com

BY THE SAME AUTHOR

The Broken Sword – *Mary Fox's first adventure*

You only discover what dangers you can overcome when you're tested to the limit...

Tudor England

When Mary Fox is ordered to marry a sadistic older man, she decides instead to strike out on her own.

As a woman in a man's world, no-one expects her to survive, but Mary is determined to prove them wrong.

Challenged to return the Broken Sword talisman and so break a centuries-old curse, she soon learns how to scheme, fight and outwit those who would drag her back to a life of servitude.

And in doing so, she becomes more than a match for any man.

Readers have said:

"Diabolically good! What makes this novel irresistibly readable is the emotional energy generated by the main character Mary Fox, her ups and downs, drawing parallels to our present times."

"I would highly recommend this book for its entertainment, historical authenticity and value."

"I thoroughly enjoyed this book. It draws you straight into the action from the first paragraph and the pace continues to the end. I found it hard to put down and was sorry when it ended. Very well written and easy to read, this is a great adventure story and I can't wait for the next one."

"If you like historical fiction, buy this book. You won't be disappointed."

mybook.to/MaryFoxBrokenSword

The Witchfinder's Well Trilogy

Part 1 - The Witchfinder's Well

What if you fell through a time travel portal and landed in Tudor England?

How long before you say the wrong thing to the wrong person? Before you're accused of being a witch?

For Justine Parker it's almost immediate. She hardly has time to find her feet in a historical world that's hostile for women, before she's on the run from a ruthless witchfinder. He makes it his deadly mission to submit her to a terrifying trial.

And if that doesn't kill her, he'll burn her to death.

Justine needs to do whatever it takes to keep out of his clutches. But she can't do it alone – as a stranger in Elizabethan England, she needs help. Handsome Sir William could be her saviour – and even her lover – but his time is running out fast. A cruel twist of history says his own death is imminent.

Now Justine has to face a terrible choice – save herself, or change history and save her new love?

Unless she can find a way to do both.

Readers have said:

"A must for everyone who loves history and a must for everyone who wants to be whisked away to another time."

"An enchanting and un-put-downable read!"

"A good tale, entertaining, funny, informative, recommended, a good holiday book, one to go back to again and again."

" I couldn't put it down... a well-written book. Total enjoyment!"

mybook.to/WitchfindersWell

Part 2 – Alchemist's Arms

Lady Mary de Beauvais seems to be the perfect 16th century woman, but she hides a dark and terrible secret - she is actually a time-traveller from 2015 called Justine Parker. So when she discovers there's another traveller from her own time, she sets out across Elizabethan England to find him.

But it's a search that leads her into dreadful danger – threatening not just Mary's own future, but the life of Queen Elizabeth as well. So Mary is forced to face her fears and take control – if she wants to save herself and those she loves, in this *"gripping adventure thriller"*.

Readers have said:

"Thoroughly recommend it."

"...this marvellous book was a winner for me... There's a good feel for the time and era, so history buffs will enjoy the rich tapestry of detail in this book."

"The numerous twists and turns keep you on the edge of your seat."

"Well written, kept you wanting to read page after page in one go!"

mybook.to/AlchemistsArms

Part 3 - The Sovereign's Secret

England 1575.

After involvement in an audacious assassination attempt on the life of Queen Elizabeth has tested Lady Mary de Beauvais to her limits – and beyond – all she wants is to do is live a peaceful life with her family.

Unfortunately her time-travelling past catches up with her, and she now faces the greatest threat to her life in Tudor England. That is until Francis Walsingham, the sinister spymaster, offers to send her on her most dangerous mission yet.

Can Lady Mary find the courage, the strength and the sheer determination to win through finally?

Whatever happens, history is going to change.

Readers have said:

"I liked that Lady Mary is a kick-ass heroine and the story has the odd bit of humour. The book is well-written and the historical detail seems pretty accurate."

"Be prepared for the fulfilment of the warning on the cover of "This time history is going to change." It's fun to see how [Jonathan] Posner brings this about."

"From the first page I was hooked. Well written, the book was full of excitement and at times I couldn't put it down. Most enjoyable."

mybook.to/SovereignSecret

Prequel - The Lawyer's Legacy

This fast-paced, action packed, historical thriller introduces Robert Wychwoode, the lawyer and spy-master of *The Witchfinder's Well* trilogy.

What if you uncovered a traitorous rebellion – but nobody believed you?

1535. Tudor couple Ophelia Williams and Robert Wychwoode make a great crime-busting team. They've cracked open a Cornish rebellion against Henry VIII.

But when it comes to stopping it – then they're on their own.

There's no doubting their bravery. Or their relentless determination. Or even their cunning and ingenuity.

But will it be enough?

Because the price of failure is death.

Readers have said:

"...it kept me on the edge of my seat and I just wanted to keep reading. Couldn't put it down!"

"Most enjoyable Tudor historical fiction."
"This was a fun read, especially in following the escapades of a 16th century woman who learns espionage…"

"…without giving anything away, there is an episode on board ship that had me on the edge of my seat. Well-researched and well-written; a joy to read. Highly recommended."

mybook.to/LawyersLegacy

All Jonathan Poner's books are published by
Winter & Drew Publishing Ltd.

winteranddrew.com

www.ingramcontent.com/pod-product-compliance
Lightning Source LLC
Chambersburg PA
CBHW061100210726
48294CB00001B/229